THE SECRET OF THE SARAH M.

ROBERT J. WATSON

Cover Photograph from Stock
Design by Nicola Ormerod
Copyright© 2013

Karabeth Publishing

There are several people I would like to thank mainly for their help and support. A writer might think they have written a book by themselves. But trust me we don't. In my case I would like to thank my wife Jackie and my children Emma. Stephanie. Simon. David and Rob. A massive Thank you to Nicola and Nancy at KARABETH publishing

I would like to say hello to my grandchildren mainly so that they have bragging rights in years to come. Liam. Ellie. Ethan. Charlie. Christopher. Matthew. And welcome to the newest member of our clan. Perrie-leigh Catherine Watson Congratulations to Darren and Samantha.

And of course to my best friend Gerble. Despite the many years of trying to get him to understand. He has still no idea what is the bow or stern of a ship. But a better friend no man could ask for.

Finally I am dedicating this book to the memory of George Houghton. A man who took a scared kid under his wing and showed him what a true British seaman should be. His humour and legendary cures for seasickness where rubbish. But I laughed away the bad times. Thanks George I will never forget you. May a fair wind make your voyage safe and the stars guide your wake. I hope that Annette and her family Linsey Ralph, Joanne Squire. Grandkids Poppie Annette Ralph, Samuel George Houghton - Squire, Jessica Rose Houghton-Squire. Remember the good times only

CHAPTER ONE

I felt the hand on my shoulder, shaking me gently.

"Mister Birket, do you wish me to begin, sir?"

I felt numb. I could cry no more tears. Gathering my thoughts, and what strength I had left in me, I nodded at the padre. He moved slightly to my right. Silence fell over the deck as all eyes settled on me and the padre.

"We therefore commit his body to the deep, looking for the day of Resurrection in the last day, and the life of the world to come through our Lord Jesus Christ, at whose second coming in glorious majesty to judge the world. The sea shall give up her dead, and the corruptible bodies of those who sleep in him shall be changed, and made like unto his glorious body, according to the mighty working, whereby he is able to subdue all things unto himself. Lord take into thy care the soul of Patrick Robert Birket."

Standing there on the deck of the *Sarah M.*, listening to the words of the padre, I felt detached. None of them really had any effect on me. Around me, mourners had gathered out here on the main deck of the *Sarah M.* Some of them were genuine in their grief. Others were there acting the part, waiting for the moment in which they would see what had been left to them.

I was stood there, hoping I could find some peace in my own mind. I had never felt so alone in my entire life. I had tried to bury my grief deep inside me. I had no intention of showing some of these parasites and leeches how I felt.

Six weeks and three days had passed since the attack on the ship, the *Lusitania*. My parents and my sister had been aboard when she'd been torpedoed. I could not fathom as to why they'd gone on the damned ship in the first place. Still, over the past couple of years, my dad made some strange decisions. This one, unfortunately, had cost him his life.

This final act of remembrance had been my father's last wish. Each time he'd gone away, he'd always left a letter, telling me where everything was, and in what order it should be done.

I had stopped travelling with my family a couple of years back, preferring to stay at home and work. My own vacations had been taken in more fun places where I did not have to dress formally for dinner, or take a mountain of appropriate clothing for each occasion.

The *Sarah M.*, the ship I was now standing on, had been my grandfather's ship. He was of the old school kind. Ships sailed under canvas in his day. She had been his pride and joy. I had spent many a week on her during school, and later, during academy vacations times. I knew every stick and spar of her.

She was now a relic of a by-gone era. Nothing more than a museum piece now. My father had retired her from the working fleet several years ago. This was the first time I had been aboard her in four years. She had lost some of her grace and beauty after my grandfather, Robert, had died. In his last will, he had left her to my father until I was of an age to take her over.

I had reached my twenty-first birthday two years ago. The *Sarah M.* had become mine, but it was never the same being aboard her as it had been with my grandfather. I maintained her for the sake of him, really. Thus, it was fitting that we'd gathered here today.

Grandfather had always wanted to see her back in England. It was my father who had resisted that. This had led to many a row in the house. Right now, if I'd had my way, I would have taken her out, and burnt her at sea. Maybe it was the moment that had me thinking like that, though.

The strong south westerly wind made the *Sarah M.* bob about on the water like a cork. There were not many people aboard her for the ceremony. I personally did not have a problem with this. The fewer, the better, as far as I was concerned. As it was, I was feeling as sick as a dog. It had been some time since I had been on the deck of a ship. I had not yet gotten my sea legs. The sooner we got back to port, the better. For me, it was a lost day.

I said my goodbyes the day I got the telegram informing me about the *Lusitania* sinking. After all, I now had a shipping line to run, as well as the many other businesses that the *Nelson* shipping line had built up over the years it had been trading.

The shipping line was only a very small part of the empire it had now grown into. Oil from Alaska, railways spanning the four corners of the globe, gold mines, buildings, and quite recently, arms had been added to the line. The outbreak of war in 1914 had made it a pertinent business to get into. The *Nelson* truck had been sold by the thousands to all parts of the world. Many different armies had used it. The irony of it all was that there was a great possibility that some of the components that went into the German torpedoes were made by *Nelson Arms and Logistics* right here in the United States.

The *Sarah M.* bucked as another wave crashed against her bows. I could feel my stomach churn all over again.

For God's sake! Just get the prayers over and done with so that we can get back to dry land!

Debra Carter was pissing me off in a big way. She was standing there on deck, dressed all in black, blubbering away as if she was the one who'd suffered the loss. She'd only been an acquaintance of my mother and father's. Perhaps she was making sure that the annual donation for her charity would continue to roll in through me. I honestly didn't know.

CHAPTER TWO

Why my parents had decided to go to Ireland, I have no idea. My mother had some foolish notion about seeing where my late great-grandmother had lived. If only they'd gone to the Gulf of Mexico as grandfather had normally done. Perhaps they would still be alive today.

My father was always the romantic, though. To me, he'd lived in the past for far too long. I had told him so on more than one occasion. His reply had always been the same.

My past is now your future.

The entrance hallway and the lobby of our offices were adorned with photographs of Grandfather Robert. He had been one of the founding partners of the *Nelson* shipping line, along with his good friend, Commodore William Hogarth. Their friendship had spanned across many years, going back to before the Civil War in the United States. Grandfather had told me time and time again of how they'd met in a small bar on the River Lune, in a place called Lancaster, England. The Commodore had been a boson back then on a ship called the *Stemsi*. Over the years, they had shared many an adventure.

The *Nelson* shipping line had risen in meteoric ways since the end of the last century. Both Grandfather and the Commodore had been Englishmen who had put roots down in the state of Florida. I had never met Commodore Hogarth. He had died many years ago, unfortunately.

My father often said that after his death, a piece of my grandfather died with him. I had never seen such a thing, however. Every now and then, I would see a tear in his eyes as he told me of the Commodore. He had taught Grandfather all he knew about the sea and then some.

Grandfather had started his journey as a galley boy on the *Stemsi*. Thanks to Commodore Hogarth, he'd climbed through the ranks, eventually captaining the *Sarah M.* Perhaps that's why he loved the ship so much.

As I was growing up, I had climbed every part of her rigging. Somehow, when I'd gone to the academy, things changed. I lost my interest in ships and the sea. I'd always hated the regimental way I had been treated at the academy as I'd always been a free agent when I was with grandfather aboard the *Sarah M.* I loved being below decks with the ordinary sailors. By the time, I went to the academy I could cuss with the best of them. This was frowned upon by all of the instructors at the academy.

My father hated parent days. He would be first inside the captain's office to get my review. Each time he left the office, his face was clouded over like thunder. In the early years of me being there, I would hide behind my mother. She would make sure I did not get the balling out I was due. Family honour was at stake, he would shout. Mother would protest that I was only a child.

I think my father got his sense of honour from Grandfather Robert. Although Dad had sailed on the *Sarah M.*, he never made the rank of skipper. He had shared his memories of those days aboard the ship as first officer. They were never as exciting as when my grandfather talked to me about his days.

Father would always go on about the sense of honour he had been instilled with. I never got this impression from Grandfather. It was a tough and hard life. Treat the men right, and they would treat him and the ship in the same way. Dad worked the men like dogs. Grandfather, by all accounts, had pulled him aside on more than one occasion about the way he dealt with the men.

Maybe that was one of the reasons he came ashore, and ran the company from the office. In some ways, I was sure this sense of family brought about the deaths of my parents and my sister.

Dad had shares in the *Cunard* line. This was the parent company of the *Lusitania*. My family had travelled to Ireland in the early part of April in the year of 1915. The outward voyage had been on the *S. S. William Hogarth*. The name of the ship was yet another throwback to a by-gone era, named in honour of the founding partner of the *Nelson* shipping line. The family had state rooms aboard her that were kept in a state of readiness for them. It was by chance, that the *S. S. William Hogarth* was bound for England. Normally, she would have sailed between the mainland United States and the Caribbean.

Dad liked to travel in style. The *William Hogarth* fit this bill for him. The *S. S. William Hogarth* was not the biggest vessel in our fleet, by any means. At eighteen thousand tons, she was a multi-purpose vessel, carrying both cargo and passengers alike. Her maximum capacity for passengers was two hundred and fifty. All of her cabins were fitted for the more discerning of passengers.

Food and wine of the highest standard were served to everyone who could afford it. More often than not, it was his many friends who used her to take their mistresses on that little private holiday that had been promised to them for services rendered.

The *William Hogarth* had a top speed of around twenty knots. She could make the voyage to England in a matter of days, although it was never shown on the ship's manifest. The bulk of her cargo was made of munitions manufactured by *Nelson Arms and Logistics*.

The war in Europe was going badly. Thousands of troops from all sides had been killed. Fresh troops and weapons were needed. There were rumours of the United States joining the war. Until that point, companies like the *Nelson* line would continue to supply arms to the British and her allies, by any means necessary. Even my father did not know the *William Hogarth* was carrying arms on this voyage.

It had been my decision to ship them on the *William Hogarth*. I had been against her berthing in Dublin. The company would face a heavy fine if her manifest showed a different cargo to what she was actually carrying. The Irish had a certain loyalty to the German high command. If the ship was searched by their customs men, then we would be in a world of trouble.

Her one night stop-over in Dublin was requested personally by my father. His little joke of, 'Well, I own the company, so one extra day will not matter,' was seen as highly humorous by many. Personally, I thought it was just a waste of company money and the ship's time. He was the boss, however, and what he said was the only thing that mattered. To me, her cargo was more important.

By the time, it landed in Liverpool on the west coast of England, it would have profited the company to the tune of three hundred thousand dollars. While they were away, I got daily telegraphs from them at sea, mainly from my father wanting to know how things were running.

After spending two weeks in Ireland, they took passage home on the *Lusitania*. I still had the telegram from my father in my wallet. I had no need to read it, for I knew every word by heart now.

Ship left on time. Please have carriage waiting on arrival. Father.

On the 7th of May, 1915, at ten minutes past two in the afternoon, a torpedo from a German submarine slammed into her side. In less than twenty minutes, the giant liner had slipped below the surface with the loss of over one thousand and nine hundred people.

Her course had not been secret, but it was thought that at a top speed of over twenty-one knots, she would be able to evade any danger presented to her. The captain would take evasive action by zig-zagging across the water. In the case of the *Lusitania*, she had not. She entered what was known as the killing square at full speed, keeping her course true.

The area had been named the killing square due to its being on the main shipping route between the United States and the U. K. mainland. German submarines would sit there, and wait for allied shipping.

At the enquiry, initial reports suggested there was secondary explosion from within her hull. This could have been caused by a number of things. Her boilers could have blown up, but more than likely, the torpedo had hit one of her hidden magazines. This would definitely explain her sinking so quickly. Her hull would have been ripped apart in double quick time. There would have been virtually no time to get her water tight doors closed

Again, this was no surprise to me. In fact, it as more of a surprise that she had not blown up immediately, considering the amount of munitions she was packed with. The specially fitted munitions magazines she had installed two years previously had not helped her one bit. Double bottomed munitions magazines down in the bilge area would soon flood with water. This would make her unstable above the water.

As far back as 1910, the prospect of war in Europe was never far away. Wars did not start overnight. It took planning, arms, and men to make a war. Following the sinking of the *Lusitania*, it was thought that the United States would enter the war on the side of the British and her allies. Most especially after it was revealed that over one hundred Americans had died aboard the liner.

President Roosevelt resisted the calls, appealing for calm instead. Many congressmen openly criticized him for his lack of action. Others supported him. He was no one's fool. He would seek council from as many men as possible before committing the United States to war.

My father had dined with Roosevelt in the autumn of 1913. He'd attended a black tie affair held in the White House for both politicians and some of the most influential business men in the country. Some of these men had the ear of the president. It was enough that my dad was invited to such an occasion.

I could see the pride on my dad's face as he dressed that evening. Like everything my dad did, this evening was planned down to the last detail. He had counselled against entering the war back then. This was because the United States was not ready for war. Her army was small compared to other countries. If the United States were to go to war, she should be ready and able to fight, and to win.

The country needed new arms. Modern weapons and men who knew how to use them. All this would take time.

CHAPTER THREE

I, like many aboard the *Sarah M.*, had been glad to see her slip back alongside her moorings. For a select few aboard, there would be drinks and food served below deck in the officer's mess room. Others slipped down the gangway into the waiting cars. A more informal gathering would be had at the *Sheridan* hotel later that day. The small matter of my dad's last will and testament was the most important issue right now.

It was several minutes before we all gathered below. As per my dad's instructions, every person below had been given a drink of their choice. Once the stewards had been ushered ashore, Conrad Greenburg held the scrolled parchment almost at arm's length. A small pair of spectacles was balanced carefully on the end of his nose. Silence fell over the mess room as he cleared his throat, drawing everyone's attention.

Greenburg had been the company lawyer for many years. I had never seen eye-to-eye with him. He had a lot of influence over my dad. He was a weasel-faced son-of-a-bitch who had a permanent sneer on his face.

One by the one, the people gathered in the mess room fell silent. All in all, there was about thirty or so, all hoping to get a slice of the cake.

There were several charities of which Father had been a patron of. All of them were looking eagerly at the lawyer who would now give them their good news. Several directors from the various holding companies we had stood silently and solemnly at the back, along with the main board of directors from the *Nelson* line. All of them were sitting there with black armbands on full show. How pathetic they looked. It was not as if most had liked my dad, but then again, he paid their wages. That's the only reason they sat there with the black armbands on.

Conrad Greenburg cleared his throat once more, and then began reading from the paper held out in front of him.

I, Patrick James Robert Birket, being of sound mind, do make this bequest as my last will and testament.

The people gathered around the room shuffled about from one foot to the other. Greenburg looked around the room. The shuffling soon stopped.

To the charities listed below, I make the bequest of two hundred and fifty thousand dollars to be shared evenly between them.

These consisted of three children's homes. One foundation set up by the *Nelson* line for the family's of sailors lost at sea. One orphanage found in the Cuban islands. This had been set up by my grandfather many years ago, along with my great-uncle William. Father saw fit to keep this on as an annual gift to the people of Cuba for saving the life of William Hogarth.

To my wife, Rebecca, I leave the family home, and five percent of all my holdings in all of the companies I have shares or a controlling interest in.

This bequest was now nullified by the untimely death of my mother. Automatically, the shares would now come to me. Greenburg stopped speaking for a moment looking, around the room before his eyes settled briefly on me.

To my only son, Robert Birket, I leave the remainder of my estate. All share holdings are to be kept in trust for him until he reaches the legal age of twenty-one. Mr. Conrad Greenburg will act as his administrator.

Silence descended as Greenburg gave me one of his knowing looks. There was more foot shuffling around the room.

The total sum of personal wealth now passing to me was three and a half million dollars and some change. God knows how much all of the stocks and shares were worth. I could sit back, and have a nice long vacation until I became twenty-one. I would have to work in the office, learning more about the company than I already did.

Inwardly, I smiled to myself. Outwardly, I stood firm and solemn. Several of the people gathered in the room openly gasped.

The only other bequest was to leave the sailing ship, the *Sarah M.*, to the city of Lancaster back in England. Again, this had been a bequest from my grandfather in his will. I had never understood it when it was read out the first time after Grandfather had died. I was even more stunned at hearing it again through my own dad's last will.

Although, I loved the *Sarah M.*, I would sooner have taken her to deep water, and burnt her every stick and spar. She was now a relic from a time of long ago. The memories I had of her were happy ones. I would hate to see her rot in some dark corner of a dock on the other side of the Atlantic.

To England, she would go. I would also make a personal donation to keep her in a reasonably good state. Perhaps what I really wanted was not to be reminded of the deep pain I felt inside of me each and every time I saw her.

Sending her to England would also serve another purpose for me. I would dispatch Commodore John to sail her there. He had grown up on her as boy, and became a man sailing under my grandfather as a deck boy. He also spent a time on her with my dad. He had often given me a clip around the ear. Williams had served within the *Nelson* line for all of his working life. He was now shore based, working and barking his orders up and down the corridors of the *Nelson* line offices.

I would leave her departure to Commodore Williams. I had no doubt he would offer to take the *Sarah M.* on her last voyage. This suited me quite well. It would be his final task within the company before I got rid of the fool. It was a sense of loyalty, I think, that my dad had kept him on. He had sailed on the *Sarah M.* on those rare occasions in which Grandfather wanted to relive his days as a ship's captain.

This was, perhaps, once every year or so. Grandfather would gather a few of his close friends, and take them aboard. He'd then sail around the Atlantic for a few weeks. His friends loved the idea of going back in time, and sailing on one of the greatest ships of her day.

The *Sarah M.* had many stories told about her. Grandfather had kept her in pristine condition. She was more of a hobby ship for the past several years, no longer able to carry the big cargos the modern world wanted the ship to carry. It did not have the speed of modern steam ships, either.

Ever since the day of sailing ships had gone, John Williams had skippered various steam ships within the company, managing to bounce them off of several jetties during that time. Back in the days of sailing, John was an apprentice with romantic notions of sailing making a comeback. The days of steam would never catch on. If memory served me, and it usually did, he was a real chump, always ingratiating himself to not only my father, but the senior deck officers.

The lower ranks usually suffered for his incompetence. Two men died as a direct result of his not making fast on some of the rigging lines. The ropes had parted, knocking both men over the side. He had blamed three of the ordinary seaman for the accident. The enquiry cleared him of all wrong-doing.

His feeble attempts to keep me off of the main deck always failed. My grandfather had always wanted me on deck, learning the ways of the old school. To a degree, it became a battle of wills between us. He would always lose.

He'd climbed the ranks, taking his first officer's exam, followed by his master's exam. There was no argument about his skills when it came to being master of a ship. It was his crap decision-making that was always brought into question. He would sail in weather that no other ship's skipper would even think about going out in. The damage to a lot of the cargo on his ship sent insurance premiums sky high.

Personally, the roll of a commodore was outdated. His task could be done just as easily by a clerk for a lot less money than my father paid him. I had no doubt in my mind that Commodore Williams would love the chance to sail on a ship like the *Sarah M.* again.

He should, too. It was only fitting, as he enjoyed his last voyage with the *Nelson* line. Men like him would always find another company to take him on. Perhaps not as a commodore, but certainly as a skipper. He had many years left in him yet.

The Marconi gram would be waiting for him the very day he berthed in the city of Lancaster. I had even thought of what to say in it.

TO COMMODORE JOHN WILLIAMS,

SERVISES TO NELSON LINE NO LONGER REQUIRED.

It was short, and to the point. There was no point in messing around with the man.

CHAPTER FOUR

At the age of nine, I was sent to the *Normington Naval Academy* in Washington. For the next nine years, I was boarded there. My father had hoped I would follow the family yearning to go to sea. My mother had been in tears for weeks before I had gone. Each time I walked into the room she was in, she would dry the tears from her eyes, but the redness around them stayed. Back then, she had not fooled me.

I was soon packed onto a train. My father gave me my allowance, and shook my hand. *Grow up, and be a man, Robert. Do your family proud,* he said. The strong leather suitcase had been put in the baggage care, along with the other poor bastards that had been shipped off by their own parents. Many felt like I had. Totally lost, and scared stupid. The further along the train you went, the carriages were filled with older guys. The front carriages had full cadets in uniform.

Two of the youngest boys in our carriage had wet their trousers shortly after leaving the station. I remember being pretty close to that myself. My stubbornness was the only thing that stopped me from achieving the state they now found themselves in. For five and a half hours, we all sat in that railway carriage. No one was willing or able to talk.

At the railway station in Washington, we were herded like cattle into busses. Our tutors marched up and down the rows of boys, screaming orders at us to line up in a straight line in front of them. Only when our names were called out were we allowed to move to the line of busses to our left.

Some of the boys around me shed more tears. I clenched my fists, and dug my hands into my sides, refusing to give in to the fear coursing through me.

I hated the place from day one. The very strict regime laid down by the academy was far different from my home life. My first day was celebrated by the whole intake class being shown around the grounds in military style. On the way around the academy, we would collect our uniforms, taking each part of it back to our rooms, and placing it in a perfect position on the bed, ready for inspection later that day. God help you if you had one piece out of place. The evil bastard who was our house master and instructor might as well have given us all of our punishments, right then and there. We had no clue as to what to do.

The sadist who was to become our house master and instructor in all matter's military ran us until we vomited. Then, just to remind us that this was not something done by young gentlemen, he made us clean up our own vomit with spoons.

Welcome to Normington Naval Academy, gentlemen!

***

Within the first three weeks, I had written my first letter home, begging to be taken out of this hellhole. I waited for the weekly mail call, hoping that my parents would see how unhappy I was. I prayed they would come to get me.

It was a full month before I got a reply from my father. The top and bottom of it was that no, they would not be coming to take me away. My father felt that being at the academy was a means of character building for me. I would appreciate the academy after a year or so.

The bottom fell out of my world upon reading those words. For the first time since I had been there, I openly cried. This resulted in my having to endure the funnel. This was a special treatment to toughen students up. Eight boys from various years would line up on each side of the mess hall. The poor sucker who was to get the treatment would be pushed in at one end. The other students would then punch, kick, and abuse us until we made the other end. As if that was not enough, the recipient of the treatment would then have to stand on the table before the assembled students, and offer a short speech of thanks to them. Refusing to take part in the funnel would also result in that student following the original one through. Any breach in school discipline was dealt with swiftly, and usually painfully, by the principal.

Being sent to the gun room meant a certain beating for the poor sap that was being sent there. I had made several visits there in my early days. The gun room was a glorified prison cell. The only difference being that it had a four pounder cannon in the centre of it. Part of the student's punishment was to clean the cannon with a toothbrush. If the high standards of the school were not met by the student on punishment detail, another two strokes of the cane would be added to his original punishment.

The principal would then march into the room in full uniform. He would read the charge out to the student. Apart from death or some other equally important reason, punishment was always carried out. The academy boson would administer the punishment. The student would lie across the gun, and have to recite the points of the compass out loud to the commander after each stroke. The basics of North, South, East, and West were easy to remember. It was when you came down to the smaller points such as North by East etc. that the memory failed.

Being in pain did not do you any favours, either. At the end of punishment, the commander would shake hands. We would have to thank him. The boson would then march us out on the double, and take us back to the dormitory. We then had two days to learn how to box a compass down to by points, or else the punishment would be given again. It was a simple, but effective, method of learning.

Throughout my time there, I had never met anyone who did not get the extra two strokes. Or learn their compass points. The uniforms all students had to wear daily were made up from a mixture of barbed wire and horse hair. They were hot in the summer, and cold in the winter, and were light grey with a red stripe down each leg. Inspections were done for dress uniforms, and we quickly learned to be well-turned out during these times. Standing extra duties and being given extra study along with kissing the gun room was not the best way to spend free time.

Each evening was dedicated to prayer and silent contemplation. Silence being the operative word. Even coughing could, and often did, bring a swift slap on the back of the head by one of the seniors in the room. This period would then be followed by supper. Uniform cleaning would come after, quickly followed by the routine inspection of the dorm and bed area.

The slightest infraction of the standards would result in the guilty parties sleeping area being trashed. A further inspection of that student's bed area would take place again within the hour. Should he fail the inspection, the same treatment would be dished out until the student got it right. The rest of the dorm was treated to PT, whilst the offending student got on with the task.

I'd known, and had been part of, this treatment more times than I care to remember. The officer cadets, as they were known, would check the bed corners with set squares, ensuring perfection was a byword within the academy.

Most days were filled with sailing and navigation. A small converted lifeboat with a small mast amidships made the perfect sailing boat. The small lake at the rear of the school served as any ocean in the world. Although, it was not very challenging to navigate around.

I found the sailing and maritime instruction easy to pick up. I'd had a lifetime of it.

Captain Miller, our sailing master, would stand at the entrance to the classroom. To his left would be a mock-up of a sailing ship. As each student entered the room, he would point his cane towards various parts of the vessel. He expected and demanded each student to know every part of the ship from top mast to keel.

If you named the part of the ship he was pointing at, all was well. Should a student fail to name a part of the ship, he would feel the end of the captain's cane with the order to find out before his next class. The gunner's mate waited for the sorry student who failed the next time.

The academy itself was set in ninety acres of land. Within the first six months, I managed to find plenty of places to hide myself away from the seniors or the masters. Sometimes, alone. At other times, with several of my classmates. We always seemed to be found in a shit state, or with a cigarette hanging from our mouths. To us, it was the last place we would be found. To those looking for us, it would be the first.

By Christmas of that first year, my rear end was more like cowhide than skin, due to the beatings I endured in the gun room. My home leave that year was spent letting the skin grow back on my butt. I never told my dad about it, though. I knew what his reaction would be. My mother was more sympathetic to me, but she was always going to lose the argument with Dad.

Grandfather Robert passed away during the March of the following year. It broke my heart to know of his death. He had been such an influence on me. I was not allowed home leave to attend his funeral. Instead, I paid several visits to the gun room for dumb insolence.

During that springtime, my father, for whatever reason, loaned the *Sarah M.* to the academy. We spent four weeks sailing around the Atlantic on her. Though, my joy was tinged with great sadness. I had spent so many happy days on this wonderful ship with Grandfather Robert. I knew ever stick and spar of her. Yet it no longer seemed that happy ship I had grown up on.

I had vivid dreams of Grandfather standing on the poop deck. I was standing alongside him, watching each flutter of the sails, knowing her moods and her handling. I had spent many hours standing at the wheel, my small hands gripping its spokes while trying to steer her. Nine times out of ten, I would be thrown one way or the other as the sea bucked her to and fro.

Under the command of Captain Miller, she was a different ship. He would have her run like a war ship, and not the merchant ship she really was. I loved being aloft on watch-keeping. I had carved my name into her top mast four or five years ago. It was still there. I ran my fingers down the carving, wishing that my grandfather was still here with me. For the first time in my short life, I wished I could get away from the sea forever. My first year at the academy could not come soon enough for me.

The smell of vomit below decks from the boys who had never been to sea before was foul. I managed to get the hammock space I had grown up with way up in the prow of the ship. I was left alone there, and this suited me just fine.

The senior cadet officer on our watch, Mister, enjoyed his power a lot. He was from one of the oldest naval families in the United States. I'd vaguely known him for some years. His family had known my family through the shipping line. He was an arrogant prick, back then, and hadn't changed one bit since then. He was expected to go straight to the United States Navy, and climb the ladder quickly. In the meantime, he used the younger cadets as his own personal staff waiting on him hand and foot. A rope's end with a monkey's fist knot on one end served as his persuader to the unwilling junior cadets.

CHAPTER FIVE

By the time my third year had ended, I had become a rebel. The gun room seemed like an everyday occurrence for me. At one point, on the advice of the doctor, I had been admitted to the academy hospital because my butt was so marked from the cane. I refused to be beaten into submission, though.

More and more extreme ways to get me to conform were concocted by the faculty heads. These would include midnight runs, six or seven miles, in my pyjamas, along with a full kit bag of sharp stones that only had the effect of cutting my back so badly that I had to spend the next four days under the care of Matron Bryce in the hospital wing.

It was with her that I found the joys of manhood. It was a surprise to me what five dollars could get me. She taught me things I never knew were possible. It almost became a happy occasion to be sent to her. She was not the prettiest women I had ever known, but she had a world of experience with young and less experienced men who were only too willing to learn, and pay her the agreed amount. Her extracurricular classes were extremely pleasurable.

After three days in her small hospital ward, I would be back on my punishment routine. Most times, I would not be able to walk or run, due to my feet blistering so badly from the late-night runs I had to do in my bare feet. On these occasions, I would have to present myself every hour to the duty officer cadet of the day for a full inspection of dress and kit.

It was dependant on who was officer-of-the-day as to whether it would be a full inspection or not. Some chose to dismiss me without the inspection so that they could go back to sleep. Others saw it as their duty to have me stand at attention. They would comb my uniform inch-by-inch, looking for the smallest fault.

For two full terms, I kept up my act of defiance. It was only when my father threatened to move me one thousand miles or so south to an even stricter academy that I chose to improve my attitude.

By year five of my term, in what many of us classed as Andersonville, it brought more sea time. I found I was very capable of navigation and setting courses.

As each year passed, I found the new intake of cadets grow more and more annoying. There had always been initiation ceremonies in the academy. These usually involved scaring the intake to death with tales of ghost stories, and locking them in the academy cellar for half an hour or so. Usually one of the older cadets would have been installed down there. He would creep round the cellar, touching the young cadets with the tip of a broom, and a chain rattling along the floor soon had them screaming for *Mother*. I, myself, had lasted a full fifteen minutes down there before breaking down.

During my sixth year, several of us found that soaking the new intakes in fresh pig's blood was highly amusing. It is surprising how much of a mess half a bucketful can do to a dormitory, especially ten minutes before inspection time. Using the new cadets as a personal slave was also a great advantage to the older cadets.

For my last two years at the academy, I never once cleaned my uniform or my room. The penalty for not complying with us was simple. The offender would be strung up by his ankles over the balcony directly above the cellar. Ten minutes of that, and a beating, normally did the trick.

I never got to finish my last year at school. I was found in the gunroom by the principal and his deputy. They walked into the room just as I bound the matron over the school cannon, her bare backside still showing the whelp marks from where her friend had been whipping her. My state of undress did not go unnoticed by the principal, either.

There were two simple choices – resign on request, or be expelled. I chose to resign. I went home with a certain amount of disgrace, but feeling very smug with myself on the inside. The first few days at home were spent in silence. My dad refused to talk to me at all. I can't say I was unhappy about that. I knew the lecture would come sooner or later from him.

Eventually, he summoned me to his study. One of the servants came to get me. By the time Dad finished with his lecture, I was left in no doubt about my future.

For the next year, I was packed off to Texas to work on one of the new oil fields the company had bought into. There was no arguing with him. It was Thurber Texas, or make my own way in life.

I arrived in Thurber on an extremely hot day. Dust covered everything. The rig was also twenty miles west of the town.

I was picked up by Hoots Bransom, a gnarled old guy who had spent most of his life out in the wilds searching for the *black gold*, as it was known. Apart from telling me his name, he had nothing else to say to me on the road out to the rig.

Once there, my gear was thrown onto the deck, and I was shown where to stow it. I had ten minutes to get changed into working gear, and get on the platform in order to receive my orders. This was not going to be a summer vacation. I was sure of that. The sickly smell of crude oil made me want to vomit. Rig four-nine-two was only a small part of the oil field here. As far as the eye could see, there were wooden rigs dotted about. Trucks and men moved about like ants.

The hut I was staying in was nothing more than a shit hole several men slept in there. This was nothing new to me. I had shared dormitories before. I made my way to an empty bunk just in time to see a rat scurry out of a hole in the corner of the hut. Dad knew exactly what he'd done when he sent me here. I'd never been in such an environment in my life before.

The door to the shack flew open, and another bearded wonder stood there. An unlit cigar hung from his lips. His stature filled the doorway. The ten gallon hat he had on covered the rest of the door, almost blocking what daylight there was outside.

"Are you going to just stand there, you lazy son-of-a-bitch? Or are you going to get some God damn work done today?"

My stammering reply of, "I had just got here," did not stop him from carrying on with his rant.

"You're not here on a God damn holiday! Your daddy told me to treat you like the rest of the men working here, so move your God damn lazy arse out of here, and get out to the rig now!"

The hairs on the back of my neck began to stand on end. Throwing my kit bag on the empty bunk, I began to pull out the heavy pair of boots and denim jeans. I heard his heavy feet stomp over the wooden floor. A heavy pair of hands grabbed my by the collar of my shirt.

"Don't you God damn turn your back on me, you son-of-a-bitch!"

The forward motion he had made threw me across the small cot. I ended up in a heap on the wooden floor, looking out of the escape hole the rat gone had through a couple of minutes earlier. I lay there, catching my breath. For a moment, his cursing did not stop.

"One minute to get your arse outside, Greenhorn!"

Clearly, he was not a man to see reason. The door slammed behind him, and I crawled to my feet. As quickly as I could, I changed into the work clothes I had been given, and made my way to the platform.

The roll of a greenhorn was basically a shit kicker. And shit that needed kicking called for the greenhorn.

For three days, I moved drilling pipes, moved oil drums, humped drilling bits, and cleared blockages. I worked from dawn till dusk. Sleep was impossible. Men banged about outside the rigs still working during the night. What was left of my shredded hands was so blistered, I found it hard to grasp anything at all.

My new best friend screamed at me every chance he could for just about anything. As often as he could, he was only to willing to take me behind the rig, and show me the error of my ways. I declined his kind offer each time.

By the time Saturday came around, I would have been happy to die, right there and then. I had never felt so tired before. We now had the day off. Most of the men on the rig got spruced up, and headed to town. All I wanted to do was sleep. My new best friend, Red, as I found out he was called, was staying on site. I was not going to stay around here with him. I hopped on the truck with the rest of the men, and headed for the bars of Thurber.

The town was heaving with rig workers, all willing to spend their money on cheap booze and cheap women. I followed the crowd into *Ma Mclusckie's* place, a wooden building that would not look out of place in the Wild West. We had to fight our way to the bar. Over to the left of it, several card tables were surrounded by men watching the players win or lose a week's wages.

Before I could finish my first beer, a fight broke out around one of the tables. More and more men became involved in the fight. It seemed like the only way the men could entertain themselves was to fight. Apart from the whores who now lined the upstairs balcony, screaming encouragement to the men below, mind you.

A fist landed on the back of my head. Instinctively, I threw one back. All hell broke loose at that point. Tables, chairs, and windows were now flying through the air. Some of the whores who had been trapped downstairs when the fighting broke out began screaming and searching for cover.

I felt another blow to the side of my head. Stars floated across my eyes, and then an inky blackness took over. I had no idea how long I'd been out for. I tried opening my eyes. The right one remained tightly closed, and I could feel the bruising around it. The fighting had now stopped, and I found myself outside. My clothes were wet completely.

I soon found out that the only real medical treatment out here was the horse trough. If that did not bring you around, you were either dead, or too ill for the horse trough. Several of my work mates were alongside me, all having received the same treatment I had.

A bottle of whiskey was thrust into my hand as an after-care treatment. I took a large mouthful of it. I could feel it strip the inside of my throat as it went down. Several mouthfuls later, I was cured. All the pain had gone. I was left with a silliness about me I had never felt before. The sun was going down before we headed back to the shack. For the first time in days, I slept.

Sunday had always been the Lord's Day. Most of the men I'd been in the bar with, and who, no doubt, had spent a lot of their hard-earned wages on booze and whores, now got into their Sunday best, and went to the open church. The local preacher fired hell and damnation at them for over an hour. I'd stopped attending church some time ago. I had my doubts about the existence of a god.

Monday morning came only too quickly. Red began ragging my arse as soon as the sun came up. I was still a lazy son-of-a-bitch who was good for nothing in his eyes.

It was during one of his rants that I took my eye off of the job in hand. One of the drilling pipes swung around, and out of the sling it was in. I could not hear the warning shouts from Billy Rivers. By the time I'd swung around, the drilling pipe had already smashed into my lower leg. I was knocked off of the platform, landing on my back eight feet below. My right leg was twisted beneath me. The pain was making me black out. I don't think the horse trough would work this time. It did not take a genius to work out it was broken.

Red was still screaming at me to get back to work. "You're not dead yet, and you have another leg. Get on with it!"

My days as a redneck came to an end. The telegram sent to my mother saying I was seriously hurt had her on the next train down to Texas. It was the best ten dollars I had spent making sure Billy Rivers had sent it to her.

CHAPTER SIX

The Germans had been using submarines to fight the war at sea for some time now. The principle was pretty simple. If you starve a nation, such as England, and don't allow ships in or out, sooner or later, they would not be able to supply the army. Or the nation. Sink their ships, and you could win the war. The United States, at this point, was still sitting on the fence.

Negotiations between the United States and the German high command resulted in a halting of the use of the submarine in war. The Germans, however, did not keep to their word, citing various ships as troop and arms carriers, therefore making them legitimate targets.

On April 6, 1917, the United States entered the war. This followed many weeks and months of electioneering by President Woodrow Wilson. His election promise of non-aggression or interference in the war had now been broken. The United States was unprepared, and undermanned. Its army totalled less than three hundred thousand men with less than four hundred aircraft, and even less weaponry to fight the war. Many Americans felt that the United States should remain neutral.

The barbarity of the war filled many pages of the newspapers. *Trench warfare* was one headline. Troops being gassed, and the loss of life, headlined the papers almost every day. Hundreds of thousands of troops were being killed daily.

As far back as 1915, companies such as the *Nelson Company* were contracted to develop new methods of production. Written plans had been submitted twelve months earlier to the war department, specifying as to how production could be improved. New weapons were already under development. Yet it was not until America had entered the war that our plans had been looked at.

Half a million men would be called up to fight. This meant employing women to do the work of the men. By the end of 1917, *Nelson Co.* had over two thousand women working within its ranks making munitions and trucks.

Many of them constructed the new *S. K.* tanks. Not only did the *S. K.* have five inch turret cannons, but it also had four machine guns on each corner. This gave a vast amount of fire power to the personnel inside.

Half-inch plates around the turret gave the men inside greater protection. The age of tank warfare had arrived. These would lead the ground troops into battle, clearing a path for the armies to charge through. The ground troops would still have to fight for every inch of ground, however the new tanks would take the ground easily.

I had never thought of getting involved directly in the war. However, on the 17th of May, 1917, I received a letter from the Department of Defence. My reservist listing had been activated. This was news to me. I had no idea I was on the reserve list. It turned out that even though I had resigned from the academy, I remained on their list.

In some ways, it was a blessing in disguise. I spent many months arguing with Conrad Greenburg. As my guardian, he also took my place on the board. Greenburg resisted every attempt I made to make the company more profitable, or change things I felt needed to be done. His focus was on the war effort. I was nothing more than a puppet in and around the offices.

By the 29th of May, I was in the naval base at Norfolk, Virginia. From there, I joined the *U. S. S. Fanning* as Ensign Robert Birket. In many ways, it was like being back at the academy as a shit kicker with a rank. Our mission was to protect the merchantmen sailing the Atlantic.

Through September and October of that year, the nearest we came to seeing a German U boat was a pod of whales. This changed in November. We had been keeping station several miles off of the coast of Ireland when a U boat was sighted.

"All hands to action stations!"

The U boat had come up to get a bearing on the *S. S. Welshman*. Her intent was to sink the merchant ship upon sighting us. She began venting her tanks, ready to dive. Depth charges were dropped over her. It didn't take too long for her to surface again.

From what I had heard, being in the middle of a depth charge attack was one of the most scariest things any man can deal with. U boats are nothing but coffins that sink on command. A depth charge exploding near you shakes the boat so hard that it can literally rip it open. You have no idea where, or when, the next bang is coming from. All you can do is pray to whatever god you believe in.

The U boat surfaced, and we began to open up with our stern gun on her. The German sailors came on deck, and began firing back at us. Their shots missed us easily. The U boat crew surrendered after they saw the futility of their efforts. Her skipper was not crazy enough to hand over a perfectly good boat to the U. S. Navy. He opened her water intake valve, allowing her to sink into deep water.

The operation changed now from an attack to one of a search and rescue for survivors. It never failed to amaze me that we spent so much time trying to blow ships out of the water. As soon as the battle was over, we then took on a humanitarian act to save the very men who had been trying to kill us. Many of us had heard of U boat commanders shooting enemy sailors in the water, though I had no proof of this.

That was the only action I saw during the war. Convoy duty was not the best action in the world, but it beat the crap out of the boredom I was feeling in the offices of the *Nelson* line.

After the end of the war, I stayed in the Navy until the end of 1919.

I'd achieved the rank of Lieutenant Junior Grade.

CHAPTER SEVEN

Following the end of the war, Congress discussed what was to be known as the *Falstead* act. This was a national order to stop the making and distribution of alcohol. That act was ratified on January 19, 1919, under the eighteenth amendment of the Unites States Constitution. It became enforceable on January 20, 1920. Alcohol with strength of over 2.75% became illegal.

Many citizens accepted the act. Others took it as the chance to make their own fortune. Two bit hoods, cheats, and con men all saw the chance to make money. Cheap alcohol was re-brewed to make fuller strength booze, and sold to mugs across the U. S.

Stills were erected in the most unlikely of places. Territories were also fiercely guarded to ensure that only the gangs who ruled that turf only sold their own booze. Murders and beatings became an everyday event. Before the *Falstead* act came into being, New York was a hive of clubs and bars. Many of these disappeared for the man on the street.

Private clubs opened, as did speakeasy joints. Most of them were hidden from the view of the cops and federal agents who were placed about to find the booze, and cut off the lines of distribution.

Bribery and corruption ran rife in the police stations. The ordinary cop on the street would turn a blind eye for those few extra bucks in his back pocket. Judges, attorneys, and high-ranking cops were paid large amounts of cash to turn a blind eye, or tip off the hoods that ran the rackets. For many of the officials, the money was a better option to take than the blackmail threat that hung over them. Nearly everybody had a skeleton or two in the locker. The crime bosses could easily find these out. If the blackmail did not work, a man's family would be targeted. Their kids would have accidents. Wives would be attacked. They soon came around to the right way of thinking.

The daily drudgery of office life was not for me. I craved more excitement. The obvious one was to become a member of one of the speakeasy joints. This was easy enough for me. Many of my pals in the business world had joined them once the *Falstead* act had come into force. I had no great fears of arrest from the cops. Money always talked.

Security and lookouts gave those of us in the joints a high degree of protection. Like everything else, it did come at a price. Membership to some of the joints was free. However, the drinks were expensive. In other bars, the reverse was the reality. The managers of the bars were glorified hoods trusted by their bosses to run a square joint. Those who chose to make a quick buck from their bosses by crossing them were dealt with quickly and severely. Usually a bullet through the back of the head, and their bodies dumped in the river.

For less serious infractions, a broken knee cap from a well-used baseball bat would have the desired effect. I became a regular at the Blue Flamingo club in Lower Manhattan. It was not one of the high-end joints I'd visited. The higher end clubs had far too many men from the business world. I wanted some excitement in my life, away from the office and work.

I had heard about the owner of the club as his reputation preceded him. I, for one, had no wish to cross him at all. I had also seen one of his men after he had scooped fifty bucks from the till with a broken leg, and a face that looked like it had been trampled on by a herd of cows. The poor sap was forced to continue to work with his injuries, too. Partly to pay the cash he had taken back, and partly to serve as a great advertisement to others who worked for Zuckerman. After all, what better deterrent do you need other than a walking victim?

My own first meeting with Dwight Zuckerman was in the early spring of 1922. Zuckerman walked in with a broad grin on his face, and three of the biggest men I had ever seen shielding him. The big Cuban cigar he held between the fingers of his right hand complimented his look. The tailor-made suit and Italian shoes gave him an air of breeding.

It was only when he spoke that his New York accent came through. More than likely, he had dragged his way up from the gutters of the Lower East Side of Manhattan. Brute force and a ruthless streak running through him was his schooling. You didn't need too much of an education to pull a trigger, or to order a shooting to get on these days.

I had no doubt in my mind that he was totally ruthless. Despite the broad grin and happy-go-lucky manner, he made a point of getting to know his customers. One of his goons kept notes on the high-ranking city officials. On that night alone, he had two police chiefs', two district attorneys, and a handful of assistant district attorneys at the establishment. Over the next few nights, he would get to know several judges as well.

There is an old saying, *Once bent, it stays bent.*

Zuckerman would, I had no doubt, ensure that these poor bastards remained bent and in his pocket. Along with membership to the clubs came other perks. Women – these were handed around like dolls to the more influential customers. Married or single, it didn't matter in these places. I had never married, or contemplated it, for that matter. It was uncomplicated sex for me, and I preferred it that way.

Zuckerman always kept his girls clean. It wouldn't have done his reputation any good for it to get around that his girls were clap ridden sluts. No one messed with his girls, either. One whiff of trouble from a member, and they were shown the error of their ways.

I guardedly had an underlying respect for the man, even to the point of liking him. As I got to know him, I was invited more and more into his inner circle. We even had some business together. The *Nelson Co.* had several rat infested warehouses on the Lower Hudson River.

Zuckerman was only too willing to pay the going rate for them. I had my suspicions as to why he wanted them. It's sometimes better not to ask a man like him what for, though. Knowing too much can have a man separated from his head, or given the permanent use of a walking stick. I took his money, and had his business down as import and export. This was not a lie.

By the end of 1922, Zuckerman had rented over ten properties from us. How many others he had on lease, I had no idea. His rent was paid directly to me. The company sent collectors down to each site, but more often than not, they would come back empty-handed. One or two even arrived back at the offices with bruising and other injuries. It was better to let him pay me directly as it was less complicated that way.

He didn't want the police or anyone else involved in our dealings. Already, it had taken several payoffs of substantial amounts to keep our collectors from calling the cops. Not that the cops would have done too much about it. Most were in Zuckerman's pocket in one way or another.

Zuckerman's reputation began to spread over the next year or so. Money bought power, and he now had plenty of both. He was never a man to mess with in any form. His booze empire was growing quicker than he could supply people, as such was the demand for illicit booze. As his empire grew, so did his payoff bill. More judges, more cops, and bent district attorneys had to be bought.

Apart from his distilleries that were spread out over the whole of the New York state, he was also shipping booze in from Canada. Convoys of trucks would drive into the heart of New York. Not one of them were ever checked or stopped by the cops.

To expand his empire further, Zuckerman approached me with the intention of chartering a ship from me. Bringing booze in from Europe would give him a greater profit.

After thinking about the proposal for a day or so, I had to tell him that I could not charter a ship to him from the *Nelson* line. This would have been too great a risk to the line itself. If the ship was stopped by the Coast Guard, it could have been impounded. There were many of our shareholders and directors who were strict churchgoers, and their belief in God would never allow them in all conscience to deal with such a well-known hood.

Zuckerman's theory was to bump the directors off, and put in place ones who would see it from a commercial point-of-view. I did point out to him an alternative to his outrageous idea, however. This was for me to buy a ship, and set up a small shipping company in my own right, the reason being for tax purposes. The paperwork could be worded as such that we were shipping engine parts or anything like that to the United States from any part of the world. It kept everybody happy that way. The last thing we needed was for the government men to start poking their noses around, but not all of them were corrupt.

Following the end of the war, there were always ships lying idle in some port or another along the length and breadth of the United States. Many had writs nailed to the mast. This usually meant the owners were in debt to someone or another. For me, being in the shipping industry made it easy to find out who owned the vessels in question. Within seven days of my talk with Zuckerman, I had found a ship that fit the bill perfectly.

The *Clemmy G.* was such as ship. At eight thousand tons, she was ideal for my new venture. Knowing that I was about to step outside of the law gave me a degree of excitement I had never felt before.

The *Clemmy G.* had been left idle for the past year or so, thus picking her up for very little money was easy. Crewing her was easier still. Sailors left over from the war were only too willing to ship out on a tramp steamer.

Promoting one of the clerks from the *Nelson* line to chief clerk of the new *P. B.* line saved me from doing the donkey work. The *P. B.* line was nicknamed the prohibition booze line by Zuckerman. The name soon cottoned on around the Gin bars and speakeasies of Manhattan.

Even before we had made our first voyage, orders were being taken for certain types of booze.

Brandy and champagne was the main order from the judges and politicians. Others wanted good Scotch whiskey. It didn't matter to me or Zuk, as he now liked to be called. It seemed that every big shot had a nickname. Zuk saw himself as a big shot in New York. Compared to many, he had made a name for himself, but it was made via the use of violence, and a ruthlessness that was seen by many, dished out upon an equal amount of people who crossed him.

In the lower basement of his club, the dark bare-walled room was his punishment room. Those who visited it never went back. Unless, of course, you were on a friendly guest list. I, along with several others, visited the room one night to watch him deal with some punk who had crossed him.

His reluctant guest was already there tied up on a meat hook. His shirt ripped open. One or two of Zuk's men had made him feel welcome by breaking his ankle bone for him with a baseball bat. Blood poured from the bridge of his nose, and was running down his chest. Low painful groans came from his lips. When his eyes opened, they were filled with fear. Knowing Zuk was nowhere near finished with him made his fear even worse. The man's crime – he was selling cheap homemade beer to his brother-in-law who owned a small bar in the Bronx area.

Zuk nodded his head towards two of his boys. They obliged by forcing the poor bastard into the hard wooden chair. A funnel and rubber hose were then pushed into his mouth. A gallon of beer was poured down the funnel and tube into his gut. Each time he spilt a drop, he was given a beating. Eventually, he pissed himself, partly from fear, and partly from the beer that had been forced into him. Zuk made him clean it up by licking it off the floor. His final lesson was to have each finger broken individually, and his right knee cap rearranged with the well-used baseball bat.

"Take our guest home, boys."

The two henchmen dragged the screaming, sobbing sap towards the side door. A trail of piss, blood, and puke followed in his wake.

"Stop!"

Everybody turned to look at Zuk.

"You haven't thanked me yet, Irish, have you?"

Luigi, the taller of the two henchmen, leaned forward, and slapped the back of the head of Irish. His thick Italian accent broke over the sobbing, trembling body of the man on the floor.

"Come back here, and thank me."

The menace in Zuk's voice was very real. I looked at the poor bastard on the floor. His face said it all.

The room was silent as the order was barked out. I had never felt such excitement in my life before. To witness such an act of pure violence had me shaking in my shoes. Irish moved slowly across the room, his battered body aching with pain. His broken, twisted right leg trailed behind him. Each movement must have been torture for him.

The alternative to this would have lead to more pain, or even his death. There was a coldness to Zuk, and yet like me, he was enjoying such power over another man. Irish dragged himself the ten feet across that cold, hard concrete floor through his own piss, blood, and vomit.

"Thank you, Mister Zuckerman."

The smile on Zuk's face was priceless.

I stepped forward. Placing my right foot on the broken left hand of the Irishman, I pressed down gently on the shattered bones. This brought forth the most horrendous scream I had ever heard.

"Have you no manners, man? Were you never taught to look at a man when you say sorry?"

I pressed down harder, bringing even more pain. His pathetic head lifted. Through the pain, he squealed his thanks to Zuk. I raised my foot, allowing him to move his hand back out of reach. If there was hate in this man's face, he did not show it. Pain can hide many things if it needs to.

The two boys dragged him out the door. A nod of approval from Zuk brought a smile to my face. The whole episode had aroused me so much that I could hardly wait to get back to the bar, and choose my companion for the night.

CHAPTER EIGHT

I lay there, watching the smoke drift up to the ceiling from my cigarette. I was feeling pretty contented with myself right now. I was happy with the life I was leading. Some would say it was a double life, though I didn't really care what people thought. I had, for some time, been sick and tired of the daily crap from the office. I could now do as I wanted. I had the protection, and to a degree, friendship of one of New York's top men.

A light breeze blew in, ruffling the drapes, and breaking my chain of thought. Lights from the street below coloured the smoke, turning it from green to yellow. The bathroom light was still on. Its faint glow cast shadows around the large bedroom.

The night was hot and sticky. Noise filtered in from the street below. It might have been close to two o'clock in the morning, but the streets below were still busy. Men were shouting at other men. Hookers were laughing loudly on the street corner, calling prospective tricks to come, and have some fun with them. Men called back to some of them by name. Deals were made between them. The cheap whorehouses would have another customer for a short time, and then it would all begin again.

Zuk controlled most of the hookers around this area. There was not a lot he didn't control. Along with his growing booze empire and hookers, he ran the protection racket. This meant that the businesses in the area paid him a fee on a weekly basis so that accidents to their person or family, or even their building's, did not catch fire or were injured.

Those that did not pay would have their premises visited upon, usually on a Friday night. The place would get ransacked. It was no surprise that those who did not subscribe to his protection scheme always got hit. Once the news got out that the places kept getting trashed, people moved on to other areas of the city to spend their hard-earned wages. It was easier to pay for the protection than to say no. The dives and speakeasies were forced to sell his booze at his prices. Failing to comply would result in a beating, or a sudden firebomb going through the windows or doors.

Zuk also ran the numbers racket. This, in his words, was a license to print money. His sellers would work all over the area. Bars, hairdressers, cafes, even the drug stores ran the numbers game for him. The system was that easy. People got to pick three numbers from a list going from one to one thousand. If the numbers matched three printed numbers, the person would win. This very rarely happened, though, as the numbers racket was fixed by the mob.

The black community who did not have a pot to piss in would take any chance to have a little bit of luck, now and then. The numbers game was a little bit of a hop for all. Now and then, a winner would be paraded in the papers. This gave more hope to the local Joe on the street. Usually, the winners were members of Zuk's mob. Many knew the racket was rigged, but when you don't have enough money to feed your family, any bit of hope is better than no hope at all.

Despite his ruthlessness, I did quite like Zuk. He had a charm about him when he needed to lay it on. To his friends, he was generous and protective. Just the mention of his name had others quacking in their shoes. He was nobody's mug, though.

In the back of my mind, I always kept in mind not to cross the line with him. I also couldn't work out why he had struck up a friendship with me. We came from two different worlds. I had been given a charmed life in many ways, never having seen what hunger or real cruelty to a child was. My education, even though I had hated it, had been paid for by my parents.

He had come up the hard way, born as the son of an Italian immigrant. His old man had worked twenty hours a day sometimes to put a meal on the table, working in sweat shops making suits for the likes of me and my dad. Zuk had not had it easy at all. As in all walks of life, the big took of the small. The only way of keeping what you had was to fight for it, and fight hard. His schooling was from the street, not the books I had read. Betting slips as a bookies runner were his math's teacher.

I could see why he wanted the wealth he had now, and no one was going to take it from him that easily. He had already proven that point, time and time again. How many he had killed, I did not know, but it had to run into the tens, if not dozens, of people who had tried to get in his way or take over his turf.

CHAPTER NINE

Rochelle had fallen asleep. Her naked body was still moist with sweat. Her dark brown hair was sticking to her forehead as she slept next to me. I enjoyed her company. She was nothing like the girls on the street below. She had class, and was well-educated. She also had that ability to make men turn their heads, and stare when she walked into a room. Her deep blue eyes sparkled like diamonds when she smiled or laughed.

In the next room, the head of the bed bounced off of the wall noisily. I had to smile. Nancy was entertaining again. I had spent several nights with her over the past few months. Nancy liked it rough and hard.

That was not my bag, but Judge John Stevens obviously liked her style. The loud groans of delight and pain bounced off of the walls as she called him every son-of-a-bitch there was.

Rochelle was different. She was gentle and caring, always happy to please her man. She took time to prepare for a date. Her trim figure would grace any room she walked into, and she knew it. She had turned the heads of many men, and wives had slapped husbands for openly staring and smiling at her when she walked into the bar below. Her dress sense was elegant, and her tanned body had a slight smell of expensive perfume.

I felt her body tighten as my hand ran down the inside of her thigh.

Her right hand moved from under her head to cover mine as she slowly moved it up to her breast. Rolling towards me, her eyes opened wide, and a seductive smile spread across her lips. I wanted her, then and there.

She wrapped her arms around my neck, and pulled me towards her. Her soft lips met mine, and we gently kissed. My tongue found hers as our passion grew. Pulling her tightly to me, our kisses grew harder, and gentle moans of pleasure echoed round the room. I liked kissing her, and she was passionate with her kisses.

Rochelle broke our kiss, and moved her now swollen lips to my neck, kissing and licking, as her hands began to stroke my body. I was now tingling with mounting pleasure. Her firm breasts pushed against my chest. Kissing her neck, I trailed my hand down her chest, my fingers lightly brushing her nipples. I felt them harden under my touch.

A low groan from deep within her throat made me smile inwardly. My right hand continued its journey down her soft body, and as I reached her thighs, she sighed with pleasure. Her legs parted, allowing me to stroke her womanhood. Moans of pleasure escaped her lips, and she lifted her body slightly to push against my hand.

Rochelle ran her hand down my body, and her fingers closed around my hard cock, making me catch my breath as she caressed me. Taking me by surprise, she took charge, and pushed me back against the bed. Her lust filled eyes held mine as she lowered her head, and began to softly kiss, and lick my neck and chest. My whole body is on fire with passion for her.

Trailing her tongue down my belly, I could feel her hot breath on my now throbbing cock. She rolled her tongue around the tip, and I gasped. The pleasure was immense. Her lips closed around me, and she gently sucked me in. Up and down, her mouth worked me. My pleasure mounted, and I was ready to explode. She released me, and started to work her way back up my quivering body.

Sliding her body against mine, she took my hands in hers, and forced them above my head. Moving her body expertly, she slid herself onto my hard cock, and the sound of pleasure escaped our lips. For several seconds, she remained still. Unspoken words passed between us as she slowly started to move her hips.

My hands moved to cup her breasts, and I gently pulled on her hard nipples, Rochelle threw her head back as she started to move faster. Her eyes never left mine. Taking my hands from her breasts, and forcing them back onto the pillows, she ground down on me, harder and faster. Our groans of pleasure became louder, breaths harder. Her thighs gripped me tighter, and I felt every muscle in my body tighten, ready to explode. With her head thrown back, her excitement grew. My body thrust upwards to meet hers. Wild rampant passion took over as we both cried out, and exploded together.

With a final gasp, her sweat soaked body fell forward onto mine. She held on tightly to me as every muscle in our bodies began to relax. For the next few minutes, we lay in each other's arms, breathing heavily. The one thing I liked about Rochelle was the fact that she didn't have to say much after we had sex.

I had never gone in for all the complicated crap of *I love you*. It was what it was – steamy sex. By morning, she would leave, and so would I, until I wanted her again. Zuk always picked up the tab for his good customers.

I hoped he paid her well for her services. She was not the sort of girl you would take home to meet your family, but right then and there, she was all I needed and wanted. I liked having her around me. She had the knack of changing any atmosphere in any room. I also found her very easy to talk to. I'd always been a shy person. Somehow, she was able to see through this, and get me to open up.

CHAPTER TEN

For some years now, my love affair with the sea had been over. There was no great pleasure in being thrown about from arsehole to breakfast time anymore. Back when I had sailed with Grandfather, it had been a great adventure for me in feeling the spray of the waves batter my face. The spray would make a thousand rainbows before my eyes. To me, they were magical times.

However, the draw of me breaking the law in going personally to buy the contraband for Zuckerman was too much of a lure for me. It was on his express wishes that I went. You didn't argue with the man when his wishes were voiced. Although, he made it sound like you were doing him a favour, when what he really meant was, you are doing things, regardless of what you want to do.

He chartered the ship as any normal company would do. As far as the customs men and the dock workers were concerned, we would be shipping machine parts back to the United States. Zuk financed the deal. Twenty grand in used notes was packed into a strong box, and loaded aboard the *Clemmy G.* The chartering of the ship was dealt with in the usual way. Strictly cash. This was handed to me by Zuk on the 18th of October, 1922.

The *Clemmy G.* sailed on that night's tide from Lower Manhattan.

The ship itself was nothing much to look at. She looked like any other tramp steamer going about her business. This was to our advantage. The less conspicuous she was, the better.

Her rust-streaked hull slipped from her moorings, steaming slowly down the Hudson towards the open sea. Zuk had come down the quay side to watch us go. A small bevy of girls on his arm were giggling loudly as we left. Even for him, twenty grand was a big outlay. I guess he wanted to be sure that to the point of sailing, it was his money. As soon as we let go of the last stern line, it was mine. If things turned to rat shit, then I would owe him twenty big ones.

With this in mind, I had also ordered two other boxes to be loaded aboard, and put down below in my cabin. Both boxes had been filled with the new Thompson machine guns. Not that I expected any trouble on the voyage out. It was the homeward voyage that would bring any unwelcome visitors to us.

Zuk might be a big shot in the New York state, but there were always others willing enough to make a name for themselves by stealing his booze. *Better to be safe, than sorry,* was the motto I always used.

Rain battered the bridge windows, driven by an increasing south westerly gale. This was going to be no picnic in the park. We left the mouth of the river, heading east. After an hour, we were in the open sea. The sea was running on our beam, and the ship rolled and pitched in the heavy sea.

I stayed on the bridge for a while, but the very sight of the waves breaking over our beam made me feel like crap. It was hard to tell where the sea and the skyline joined. Already, my stomach wanted to empty its contents onto the deck. I was not going to give anyone on deck the satisfaction of seeing me puke my guts up. It wasn't long before I went below to my cabin.

I had always been the same. For the first twenty-four hours at sea, I was as sick as a dog. Right now, all I wanted to do was to die. Each pitch of the ship as she hit a wave had me retching. It was the worst feeling in the world.

Great-Uncle William, as he was always known, took me to one side many years ago. He told me the cure for sea sickness was very hot, very sweet coffee. Like a fool, I rushed to the galley to pour some down my throat. Within minutes, I was puking my guts up over the port rail.

Great-Uncle William stood on the bridge, chuckling at me. He must have known what was in my mind right at that moment. His classical line of, *'You should not have signed on if you cannot take a joke, boy,'* rolled off of his tongue.

I knew I would be fine in a day or so. I always had been, but for now, I would sip cold water, splash my face off, and sleep as much as I could. I found there was no point in fighting sea sickness. It just made it worse.

I didn't always have the luxury of being able to stay in my bunk. Back in my academy days, the captain would have us all on deck. For those of us who looked like crap, it was the mast head for us. That was his cure. All it ever seemed to do was cover the deck, and sometimes the boys below, in our dinners. You did not have to hear the cursing from those on the deck below when you were up there. The shaking fists told us all we needed to know. But when you're dying, stuck one hundred and forty feet above a swaying deck in bad weather, you don't really care what is happening below you.

It was just as case of getting through those couple of days that were the problem. My boot slammed hard on the back of the door when the steward announced that food was being served. He did not come back after that. I would have shot him with pleasure if he had.

Thank God, we would only be at sea for four days. Canada had no prohibition. Moving the booze by sea was a lot easier than by using a convoy of trucks, and cheaper, too.

Another wave hit our starboard side, rocking us violently. The bucket I had by the side of my bed slid across the deck plates. To hell with it! The smart arse crewman who came knocking on my door could clean it up. After all, why should I clean it up? I owned the God damn ship.

The smell of coffee coming from the mess room soon had me reaching for my trusted bucket. God damn stupid idea at playing sailors! It was another of Great-Uncle William's pearls of wisdom.

I turned on my left side, and tried to sleep. After twenty-four hours, I managed to crawl out, and up onto the deck. The fresh air made me feel better. The stench of my cabin was becoming too much for me. Stale sweat and puke don't do your insides any favours.

Salt water splashed over my face. It felt so good to me. I stood there on deck for the next hour, managing to smoke a cigarette without heaving.

A strong smell of coffee wafted up from the ship's galley through the open hatchway. Even that smelt good. I was now getting my sea legs. More sea water sprayed over me. The sea was dark green with the tops of the waves whipped away in a haze of white spray. A thousand rainbows formed across the spray, making me smile, and remember Grandfather again.

The strong south westerly gale battered us for the rest of the day. We had made our turn north some hours ago. The sea was now running off of our starboard quarter. A following sea would push us faster, and not as violently, as a head sea would do.

By midnight, the wind began to moderate a little. The sea had lost some of its ferocity. Instead of huge mountainous waves, the sea was now a long, lazy swell. After another cigarette, I went towards the galley in search of the coffee wafting in my direction. The fatigue I always felt when I was feeling crappy was now gone, replaced by hunger and thirst.

Apart from the small light from the binnacle compass in the centre of the bridge, we were in total darkness. Two lookouts were posted in each corner of the bridge. This was a standard set up. The officer of the watch was checking his chart in the small room just aft of the bridge, and the helmsman was concentrating on his course.

At the aft end of the bridge, port side, was a small bench-type seat.

Next to that, was the countertop. I perched myself on the seat, and poured myself a cup of coffee, and lit another cigarette. The bridge lit up for a second or two as my light broke the darkness. None of the men turned to look at me. They had a job to do, thus I let them get on with it.

***

Stu Burke was the third mate on watch. He emerged from the chart room, and checked the ship's head.

"Five degrees port, if you please."

The helmsman repeated the order. This was normal practice on any ship. It ensured that the officer and the helmsman were on the same song sheet. The large ships wheel turned until the indicator showed five degrees of port wheel on.

"Midships."

Again, the order was repeated. The wheel was turned back until the indicator showed the rudder was amidships,

"Steady, as you go."

***

Stu was a very quiet man by nature. Apart from answering yes or no to me, the next hour or so passed quietly. This did not bother me in the least. I was not on a pleasure cruise. I sipped my coffee, and smoked another two or three cigarettes. The bridge now had a slight haze of smoke filling it.

Stu was a non-smoker. The door to the portside was opened, and smoke streamed out into the night air.

The sky was clearing rapidly now. We would have freezing weather by morning. Already, a shiver rippled though me from the sudden drop in temperature.

Time for bed.

CHAPTER ELEVEN

Stu had been picked for his navigational skills. He was also one of Zuk's hard men.

It seemed to be the same all over the city. If you were a sailor, and couldn't get a berth on a ship while being able to look after yourself, you worked for men like Zuk. The pay was good. The benefits were better, since you could use the street hookers whenever you needed them with as much booze as you could drink. To many sailors, this was their idea of heaven.

I knew very little else about the man. In truth, I was not that interested, either. I had seen him in action for Zuk. His favoured weapon was a set of brass knuckle dusters with spikes on the knuckle part of them. Considering his line of work, he was remarkably unscarred, unlike some of his victims. Most would end up with their faces ripped open, and a few broken ribs. If his sailing skills matched his fighting power, I would have no complaints.

The two o'clock weariness drifted over me. As the watch-keeping changed, I slipped below to my cabin. Someone had cleaned the mess up from the deck. The bucket I had been using was clean, and placed by the side of my bunk. A fresh jug of water also stood on the small table next to my bunk. I was happy I wasn't the one who had to clean the mess up.

The linen sheets were cool on my body as I lay down. The heat of the engine room filtered up through the deck plates, making the room sticky. I was not going to open a port hole, however. The swell from the sea would have swamped my cabin in seconds.

By eight in the morning, I was sitting in the officer's mess room with a steaming cup of coffee. The smell of bacon drifted through from the galley. I could have eaten half a side of it by myself right now.

There is not a lot a man can do on a ship when he is a passenger. I spent the morning walking around the aft deck. The East coast of the United States was on the horizon. The sea had calmed to almost a mill pond overnight.

The cold of the day soon sent me below decks. Ice had begun forming on the rigging. If it got too much, then the crew would be sent on deck with hammers and shovels to clear it. Too much ice in a ship's rigging can make her top heavy. If a sea began running with a lot of ice topside, she would turn turtle and sink. In these waters, you would be dead in a matter of minutes.

In my grandfather's time, it was called the *creeping sleep*, in as much that the cold sent you to sleep. One, a man never woke up from. The modern name for it was hypothermia. The body hurried to protect the internal organs by sending blood to the skin. Your internal organs went to sleep on you. Many of the people on the Titanic died from the cold, and not drowning. Creeping sleep/hypothermia – it was all the same. You're pretty screwed if you were to go into these waters.

***

I sat in my cabin smoking yet another cigarette. The door to the companion way was wedged open to allow some of the smoke out. Another twenty-four hours should see us in Halifax.

I had already worked out in my own mind what would happen when we landed there. Mat Valente would meet me on pier ten. The storage warehouse should be in view from the landing pier. There was no question of me handing any money over until I had seen the goods.

Two of Zuk's men would come with me to ensure the deal went ok. Twenty grand is a lot of money to hand over to a stranger in a strange port outside of the United States. Although Zuk was happy with the deal, and had some good things to say about Valente, I did not know him. Nor had I ever heard of him.

Thinking about the money, my foot instinctively felt for the strong box bolted to the deck. It was still there. Not that it had many places to go. All hands on the ship would know Zuk would have them chopped into fish food if a single cent went missing. The brown envelope I had been carrying in my coat pocket was still there. It had become a habit, since I put it there to keep checking. This would pay any customs men off who needed to turn a blind eye to what was happening. Since I had known Zuk, it amazed me how many officials had eyesight problems when a wad of cash was put into their grubby claws.

The Colt revolver I had tucked under my pillow would ensure my own safety if things went wrong. I had not fired a weapon since my academy days. Back then, I was pretty good at shooting. Although, the targets I was shooting at were not shooting back at me. It bothered me a bit, in case I could not pull the trigger if I was in a position where I had to. All I could keep telling myself was, *It's you, or the sap shooting at you.* With luck, it would not come to that, but it's better to plan ahead, rather than get shot.

The Colt slipped easily into my hand. Out of sheer boredom, I stripped it down, and cleaned all of its working parts. The very last thing I needed was for it not to fire at the last second.

I had a knot in the pit of my guts that I hadn't had for some time now. It was not fear, but rather excitement. I'd been bored sitting in a stuffy office for several years. Dealing with the old guys on the board of directors had not been my idea of fun.

Most of them had been living in the past. All wanted to have a say in where the company went, and how it should be run. After the death of my parents, I really couldn't have given a rat's behind as to what happened to the company. All I wanted to do was have some excitement in my life. All the money I'd had couldn't buy it.

Part of the thrill, right now, was knowing that I was going against everything my dad had taught me. His sense of honour and helping others along the way had been drummed into me. I went along with his thinking, never really believing in it at all.

It was just another way of avoiding being sent on crap sites, and working with men who worked liked dogs for a pittance. All of them thought they were going to be rich some day. The truth was, they would have to be lucky. You did not get your luck from the Saturday night whores, or the cheap Gin joints they always managed to find in whatever town or city they were in at the time.

CHAPTER TWELVE

Halifax, Nova Scotia was not what I had expected it to be. I had grown up being used to living in New York. To me, this was more like a small town than a major shipping port. From here, ships could travel up to the Great Lakes, carrying grain from the inland ports to countries all over the world. This gave me an idea that perhaps we could ship grain back to the United States, and distil that into booze. I would run it by Zuk when we got back from this trip.

By the time, we were tied up alongside the jetty head, the wind had blown up into another storm. Small ships bobbed about in the choppy waters. Big tractor tires were scattered along the jetty to stop us from being holed from the banging alongside the steel and timber framework of the jetty.

On the near horizon, rain was pouring in from the north. The tops of the hills were already covered in snow. It wouldn't be long before this came down to the lower levels. The rivers and lakes would then ice up for the winter.

I stood on the bridge of the *Clemmy G.*, watching and waiting for some kind of action from the shoreline. I was keen to get on with the business I was here for. The palm of my hand rubbed gently over the grip of the Colt pistol in my coat pocket.

Rain began pounding down on top of the bridge, making it almost impossible to hear what was going on. On the main deck, the men began running for cover as soon as the last mooring line was secure. I could just about see the big warehouse with the number ten sign on it. But as each minute passed, the rain grew heavier and heavier.

Out in the river, a ship's horn sounded a warning to other vessels. Our own ship's whistle blew. This would give the oncoming ship a navigation point to work from, and a clear warning that we were in earshot of her warning. She was going out to sea. Her whistle sounded again further out on the river mouth. Several other ships inward bound gave their warning back to her.

A care horn blew from the shore side. It was just about visible through the rain. The small black Ford drew up to the end of the jetty. I could see the four occupants watching us. The two men in the front were the bruisers. It was the man sitting just behind the driver who had the power. Smoke from his big cigar wafted out of the rear window. He sat there, calmly watching the ship as the men ran for cover.

The other three looked about, watching every movement that went on around the dockside. The boss in the back of the car tapped the driver on the back of the head. The car slipped forward another twenty feet or so before coming to a full stop. I had no reason to mistrust these guys, but when you have twenty grand on you, you have to be a little guarded. It would have been lunacy just to jump in the car right now.

They would be sitting in the car for a while yet, anyway. The inevitable customs men turned up. There should be no problem at this end, for the ship was in ballast. The skipper and his men would deal with them.

I was sitting below in the officer's mess, downing yet another cup of coffee. The door swung open. Two men walked in, uniformed and armed. After identifying themselves as Canadian customs men, they began a search of the mess room. The Canadians were almost obsessive about recreational drugs being brought into the country. In the United States, the use of drugs was on the increase. For those that sold them, the profits were high, and the users plentiful. I hated drugs over the past year or so, for I had seen what they could do to people.

For the mob, they were easy to ship, and could be hidden in smaller places on just about anything. In many ways, I was in support of the customs men checking everything.

I verified my identity with them, and told them who I was. I was left alone so that they could carry on with their rummage of the ship. It was another hour before the customs men had finished with us.

The money I had in my cabin had now been placed in a space behind the bulkhead in my cabin. Certain adaptations to the ship had been made, the hole behind the bulkhead being one of them. The other major one was a false bottom in the hold. This is where the contraband booze would be stored on the voyage back. There would also be machine parts.

There was profit in that for me as the owner, but it was also my problem to land the booze ashore for Zuk. Up until that point, the shipment was mine. Not just the twenty grand's worth I had bought, but also the street value. That would be in the region of sixty or seventy grand's worth in the bars and speakeasies.

There would be more than that if the shipment was taken by the G. men. Only then, it would be my knee caps being turned around to face the other way. The initial outlay of making the false bottom was well worth it to me.

Several ships had been seized by the G. men in the last month. The amount that slipped through the net still outweighed those being caught. One ship, earlier this year, had decided to try and fight it out with the coast guards. That was a bad mistake. The Coast Guard had a four inch deck gun. The contraband ship only had light weapons aboard her. There was only going to be one winner. A four inch shell bouncing off of your foredeck soon makes you have to re-think the situation.

I always thought it was better to prepare yourself as best you can to avoid the situation in the first place. Making hiding places on the *Clemmy G.* was my preparation for it.

Out on deck, the clanging sound of the large gangway banging onto the dockside meant I could now go ashore. I had a tingle of excitement in my gut as I pulled the collar up on my coat to ward against the cold wind. The Colt in my pocket tapped my thigh as another sign of reassurance.

The windows of the Ford had steamed up. The driver rolled his window down. Smoke from several cigarettes blew away on the strong wind.

As I stepped onto the dockside, the rear driver door opened. Mat Valente stepped out, his hat and coat drawn well up over his neck and head, protecting him from the storm. Stiffness from sitting for so long in the car made him stoop slightly until he'd walked it off. Standing about five-feet-nine inches tall, he had the walk of a boss, and the slight arrogance that comes with authority.

Ten yards away from me, his hand slipped out of his pockets. My eyes searched both of his hands for any sign of a weapon. I would never be sure I would have gotten to my gun in time if he had drawn a gun on me, but at least I had some confidence in knowing I would have tried.

"Robbie, you rouge, son-of-a-bitch!"

I had not heard anyone call me Robbie for years now. I stopped in my tracks, looking hard at the man now coming towards me. Lifting his head slightly higher, I could now make out the scar on his left cheek. A shock of blond hair was sticking out from below his hat.

A broad smile spread across my face. I had not seen Mat Valente since the day I had been asked to leave the academy. I raised my right hand above my head to let those on the ship know that I was ok. The three men on board the *Clemmy G.*, hiding behind the lifeboats, stood up, the Tommy guns now pressed against their sides.

Mat Valente raised his hand. I could not see what the men in the car were doing. In my own hindsight, I had no doubt that the weapons they were carrying would now be safely pointed away from me. It was the way it was. When you deal with hoods, it paid to be paranoid. When you're dealing with Zuckerman's money, it paid to be careful as well.

We stood there for a few seconds, smiling at each other. I had never been one for doing the big hug thing. We settled for a long warm handshake, and a playful punch on the shoulder.

Mat had always been one of the good guys at the academy, or so they thought. The thing about him was, he never got caught out by the junior officers. He always managed to keep his head down, and get on with his work. Then he would disappear for a few hours or so. The matron made a good few bucks out of him during his time at the academy. He was also a good fixer for the boys there. If you wanted it, he could get it. Maybe he had a deal going with the officers to let him be.

His only weakness was sailing. Each time he got on board a ship, he would be heaving his guts up even before we set sail. I took the rap for him puking up from the mast head on more than one occasion.

He was four years older than me, and in his final year, when I left. Apart from his poor seamanship, he excelled at everything else he did. In my early days at the academy, he had tried to straighten me out a little. He failed on that one, though. I cannot say we were the best of buddies, but I grew to like him during the time I was there.

CHAPTER THIRTEEN

The large warehouse at the end of the jetty was a hive of activity. Crates, stacked six high, were being moved from one part to the other. I did notice many of the crates marked machine parts. I had to smile. There was a hell of a lot of machinery going into the United States.

Mat guided me to his small office. It was nothing like I had expected.

My own set of offices back in New York were plush and efficient. Here, a simple desk stood in one corner of the room, cutting the room off. Two black telephones sat on the desk, ringing loudly, and constantly. A slender black-haired girl was trying her best to answer both of them without much luck. A few strands of her hair hung down over her forehead every few seconds as she attempted to brush it away. It would fall back almost at once.

A dozen sheets of paper had been scattered over the desk. She was hurriedly trying to scribble on one particular sheet, whilst holding the phone in her other hand. A narrow harassed smile appeared on her lips as we entered the office.

The smell of a thousand cigarettes hung in the air. The once white walls were now a sticky brown colour. The phones on the desk began to ring once more. The harassed office girl sighed deeply before answering. A well-rehearsed and well-used tone of voice was given to the voice on the other end of the line. No sooner had she finished one call, when she had to go through it all over again on the other line.

"Business is good for you then, Mat?"

"Well, I can happily say, Robbie, that your prohibition was the best thing to happen to us Canadians." A broad smile was now wide across his face.

Leaning over the desk, and opening the drawer, Mat pulled a bottle of Scotch up onto the desk top. "A drink, Robbie?"

I would have loved a decent drink, but not now. I wanted to be clear while we worked on the deal. "Just coffee for now, Mat. Maybe later, when we've talked."

For the next thirty minutes or so, we chatted about old times, and laughed at our exploits at the academy. His family had been in the iron and coal mining industry. However, like me, he had become bored with the mundane crap of office life. Import and export was his own little pigeon.

He was far removed from the devout Christian values he had been brought up in. That's the way he wanted it to remain. Standing up from his well-used leather chair, I got the fifty cents tour of his operation. It was also evident that he did not want the hired hands to know too much of his business. His voice almost dropped to a whisper whenever someone was close to us.

The warehouse was much bigger than I had first expected. There were hundreds and hundreds of barrels. Some were marked whiskey, others gin, and brandy. Export only was stamped on them.

The front left side of the warehouse was marked with a red tractor part on it. *S. S. Clemmy G.* was chalk written across the top of each crate. Even though there had to be thousands of crates with the same markings, it still did not fill the part of the warehouse it was stored in.

The middle of the warehouse was stacked with even more crates. All were to be shipped to Chicago. There was only one man who had the outlet for this amount of booze – Al Capone. He was one of the most feared crime bosses in the United States. Even Zuk blinked when the man's name was mentioned. I knew better than to start asking questions.

"We can start loading for you in the morning, Robbie. We have a few truck loads to get out tonight."

Again, I was not going to ask any questions. The less I knew, the better.

"That is, once we have concluded our business."

Mat held his right hand out in front of him, his thumb and forefinger rubbing together. It was the international signal for money. I nodded my head towards the *Clemmy G*.

Rain hammered down onto the warehouse roof, making it almost impossible to speak or be heard. We pulled our coat collars up high around our necks, and ran towards the ship.

Back on board the *Clemmy G.*, and in the comfort of my cabin, I paid Mat the twenty thousand bucks, the price that had been agreed on. With the profits of this cargo alone, we should be able to double the amount next time.

Mat did not bother counting the money. There was no real need to. His accountant would do that for him. If it was short, then next time, he would make sure it was counted. The bottle of Scotch he had in his pocket was now put on the table.

"A drink, Robbie, to celebrate what could be the beginning of a good business for us all."

I was not going to turn it down now. We sat there, drinking and reminiscing about our times at the academy for another hour or so. It was dark by the time we both left the ship.

CHAPTER FOURTEEN

I spent the evening and night at Mat's home. It was so much more comfortable than staying aboard the *Clemmy G*. The ship's crew would be shore bound. That meant booze fights and whores. After they'd had their fill of all three, they would fall back aboard the ship. My cabin was just aft of the gangway. The noise they would make would be enough to wake the dead.

Mat's house was set back into the woodlands of Halifax, purposefully built to his design for comfort and privacy, and was very handy for his workplace. It was about a thirty minute drive away. I think what he had done was set a construction crew down in the middle of the forest, and said, *'Build here. One road in, and the same road out!'*

Mat had moved out of the family home a year ago. This was his retreat. This place was a birthday present from his parents.

I'd hoped to see them again after so many years. I'd liked them when I was back at the academy. His mother always made a point of talking to me, and offering me words of encouragement in my first year. However, it was the time of year in which they took their own vacation, and were cruising on the family boat. They, like my parents, would sail down to the Caribbean for a couple of months.

Looking around his home, it made me think it was time for me to move from the big family home outside New York. I could find a place in the city more suited to me.

Dinner was spent in the company of two local girls. Mat had never married. Like me, he enjoyed playing the field a bit. The girls were not the brightest pair of bulbs in the box. Both were very good-looking, however. They were only too willing to jump into the sack with either of us.

CHAPTER FIFTEEN

The loading of our cargo took Mat's men three days. The secret hold had to be opened up. This had been built to blend in with the rest of the ship. The shape of the ship had been followed by the shipyard. For all intents and purposes, the hold ceiling looked perfectly normal. The space below would be filled to the brim with contraband booze. Unless the customs men ripped the ship apart from stem to stern, they would miss this compartment. Once the planks had been put back, black grease and paint were rubbed over the bolt holes to disguise them. A legitimate cargo of machine parts and other general cargo were loaded as normal on top.

The *Clemmy G.* had not been the only ship carrying bootleg booze to the United States. Two other ships had been at anchor for two days. The *Santiago* was loading up with one hundred thousand dollars worth of booze for the Chicago mob. She had no need for false bottoms or added security. Her owner had enough power and money to make sure she would never be stopped.

Al Capone was the biggest of the mob bosses. Though, not many people hadn't heard of him. Ruthless beyond words would have been a compliment to the man. No one messed with that guy's business. Some had tried, and many had died. He ruled with a fist of iron. His close lieutenants were equally brutal and loyal to him. His fortune had increased from prohibition. His payoff bills to cops, judges, and politicians ran into the hundreds of thousands of dollars. People dealt with his outfit, or died. It was as simple as that.

Capone had been born in Brooklyn, New York. His notoriety was known in the United States from an early age. From what I could gather, he was happy to trade on that fact to instil fear into others. That was until he could put the fear of God into others under his own name.

Some said his income was over a million dollars a year. How much of that is true, I do not know. He was not a man who liked to be kept waiting. Thus, having one of his ships waiting at anchor was costing him money. He still had strong connections in New York with bent cops and gangs only too willing to bump someone off for a few bucks. That itself was encouragement for us to get the hell out of there as soon as possible.

It was fair to say that Zuk had some heavy connections in the city, but Capone was in another league. Like Capone, Zuk had been born in New York, and had grown up in the gangland areas. Rumour had it, he had killed his first man at the age of twelve. I had no reason to disbelieve that rumour. He was certainly ruthless and dangerous.

Another rumour had it that Capone and Zuk had crossed swords at an early age. Both had been in opposing gangs. Turf wars were not just about land or keeping others out of one area or another. It came down to power. Power to run that piece of turf. Power to blackmail, and power to make money from corruption.

This put money in the pockets of the gangs. Families could be fed. The foot soldier was only too willing to risk the electric chair for this. Once you were in the gangs, you never left. Several had tried, and some had turned stool pigeon. The bosses would have a contract taken out on these individuals. Some would end up in the East River, while others simply disappeared. That was a strong deterrent to others.

The gang mentality was to stab or shoot first before the other sap does it to you. Prohibition had been a good friend to those that had the leadership mentality in gangs. From little acorns grew strong trees.

The step up from petty robbery and protection was easy to make. Once you had a district living in fear of you, you could then make them do whatever you wanted to do. The profits from bootlegging only enhanced the fear. The bribes paid to the local cops would also see any informants dealt with quickly.

CHAPTER SIXTEEN

The Colt I had in my pocket had been given as a gift to me by Zuk. In his words, it had done its job well many times over. I had wondered, at first, how many people it had killed. When he was making his mark in New York, he had killed women and children to make his point to unwilling victims.

To me, it was a tool of the work I was now immersed in. I still got a thrill from it each time I held it. Although, I had no need to use it yet. Zuk's boys looked out for me, thus far. It was just another perk of being associated with him, I guess.

The knock on my cabin door halted my thinking. One of Zuk's men stood in the doorway.

"Skipper wants you on the bridge, pal."

Hellerman had not been brought on this trip for his sparkling conversation. Or his rapid mind. He had been brought up like many men in the back shit streets of the Bronx area of New York. He had found out at an early age that he could fight. He fought his first pro fight at thirteen. That's where he got his nose rearranged for him. He still went on to win the fight.

For the next ten years, he fought all comers. At one point, he was looked at as a serious contender in the middle-weight division before the mob took over his management. That was his downfall. Fights he should have won were lost fights, and those he should have lost were won. He became a journeyman in the world of boxing, from the lights of New York to back street garages.

When the fights began drying up, he became a bouncer in one of the private clubs in the area. Zuk took him on as a debt collector. His loyalty to Zuk was unquestionable now. I had seen his handy work. His brain might not be in gear completely, but his hand speed and punching power were still there.

A slight nod of my head acknowledged him. Slipping on my sea boots and overcoat, I climbed the stairs from the lower deck. I bounced out of the bulkhead as another wave hit us across the ship's beam. My shoulder slammed hard against the metal plates. I cursed loudly at the weather and the sea. Brains stood there, feet firmly planted on the deck, smirking at me.

I stood my ground until the ship came back to a more even keel. Brains walked ahead of me, his arms pushing against the bulkheads as he made his way towards the aft, away from me.

Trying to climb stairs in seas like this was as bad as running through wet sand. I had done some of that back in my academy days. I hated it then, almost as much as I hated it now.

I took the port side door onto the bridge to avoid getting a soaking for my troubles as well as more bruises to my body. The navigation chart of the Atlantic slipped across the chart table as the wind rushed across the bridge. This brought a scowl from the skipper.

Nuts to you, pal, I thought.

"You wanted to see me, Skipper?"

"Not really, Mister Birket."

Sarcastic bastard! I stood there looking at him, hoping that the irritation showing upon my face would be clear to him.

"We have a United States Coast Guard ship on our port bow. I thought you should know, seeing as you're the owner of this vessel, and considering the cargo we have aboard."

I was already looking through the binoculars as he spoke to me.

"How far off shore are we, Skipper?"

"Four miles."

I let out a slight sigh of relief. There was an ongoing row about when a Coast Guard ship could board another vessel. Many claimed that three miles out was, and is classed, as international waters, therefore the Coast Guard had no right to board us.

"Then stay on your course, Skipper. We are in international waters. Screw them."

The look of contempt I received from him said it all. *You might be the owner, but I am the skipper, and I decided what to do.*

The signal lamp flashed from the Coast Guard.

CLEMMY G., WHAT IS YOUR DESTINATION?

"That's the third time they have asked us, Mister Birket. If we tell them, New York, they might follow us until we get into U. S. waters, and then board us. If we tell them another destination, they might do some checking with the Canadian people."

"This could give us a problem."

It had always been my belief to not try to bluff with a stacked hand. It would cause less crap in the long run.

"Give them our destination, Skipper, and let's see what happens."

A few seconds later, our own signal lamp fired up.

COAST GUARD CUTTER. INWARD BOUND FOR NEW YORK. CARGO, MACHINE PARTS.

It was a case of, *'Let's wait, and see what they would do.'* There was no real reason to order us into U. S. waters. A single flash from the Coast Guard was acknowledgment to our signal.

For the next twelve hours, the sons-of-bitches stayed with us. They were one mile ahead of us, at the most. All we could do was stay on our course. The storm blew even harder. Huge waves now crashed over us. Below decks, the sound of crashing packing cases in the hold echoed around the bridge.

Several of the hands were sent below to lash them down, and report how badly the cargo had shifted. We could now use this situation to our advantage.

"Skipper, signal the Coast Guard. Tell them we are heaving to due to our cargo shifting. Let's see if they want to stay with us."

"Port twenty."

There was no reply to my suggestion. The order had been given by the skipper. Slowly, the ship's head turned into the heavy sea. Once we'd turned around so that our stern was to the sea, she settled in the eater.

Two rings on the ship's telegraph ordered the engines to be reduced to dead slow ahead. She would now ride the waves instead of battling through them. This would allow the men below enough time to lash the cargo down. I carried on, looking at the Coast Guard ship. Her signal lamp fired up.

CLEMMY G., DO YOU NEED ASSISTANCE?

Our reply: *No, thank you. Situation under control.*
Two minutes later, another flash of their signal lamp was received.

GOD SPEED, CLEMMY G.!

The Coast Guard steamed away, pitching and rolling on her beam ends. I allowed a small smile to spread across my face.

The *Clemmy G.* was now riding the waves well. The trick now was to get her to ride the waves, and not punch through them. Some of the men were now stripping back the sheets over the number one hold in readiness to go below. Once the hatch boards had been stowed safely, I would go, and inspect the damage myself.

Mister Simmonds, the second mate, was already wearing his bad weather gear, waiting for the right time to go out on deck. Two of the men on the open deck had begun bringing in ropes from the forecastle head. A small cargo net was dropped several feet into the hold. I slipped below decks to pull on my own wet weather gear. The ship had steadied enough now, and was pitching along with the waves. I left my exit from the bridge until the rope ladder had been made fast to the ship's side.

The wind must have been gusting at eighty miles-per-hour. Freezing spray battered my face as I clung on for grim shit to the grab rails. Twice, I fell flat on my arse while walking along the main deck. I could almost hear the laughter coming from the bridge.

The hard part came as I tried to climb down into the hold. The rope ladder swayed back and forth. At one point, I closed my eyes, and waited for my body to be smashed against the hull of the ship. It did not happen. Without thinking, I dropped the last five feet from the ladder to the ceiling of the hold below me. I did not give a rat's arse if anyone had been below me. I would sooner have landed on top of someone else than have my face smashed in.

The pitch of the ship rolled me back ten feet before I could grab a hold of a packing case on the port side of the hold. I let out another stream of obscenities as I came to rest against another packing case. The shoulder I'd hit below decks slammed hard into the corner of the case. If anyone had seen me, they did not make any comment. Maybe it would bring a lot of laughter at the next meal time.

The men had worked quickly in setting up lights. I wanted to see how much damage had been done to the precious cargo. It was several hours before enough space was cleared to lift some of the boards covering the booze. Everything else seemed ok. No one had to be a brain surgeon to work out that we had some damage done to our cargo of booze. The strong smell of Scotch wafted through the holdout. We would have to spray some disinfectant about to cover the smell when we arrived in New York. The smell might bring some of the government down to have a better look at us. We knew that the government had men working on the docks spying. For them, this would be an easy catch.

Four cases of Scotch had shattered. Already, the men were drinking what was left in the bottles. I couldn't blame them. Right now, it seemed like a good idea to me. If you can't beat them, join them. I did this willingly. To hell with the neck of the bottle being shattered! You had to be pissed, or just plain crazy, to be down here in this weather.

I stood back from the men. I did not want to get in their way as they struggled with the moving cases. I would only have been a hindrance to them.

One barrel of Gin had ruptured. The smell of Gin made everyone's eyes water. It was more like rubbing alcohol than real Gin. This would be distilled again, and bottled. It was another good profit for Zuk.

If this is all that had been lost to the storm, I would be happy. Taking another slug of Scotch, I began to climb the ladders back onto the main deck. A nice warm feeling was now spreading through my body. My head poked out over the hatches. Spray hammered my face again. I would leave the main report to the third mate. He knew more about things than I did.

By the time, I reached the bridge I was soaked. I took enough time to inform the skipper what I had seen. As I'd expected, he took no notice of me. After all, I was only the owner of the ship. Slipping below decks, I changed into dry clothes, and went back up on topside. The third mate was now giving a more accurate report to his skipper.

We had actually lost twenty cases of Scotch and two barrels of Gin. The men were securing the rest of the cargo down. It could have been a lot worse.

I was still pretty pissed off, though. I would tell the skipper so when I had the chance to get him alone. Right now was not the correct time. He should have made sure the cargo was secure before we left Halifax.

For the next six hours, we sat there, riding the waves. As soon as the last man had come up topside again, the hatches were secure.

"Starboard, twenty. Resume a heading of south-southeast."

Soon, we were back to being rolled around from arsehole to breakfast time on our beam ends. I was not going below again just yet. Planting my feet apart, I stood at the back of the bridge, rolling with each wave as it crashed over our beam. Sea water rolled furiously across the hatch covers, and down the other side, before running out of the scuppers. Below decks, in the galley, crashing pots and pans rolled over the deck. The cook, if that is what you can call him, would not be happy right now. The crap he served up left a lot to be desired, but when you're hungry, you will eat what is put in front of you. Most of the crew wouldn't have minded what was put in front of them tonight. The better part of the team was stewed to the gills from the free booze that had come their way.

At eight o'clock the following morning, the wind finally began to moderate. This was lucky for the crew. The greasy thick breakfast they had eaten, and the booze had come back to haunt them. Several were praying to Neptune, the god of the sea. Their breakfast was the sacrifice to him.

This was still a working ship, and Prentice, the boson, took extra delight in giving them all a hard task to do during the morning. By lunch time, most still looked as green as the sea itself.

I still found it hard to fathom why anyone would do this work for a living. My grandfather had loved the life, and so had my father. *Screw this game,* was my attitude. I was more than happy to be a passenger right now.

Twenty-four hours after we had seen the Coast Guard ship, she rejoined us. Her signal lamp was flashing long before she was fully insight.

CLEMMY G., WHAT IS YOUR SITUATION?

Our reply was short, and to the point. There was no need to invite them to supper.

U. S. COAST GUARD SHIP. CARGO NOW SECURE. SHIP SEAWORTHY. PROCEEDING ON COURSE. END.

We were still four miles out from the U. S. coast, so we had no great worries about being boarded. It was just a matter of making sure we did not act out of the ordinary right now.

The Coast Guard continued to head towards us. I could see at least two sets of binoculars trained on us. There would be at least two more. The hands working on deck downed tools, taking the time to give a wave to the ship now abeam of us. Several sets of hands waved back.

Making a slow turn to starboard, the Coast Guard sailed off into the Atlantic, steaming at full ahead in an easterly direction. With luck, that would be the last we had seen of her.

Our plan was to remain outside the three mile limit until we were off of the coast of New York. This served a couple of purposes. The first would keep the Coast Guard off of us until the last possible moment. The second was a little more sinister. With the amount of bootleg booze we had aboard, it was always going to be hard keeping it a secret. Zuk's rival mobs would be only too willing to give a few lives up in an attempt to take it off of us.

Zuk had done something similar to another hood named Snakes Brown. Brown was one of the new kids on the scene, trying to make a quick name for himself. He worked the lower east side of the Hudson. He had tried running the bootleg cargo the same way we were doing now, but Zuk had eyes in every camp.

Once he found out about Brown's endeavour, he sent two boats out to intercept the ship. Brown had made the big mistake of coming inshore. A dense fog had settled over the entrance to the river. This made it easy for Zuk's men to slip aboard. The order he had given was simple. Clear the ship of booze at any cost. His men did not let him down.

The cost was cheap to his own men. Only two were killed, and one injured. The crew of the contraband ship were killed, and thrown over the side, every last one of them. The bodies soon became shark food. You don't tend to find many bodies after the sharks have had their fill.

The ship itself was left to drift. She was just a container to carry the booze in. Now, the container was empty, and there was no further need for it. The story ran in the New York Journal for over two weeks, likening her to the Marie cyclist.

Zuk had taken over six thousand bucks worth of booze from her that night, making a fine profit from the sale. The *Clemmy G.* would not fall into a similar trap.

Snakes Brown had made it common knowledge that he would get even with the bastards who had taken his booze. Zuk was on top of the list.

Zuk's arrogance and his own self-belief in the power he wielded only brought a smile to his face. His plan was to hit Snakes Brown before Snakes could get to him.

Open warfare broke out in New York. Two of Brown's speakeasies were firebombed on a cold winter's night. Snow had been falling, so all of the windows and doors had been shut tight. Fourteen customers were burned to death inside the place. Five of Brown's heavies also died that night.

The fire had been started in the cellar. Twenty gallons of gas had been poured down the opening. To make sure it went off with a bang, a grenade was then thrown in. The poor bastards did not stand a chance. Their chances were lessened even more by the hail of bullets that went through the main door just before the grenade went off. That would ensure everyone stayed inside until it was too late to get out.

Mysteriously, the fire department did not show up at the joint until thirty-five minutes had passed after the fire broke out. To me, this was no surprise. The fire chief had been bumped up onto the higher guest list of Zuk's Green Parrot club. Several of Zuk's girls had paid a lot of attention to the fire department's chief over recent weeks. I did hear that the fire department went to the wrong address, at first. How true that was, I do not know.

Snakes Brown swore revenge. Six months after that incident, Snakes made the return call. Zuk had been out of town on business. Danny Strain had been left in charge of the club. He was one of Zuk's lieutenants. He was a no-nonsense sort of a guy who took his responsibility very seriously. Danny had grown up with Zuk. He, too, had killed his first man by the time he was sixteen.

The fights he had been in had done him no favours. Several scars showed above his shirt collar, and the bridge of his nose had been broken at least once. As far as I could tell, he was happy to hang onto Zuk's coattails for the ride. At six-foot-one, he was a formidable man to come up against. His favoured weapon was a gold-handled flick knife he kept tucked into the waistband of his trousers.

At work, his normal place would be at the far left hand corner of the bar. That way, he could see all that was going on around him. Despite his battered looks, he always had a bevy of girls around him. In return, they would get plied with good champagne and his protection. Danny liked to throw his money about like confetti. The girls loved that as well.

***

On the night of the attack, the Green Parrot had steadily begun to fill up with the usual crowd. Danny smiled, and waved at me as I walked into the joint. The seat I normally took was free. Not many people would sit in reserved seats.

Rochelle smiled as I sat down. She had a new gown on, a figure-hugging satin number. She looked good, but then again, she always looked good. I sat down with my back to the wall. I had gotten into the habit of doing this. Somehow, it seemed safer that way. I could see everything that was going on around me.

Rochelle picked her glass up from the bar, and glided across the floor to where I was sitting. Her smile was like a breath of fresh air. I did not have to invite her to sit down. She slid into the plush leather seat alongside me. Her eyes had a mischievous look about them. This was nothing new to me. Each time she saw me, her eyes lit up in the same way. Placing her glass delicately on the table, she gently kissed me on the cheek. Her kiss and closeness caused a tingle to ripple down my back. I moved my mouth round to meet her soft lips, and we gently kissed.

Her hand slid under the table, and she ran her fingers along my thigh towards my groin. I pulled her closer to me as my breathing grew ragged, and I let out a small groan of pleasure. I felt her lips part as she smiled at the sound of my pleasure.

Moving her lips round to my ear, and she gently whispered, "Later." Her smile was pure seduction.

Pouring two glasses of Bourbon, she stroked her hand down my cheek. Her right hand was still resting on the inner part of my thigh. Her fingers were gently stroking me. She did this for several seconds until she got the reaction she wanted from me. The bulge in my trousers told her all she wanted to know. Her smile broadened.

"Shall we take this some place more private?"

Downing my drink in one gulp, I stood up. Rochelle took my hand, leading me to the far end of the bar, and the stairs that would take us up to the private apartment above the club.

Danny raised his glass at me, nodding slightly at me as we walked past him. I allowed Rochelle to pass by into the doorway that led to the stairs. She brushed her hand along my groin as she did so. If I could have, I would have taken her right there on the stairs. She also knew this, and stepped away from me.

My hand dropped to my side as she stepped onto the first step. The shoulder strap of her dress has fallen down onto her arm. Her tongue gently rolled around her lips as she pulled it back over her shoulder. Her hand rolled over her breast, and down to her stomach as she continued to look at me. Her eyes were filled with lust and wanting. My heart was beating faster and faster.

Letting her climb the first two stairs, I watched her. Her gown hugged her curvaceous body. She knew how to carry herself. She also knew I was watching her. This made her show boat to a degree. Her butt wiggled from side to side as she floated up the stairs. She looked back down the stairs at me. I had not moved from the spot I was rooted to. Her lips parted slightly again, her tongue gently licking them. Her eyes widened as I began to follow her.

The door to the bedroom closed behind us. Rochelle stood there in the centre of the room waiting for me. The strap of her right shoulder had slipped off again. She lowered her head gently so that it was touching her chest. She knew exactly what she was doing. I wanted her naked, then and there. I had seen her little routine before, and it would be another minute or so before her dress would touch the floor. I could feel my excitement mounting as she stood there watching me. The side zip slipped gently down to her waist. The dress dropped lower over her shoulders. Her left hand came up to stop it from falling over her breasts.

The loud bang that came from the bar blow startled both of us. Straight away, I knew it was gunfire. It did not take a genius to work that out. Several rounds cracked out. The sound was now automatic, and screams filled the air.

Grabbing my Colt from the small bedside table, I swung the door open. The gunfire was louder now that I was in a more open position. With my heart racing, my instinct was to get downstairs as quickly as possible. My brain told me to slow down. There was no point in rushing around a corner into a bullet. Whatever it was that was going on would not be over any quicker if I was dead.

Rochelle put a trembling hand on my right shoulder. I brushed it off.

"Get back to the room," I hissed. "Shut the door, and lock it. Then find some place to hide. I'll be back. Don't let anyone in if it isn't me."

I slowed my pace down. Several weapons were being fired now. I had the Colt at arm's length now, moving slowly down the stairs. The barrel was pointing directly out in front of me. The safety catch was off, and my finger was hovering over the trigger. No matter what I did, I could not stop the rush of adrenaline throughout my body. The barrel of the gun was shaking.

Taking a deep breath, I kept telling myself to move forward slowly, checking every part of my vision. I stopped, and lowered the gun. Closing my eyes for a split second, I took a deep breath. Once I was steady, I raised the gun in front of me once more. The shakes had almost stopped.

I was halfway down the stairs now. I wanted to push myself hard against the wall. That would have cut down my field of fire. With the Colt still held out in front of me, every step of the stairs screamed out under my foot. There was more fire coming from the bar. The familiar sound of a Thompson machine gun cut through every other sound. Screams grew louder with every step I took.

Rochelle's hand was still on my shoulder. I really wished she'd stayed put. Unfortunately, it was too late to worry about it now. She was past the point of no return. Should anyone have come around the corner at the bottom of the stairs, she would have been an easy target, as there was no hiding place in sight.

Her nails dug deep into my shoulder. Like me, she was scared shitless. My brain kept telling me to run away. I knew I could not. The place was being attacked. Whoever it was would go through it like a dose of salts that would include the upstairs. At least, I had a fighting chance to make a stand.

A bloodstained body thumped against the wall below me, slumping to the floor. A pool of blood dripped across the marble floor. The two holes in his head had dropped him. His hand still gripped the machine gun. He was not one of Zuk's men. Behind me, Rochelle screamed as she saw the body lying there. Her breath was now short and rasping.

"Get back!" I ordered.

Fear had taken her over. She was going nowhere, apart from the same direction I was going in. Never taking my eyes off of the scene below me, I could feel her breath on the back of my neck, and her fingers were still digging into my shoulders.

Taking another step forward with the Colt still clutched tightly in my hand, a face I had never seen before came into view at the bottom of the stairs. A machine gun was pressed tightly to his shoulder. He was taking in everything around him.

Several rounds slammed into the walls around him. Taking one round to his lower leg, he dropped, and a scream echoed throughout the room. Rochelle screamed again. Turning his head towards us, his eyes opened wide. I gave him no time to turn the gun on us. I squeezed the trigger.

Smoke filled my eyes. He screamed as I fired again. If he was screaming, he was still alive. I was now shooting through a smoky haze. The screaming stopped. I was not going to fire again. I only had the clip of bullets in my gun. I would pick his weapon up once I got to him. For now, I had no idea if he had an empty weapon or not, save for what I had, and hoped for more.

The smoke cleared quickly. A single hole in the middle of his forehead had dropped him like a bag of shit. Without a second thought, I hurried down the stairs. With my eyes fixed on the door area of the bar, I riffled through his body for weapons. I was not used to shooting a machine gun, and I knew it was not a weapon Zuk would use in the bar. If one of his men saw the gun, they might just think I was one of the raiders, and open up on me. He had a hand gun tucked into his waistband, and it had a full clip in it. I tucked this into the back of my pants, and moved to the door.

The glass panel in the door had been taken out. Acrid smoke blew in through the hole, stinging my eyes. Several gun flashes erupted from both sides of the bar. Zuk's men were making a fight of it. Two men stood behind a pillar in the centre of the room, a steady stream of fire covering the bar. Two more of Zuk's men were pinned down. I could not see Danny.

I took aim at the first man behind the pillar. Aim for the body, and just hit the bastard. Squeezing the trigger, smoke filled the area again. My first round smashed into the pillar. He saw me. He turned his gun in my direction. Two rounds smashed into the door and wall. My next shot took him down. This forced his pal to move, and he was now out in the open. Several shots from behind the bar took him down.

The main door swung open. The draught blew blue acrid smoke all over the bar. A man stood nearby, holding a bottle in his right hand above his head. His left hand held the door open. The petrol bomb's fuse was already burning. If he were to throw that into the place, it would cause a world of shit for us all.

Taking a breath, I took aim at his chest area. My round slammed into his shoulder. He let go of the door, and this gave me a few more seconds. The door was now blocking his throwing arm. I took aim again. Several more rounds ripped into the wall and woodwork around me. I never took my eyes off of him. I squeezed the trigger again.

Click.

Shit! I was empty. Don't panic. Keep your eyes on him!

The door was opening again, and he was using his foot to push it open. He was a persistent bastard. The gun I had tucked into my trousers came up. I cocked the trigger back, and took aim. Another deep breath slid past my lips, and I squeezed the trigger. The round ripped into his throat.

The petrol bomb dropped to the deck, exploding at his feet. A wall of flame erupted around him, engulfing his now prone body. The fire prevented any route of escape, as well as stopping others from coming in. It was contained in an area that was mainly concrete, so the petrol would soon burn out.

Women were cowering in corners, and under tables. Most were too shocked to scream. I pushed through the door into the bar area. With the gun held firmly out in front of me, I swept it from side to side. Danny came into view. He had been at the far end of the bar. Two more incoming shots sped through the smoke. Several rounds were returned.

I saw another strange face cowering behind a table. Taking aim, I squeezed off another round. A splinter of wood from my missed aim stuck into the leather clad seat. His eyes widened as he scanned the area around him, trying to locate the new player in the game. Holding my breath just before I pulled the trigger gave my hand some control. My round struck him in the shoulder.

A loud scream of pain burst from his lips. The gun dropped to the floor as he clutched his bleeding wound. Firing again, he took the round in his leg. I might not be the best shot in the world, but at least I was getting my shots in on a target.

The fire fight was dying down now. There were a lot of bodies spread about in the carnage. I moved further into the bar area, sweeping slowly to my left. The heat from the petrol bomb halted my progress, forcing me to go back the other way. I gave the fire a quick scan. It was not spreading, and would die down soon enough. Keeping my eyes firmly fixed on the bar, I saw several men stand up. All of them were Zuk's men. The man I had shot, however, was still alive. Groans of pain sounded from under the table. It would have been better for the bastard if he had died. He would now wish he had.

I moved towards him, pushing the barrel of the gun against his temple. If he made one false move, I would spread his brains over the floor for him. He was not going anywhere. He had a round in the shoulder, and one in his leg, after all. Turning the gun round in my hand so that I had the butt facing outwards, I gave him a sound crack across the head with it. I didn't want him crawling off at all. He would have some explaining to do. His body slumped to the deck in the blink of an eye.

Two more shots rang out. Danny was shooting through the shattered windows of the club. He had no target, however. He was just pissed off. Silence fell all around. I could hear my heart beating quickly. The roar of the flames was dying down a bit, and I had no worries about it now. The bastard previously holding the bomb was now nothing more than a charred body. The smell of burning flesh would stick with me for the rest of my life. So much so, I wanted to vomit.

Unfortunately, that would have to wait. I needed to make sure that the attacks had stopped. All was quiet momentarily, until a chair on my left moved. I swung my gun round, ready to shoot. The blackened and bloody face of a woman crawled out from under the table. Her face was one of terror, but at least she was still alive.

From behind me, there was more movement. Rochelle stood there, tears streaming down her face. She looked as terrified as the poor bitch coming out from under the table. I was tempted to comfort her, but she to would have to wait. The place needed to be secured.

More of Zuk's men came out into the open. All of them held their guns aloft. Several had gunshot wounds to various parts of their bodies. At first glance, they looked to be ok. I left the rest of the checking of the place to them, and turned my attention back to Rochelle. She was in a real shit state. There was not much left of the bar, but I did find an undamaged bottle of brandy, and poured her a large glass of it. She was almost rooted to the spot with fear, and I had to force the drink to her lips.

Behind me, Danny started getting some of the living on their feet. He needed to get them out of the joint. There had been an increasing number of newspaper hacks only too willing to get the scoop on a hit like this. The judges and district attorneys would not want to have their faces plastered all over the front pages. Danny and his men were moving them to the back door, and into cars.

As for the dead . . . Well, they can tell no tales as to why they were there. I gave Rochelle a quick once-over. She had blood spattered all over her face and clothing. She was ok. I left her to her brandy at the bar. I had to help Danny. I was in this shit now, right up to my neck.

I made my way to the end of the bar. "Is it too late for a beer, Danny?"

We burst out laughing. Movement in the bar had us both hit the floor, guns swinging around to the noise. We scanned the area for a possible threat.

A man was groaning, blood spreading from a wound on his left thigh. Blood covered his face. The machine gun he had been holding lay by his side. Making no attempt to pick it up, he stared at both of us. He knew that if he moved, he would be dead. We carried on in scanning the room just in case. Danny calmly walked over to him, and put a bullet in his head. A pool of blood mixed with the rest of the crap on the deck.

The guy I had dropped saw what Danny had just done. He gasped for air. Danny saw him, and began to walk over to him, his gun held out in front of him.

"Danny, won't Zuk want to ask him some questions?"

The gun lowered, but he kept walking towards the downed man. He was not going to get off scot-free. Danny aimed a kick to his injured arm. A scream of pain rippled around the now empty bar.

Broken glass crunched under foot as we both walked around the bar.

"Jesus Christ, Robbie, what just happened?"

"Do you think the prices are too high, Danny? "

"God damn it, Robbie. You're some cool bastard! I will say that for you!"

Reaching out, I took a bottle of brandy from the bar. My hands were shaking as I took a large mouthful. It burnt my throat as I swallowed it.

Taking time to look around the joint, I felt sick to my guts. The bodies of men and women lay all over the place. Blood was spattered across the walls. Danny silently took the bottle of brandy from me, gulping down several huge mouthfuls before slamming the bottle noisily down on top of the bar. Outside, the sounds of police sirens grew louder.

"Robbie, help me get this mug down into the cellar. The cops aren't getting him."

It was only now that the man on the floor looked afraid. He had every reason to be. Men had suffered a lot more for a lot less when they'd crossed Zuk. This went way beyond crossing him. It was a fucking outrage!

The sirens stopped outside the bar as we finally dragged him down the steps into the cellar, his body slamming down hard on each step. Groans of pain echoed off of the walls as he hit them. A small trail of blood also followed us down.

The cellar was pretty much soundproof, and it was almost impossible to escape from. We threw him roughly into the far right corner of the room. I aimed a kick at his groin.

"Gives him something to think about," I told Danny.

A cop walked through the door as we walked back into the bar area. Sergeant Murtagh was well-known to both Danny and myself. He was a big Irish cop who was not afraid to break one or two heads with his stick if needed. He was also a regular at one of the lower class joints Zuk ran.

"What in God's name has gone on here?"

It's pretty God damn obvious to me, I thought.

Two hacks from the press burst through the door immediately after Sergeant Murtagh strode inside. Their camera bulbs blinded us for a second or two.

Murtagh responded in his usual style by cracking both of them across the back with his baton. More cops came bursting in, grabbing at the collars of the hack's coats, and dragging them outside of the bar.

There was never any chance of this being covered up in the first place. Now it would be front page news. Both Danny and I had been photographed. Our light grey suits covered in blood would show up no matter how poor the quality of the photograph turned out. More and more people rushed into the bar. Medics, ambulance crews, and more cops, as if there was not enough in the place already.

There was never any doubt that Danny and myself would be taken to the cop station on 94th street for questioning. This was done almost at once. In some ways, it helped. The street would be filled with hacks anytime now. All of them wanted a story. As far as I was concerned, it was self-defence.

The ten minute ride to the precinct was made in silence. For myself, I was going through what I would say. Sergeant Murtagh was busy chatting away to the officer driving to cop car. He would be a worried man right now. The last thing he needed was to be known as a customer for the Green Parrot.

91

The front entrance to the precinct already had several hacks standing about, cameras at the ready. All of them wanted that first picture for the next edition. The squad car slipped quietly down the side street into the back lot of the precinct. The light over the back door gave enough light for us to see where we were going. The cop car drew up alongside the dark wooden door. One or two of the hacks tried to follow the car. The Murtagh treatment was dished out to them.

The door swung open, allowing more light to escape. I took a deep breath as I entered the building. I was clear in my own mind as to what I would say to the cops. I had already informed Sergeant Murtagh that I wanted my lawyer before I said anything.

Pointing to my right, he guided me to a side office. A simple wooden desk marked with several coffee stains stood at the back of it. The black telephone was the only thing on it. A hard wooden chair that reminded me of the gun room at the academy sat at the opposite side of the desk.

The business card for *Jameson and Pit* was in my wallet. Zuk had given this to me some time ago. I never thought I would have to use it.

At the *Nelson* line, we had a floor full of lawyers. Right now, I didn't think a corporate lawyer would be the best person to have in my corner. I made my call to the attorney. I was not surprised to find someone was already on the way. Before the line went dead, I was told to say nothing to anyone. I was happy to follow this advice.

I paced the room for what seemed like half a lifetime, smoking cigarette after cigarette. The reflection from the barred window showed me in my full glory. Blood covered half of the lower part of my clothes. My face was also spattered with blood. A mixture of blood and dirt made my hands look black from the Cordite. I tried making another phone call to my attorney, but after my one call, the phone had been disconnected. Soon, I heard raised voices outside of the room I was in.

"I demand to see my client now!"

The door swung open. A middle-aged man walked briskly in, half-moon glasses perched on the bridge of his nose. "Mister Birket? I am Dwight Pitt, your attorney. Have you said anything to the police?

92

"Nothing apart from my name."

Looking over his right shoulder, he gave a dismissive nod to the cop standing at the door. "I will confer with my client in private."

For the next hour, I went through my story with him. He only interrupted me to ask relevant questions about my actions. The door swung open again, and a different man walked in. I knew his face, but could not put a name to it, nor could I remember were I knew him from. It soon came to me. He was Johnathon Brinkley, the district attorney.

The penny dropped. He, too, was a regular at the Green Parrot. I breathed a sigh of relief. Brinkley was one of Zuk's best clients. He had spent many a night with Nancy in the room next to mine. He was heavily into the chains and whips thing. He liked the best champagne in the joint. Zuk made sure there were enough photographs of him locked away to ensure he would stay on his side. Brinkley also projected the image of a very happily married man, and he had designs on higher offices.

He glanced at me. For a split second, his eyes opened wide before he gained control of himself again.

Several wooden chairs were brought in, and placed around the desk. Brinkley took his time, setting his writing paper and pens out on the desk before seating himself. For the next two hours, he fired questions at me. My own attorney fielded most of them.

There was not one question about the Green Parrot club itself. I think it would have opened a new can of worms up if we had gone down that street. A can of worms I am sure Brinkley would not want to open. He would have had a lot of explaining to do to his own people.

With a flurry of papers, Brinkley finally stood up. "Once we have confirmed your story with Miss Madden, I think we can put this to bed."

I let out a sigh of relief.

"You are free to go for now, Mr Birket, but don't leave town just yet."

Dwight Pitt guided me out of the room and the precinct to the waiting car. Danny was already sitting in the back seat, a broad grin on his face. I climbed into the back with him. Already, he had a bottle of Scotch in his hand. Taking a large mouthful from the offered bottle, I sat back, and relaxed. During the past hour or so, I had tried to work out why I felt so calm. I had just killed at least two men. Yet I had no feelings of guilt or shame. In fact, the reverse was all too evident. The rush of blood going through me excited me.

Back at the Green Parrot, the dead bodies had been removed. Several cops stood outside the bar. This was mainly to stop the sightseers from crawling all over the place. Even the photographers had gone now. More than likely, the story was already written with full page photographs of the murders that had taken place inside.

Danny and I felt that the time was right for us to have a talk with our visitor down in the cellar. If he was still alive, that is. To be honest, I did not give a rat's arse if he was alive or dead. We both knew who was responsible for tonight's carnage. Snakes Brown would be a marked man from now on. Zuk would see to that.

The cellar door swung open. The stench of blood struck my nostrils right away. The dim light hanging from the high ceiling barely lit up the room. Normally, Zuk would have had a stronger lamp brought in to shine into the face of whoever he wanted answers from. It gave a more menacing feel to the place.

The man was where we had dumped him, crumpled up in the far left corner of the room. I knew before I reached him that he was dead, but to be sure, I gave him a kick to the ribs. A dull thud echoed around the cellar. He would end up floating down the Hudson River by morning. He was just another statistic for the files.

CHAPTER SEVENTEEN

Three days after the raid on the Green Parrot, Zuk returned from his trip to Florida. Danny got the place cleaned, and running repairs were under way. Zuk would not want his regulars going to another bar, most especially, the important people who frequented the joint. As long as they kept coming back, he would have a lot of power over them.

It was also at the suggestion of Danny that I moved into the Green Parrot. My own home would now be a target for Brown's heavies. Living out of town with a price on your head was not the best idea in the world.

Using one of Zuk's realty contacts at the Green Parrot, I put the family home on the market, instructing him to also find me a new place in town. There were new apartments on West 98th Street, and he was only to keen to get the commission for one of those places. It would also be a safer place to be. Zuk and Danny both had joints around there, so extending their protection to me would be no hardship to him. After the fire fight at the club, Zuk felt he owed me a debt.

As far as Zuk was concerned, I had laid my loyalty open for all to see. His reward to me for this was put into effect by taking me under his wing. I became more and more involved with his rackets. I would have been lying if I said that I did not get a buzz out of my new way of life.

I had long since become bored to death by the mundane routine of the *Nelson* line. I was only too happy to sell my holding in the company to raise funds for three more ships. All were bigger and faster than the *Clemmy G.*, allowing for a greater profit from the bootleg booze we could carry aboard them. Like the *Clemmy G.*, I had the double bottoms put in the new ships in dry dock.

The *Birket* shipping line did carry some legitimate cargos. This was mainly to keep the incorruptible people who worked for the state department happy.

It was surprising how many were law-abiding citizens. For those who poked their noses in too deeply into the business, the threat of death or a family member being injured, particularly the kids, would make them back off. For those who had no family ties, a bullet to the back of the head, and a deep six coffin, did just as well. It all served the same warning to the department.

CHAPTER EIGHTEEN

By 1926, I had floated the *Birket* shipping line on the stock exchange. Even Zuk bought into the company, so in effect he was being paid twice for his shares. The major profit we received was coming from the bootleg booze we were running. There was also a small dividend coming in at the end of the financial year.

Zuk was one of those men who never forgave or forgot a grudge, and in the October of 1926, he repaid Snakes Brown back for his visit on the Green Parrot club almost two years ago. Several cars and trucks filled with men left one of the warehouses on the lower east of the Hudson River. All were heavily armed. The weaponry included Thompson sub-machine guns, shotguns, and grenades.

A tip of from one of Snakes Brown's own men alerted Zuk to where he would be, and at what time. Once the call had been made to Zuk personally, his instructions to the men where simple. He didn't want a stick or stone standing. Anyone who tried to leave the Alaverti palace had to be bumped off. As for Snakes Brown, he would be in the office above the palace. If he was not killed by the grenades or fire, he had to be killed while trying to get out of the place.

Zuk, Danny, and I would be in the company of the mayor and the police chief during the attack. They would be having dinner with us at a respectable restaurant. During dinner, Zuk would make a donation to the police benevolent fund. Five grand should be a big enough gift. There would be a lot of killing that night, so it was important to have a good alibi for that time. They did not come much better or bigger than the mayor or police chief.

It also turned out that the Paramount restaurant was owned by Zuk. This was one of his legitimate businesses. It kept the treasury men off of his back. A swanky little joint set in the heart of Greenwich Village, it was also far enough away from what was about to go down tonight.

Under the eighteenth amendment, it was illegal to sell booze to the public, but it was not illegal to give it away. To get around the law, Zuk would give the wine in his joint away. Everyone knew that a charge would be made for the booze, it just never showed up on the bill at the end of the night.

The small private room at the rear of the joint was private enough for us to be seen by the customers, yet our conversation would not be heard. A plate glass window ensured that. The setting was perfect. The whole joint was filled to the rafters. For this place, it was not unusual. At exactly nine-twenty-six, a time I had been asked to memorize, Zuk drew the cheque for the five grand donation out of his wallet, making a big show of the presentation to the police chief. Two photographers who happened to be in the joint took full advantage of the moment, snapping several photographs. The editor-in-chief of the New York News, who just happened to be a regular at the Green Parrot, would ensure that they would be printed in the next edition of his rag.

At nine-fifty, the small door to the private dining area swung open. The maître d' slipped alongside Zuk, informing him that there was an urgent telephone call for him. Danny and I looked at each other across the table.

Dropping his red napkin onto the table, Zuk excused himself for a few moments. Danny and I continued talking as if it was nothing was out of the ordinary. The police chief was as happy as a pig in shit about the donation to the fund. All Danny and I had to do was sit back, and let him talk on until Zuk came back. The mayor himself was talking about a civil honour for Mister Zuckerman. I tried my hardest, at that point, not to burst out laughing. If he only knew what was going on right now in his city, he would have had a fit.

Five minutes after Zuk had left the room, he came back. There was no expression on his face at all. The straightening of his tie was his signal that his plan had gone well.

Danny stretched out his hand to refill everyone's glasses, raising his own to make a toast to Zuk for his generosity. The three of us really knew what the toast was for, but as long as the mayor and police chief were happy, then so were we.

A second toast was made by the mayor. Before we could drink to Zuk again, the door slid open. The small maître d' stood in the open doorway, his face a little paler than it had been the last time he'd come into the room. Both the mayor and police chief were needed back at City Hall.

Zuk insisted that his own driver take them back, as he was heading back into town himself. Danny and I went back to the Green Parrot. No doubt, Zuk would give us all the gory details later that the night.

The Green Parrot was unusually crowded that night. Many of the men who had been on the raid were crammed in to the place. All the girls who worked the joint would swear in any court that the men had been there all evening. The three judges who were being entertained would also swear to it if needed. They might not want to get involved, but the truth was, they would not have a lot of choice in the matter. Several of the girls would swear that each judge had been engaged in sexual deeds during the course of the night. All three judges were highly regarded within the legal field. All three were also married with children.

As the saying goes, once bent, they stay bent. Danny and I took our usual seats at the bar. I was quickly joined by Rochelle. I had become used to her joining me now. Zuk had made sure she was exclusively mine. God help any mug who tried to get it on with her. She was now more of a hostess than a hooker. This was yet another perk from Zuk to reward my loyalty to him.

I had hardly any time to sit down, and get myself a drink, before the door to the club opened. Zuk walked in a smile on his face as wide as the Grand Canyon itself.

Danny, Jeff Kenshaw, and I followed him up the stairs to the big conference room. Jeff had been the leader of the men on the raid against Snake Brown's joint. I had never really liked the man. He was brash, and arrogant to the core.

The first time I had seen him was a year ago. He walked into the Green Parrot just behind Zuk. I would have sworn he was more of an accountant than a hired gun. Of a slim build, and only five-foot-three inches tall, he had a shy look about him. Until he opened his mouth, that is.

The ivory nickel-plated Colt he had tucked into his shoulder holster was always on show. He never missed a trick. He was around the same age as me, possibly twenty-six or twenty-seven. Like many of the men who were on Zuk's payroll, he had killed more than once. Most people seemed to like the guy, yet there was something I could not put my finger on about him.

Sitting around the conference table, we waited for Zuk to begin. Until that moment happened, we made small talk. A knock on the door stopped the small talk. Jimmy the barman walked in with three bottles of champagne. Water droplets had gathered around the top of them as the ice cooled the fizzy booze. It was only after he had set the tray down on the table, and closed the door on his way out, that Zuk spoke to us.

"Gentlemen, let's drink to the memory of Snake Brown. May the slimy bastard rot in hell!" His grin now burst into righteous laughter. "A toast also to Jeff. Not only did he get Snakes, he took out his good friend, Johnny Patterson, as well." Several bills fell onto the table near Jeff Kenshaw's hand. "Get yourself a new suit, Jeff. You have earned it tonight."

Jeff slipped the money into his pocket. "Thank you, Mister Zuckerman."

Zuk patted him like he would a puppy dog on the head. A look of pride spread across his face.

Brown had died trying to crawl out of his joint along a window ledge. Jeff had spotted him as the flames from the fire below him licked up and along the building. Two shots had dropped him like a bag of shit. Brown dropped from the ledge onto a parked car below. To make sure he would not walk away from it, Jeff had thrown a grenade into the car as well. There would be nothing left, but the sweepings of Brown himself.

Zuk ordered for more champagne to be sent up. It was going to be another heavy night. Taking great delight in telling us about the chief of police and mayors reaction, Zuk only paused to swallow a glass of the bubbly stuff.

"You should have seen their faces, fellas. They both looked priceless. I thought, at one point, the mayor was going to give birth. Apart from Brown, you got twenty-two other people, Jeff, including the mayor's assistant. Slimy bastard shouldn't have gone to his club, should he?"

Jeff sat there nodding his head at every word Zuk spat out.

Several moments passed. Zuk sat there looking thoughtful.

"Jeff, I want to rebuild Snakes' old place. How do you see yourself running it for me?"

There was no expression of surprise on Jeff's face. It was if he'd expected it to be like this.

"Thank you, Mister Zuckerman. I will try to do the place proud for you."

Zuk's empire, and that is what it was, was now growing rapidly. This was, in some ways, good for me as well. It meant the shipping line would have to bring more booze in to supply his outlets.

I sipped my bubbly, and smiled. I was not going to turn my nose up at more profits. Even if it meant keeping Jeff's bar open with it.

As it was, the ships we were running carried almost full cargos of booze. Hundreds of thousands of cases were now being shipped to several ports along the eastern seaboard. Apart from the ships I was now running, I had also bought a number of trucks. It stretched me as far as I could go financially, but the returns would be great. Neat cheap alcohol would be shipped in tankers marked as petrol if the driver was stopped, and his load checked. A dipping tank was installed in each of the tankers, and filled with petrol. This would be enough to fool snooping government men or overzealous cops. The tankers could run freely during the day time, dropping their cargo off at any location across the state.

Zuk also had men brewing neat booze out in the wilds. Hidden deep in woodland, all were almost impossible to find. Only the drivers knew how to get to them. They memorized the maps used to get there, just in case they got busted by the cops.

The fear of being busted was not a great one. Zuk had the cops and city officials in his back pocket. At the merest hint of a raid on one of his places, he would get a phone call. The operation could then be disguised in time for the raid.

Such was his operation that Zuk was now selling his bootleg booze through the tobacco stores he owned or ran. It was pre-mixed with fruit juice or non-alcoholic drinks. He even had men and women selling his stuff door to door. The beat cops turned a blind eye for a few bucks in their pockets. Many of the beat cops were regular customers of his as well. So it was not the money they took, but rather the cheap bottle of booze left in a pre-determined spot known only to the cop or the street trader.

Zuk was also clever enough to never let anything be traced back to him. At each part of the operation, he had shut off points. Only the money came to him in cash. He would then move it out of the country.

By 1927, he was the biggest operator in the state. He owned the governor, and most of his office. Most of the opposition had been bumped off over the last year. To a degree, peace had broken out.

Zuk allowed some small-time hoods to operate within the state as long as they paid their respects to him twice a year. This would be during a lavish dinner party. Envelopes would be collected before the small-timers entered the room. I never knew how much he collected, but it must have run into the hundreds of thousands of bucks each year.

Zuk was selling them his booze, and taking a percentage of what they earned as well. For this, the small-time hoods could pretty much do as they liked as long as it did not come back to Zuk, or harm his operations in other parts of the state.

CHAPTER NINETEEN

Despite all of my own wealth, and to a degree, the power I wielded, I found that I was becoming bored. The excitement of the early days of being with Zuk had left me. My trips to Canada had become more frequent, but even this was becoming mundane. Ever since our first encounter with the Coast Guard, we had been left alone. No doubt, Zuk had bought them off as well.

My old academy friend in Canada and myself often talked about running booze ourselves. The profits were much bigger, and the thought of running alone did bring some excitement back into my life.

My biggest problem to this idea was cash. I had committed all of my own spare capital into the trucking and shipping business. Raising the seventy-five grand I would need to put the idea into action was the only thing really holding me up.

Mat Valente already had buyers back in the Unites States lined up. Among them was Al Capone. The mention of his name would send a shiver down my spine. The risk of running booze for Capone was bigger, but so were the profits and the thrill. Politically, things were also changing. The day of the hood was now under threat. Politicians who were a new breed wanted change. The old guards who were on the make tried to make their stand, but the threat of being exposed was becoming greater. So was the cost of their silence and cooperation.

Local elections were built on the promise that the hoods and gangs of the country would be swept off the map. There were also murmurings about the *Falstead* act being repealed. Many people on the street were getting sick of the act. As had been proven over the past few years, the only people who benefited from it were the hoods.

CHAPTER TWENTY

I'd pretty much decided to go along with Mat Valente's idea to run extra booze from Canada. I raised the money for my end of the deal by borrowing against some of my company shares. These would be used as my bond. The stock market was going crazy in the early part of 1928, so I had no real problem about raising the money. I sailed on the *Clemmy G.*, so as not to raise any suspicions from Zuk. I was fully aware of what would happen if he found out I had crossed him.

I had also sent a message to the skipper of the *Tarnvick*, the newest ship in the *Birket* line. His orders were simple – proceed to Halifax, and load up with machine parts, then take passage to Washington. There was no point in adding to the danger of making this run by coming back to New York. Capone's own men would see to the rest of the deal once the ship had berthed.

By the time I had done my third voyage to Halifax, Canada, I was quite enjoying the peace and quiet. New York was never quiet. Someone had said it was the city that never sleeps. This was true. During the day, office and store workers hustled and bustled along the streets. At night, the speakeasies and clip joints came alive. Cheap hookers filled strip joints, spilling out on the streets to make their scores. Cheap motels provided some privacy for them as they entertained their mug punters. A few dollars would provide the men with their pleasure. Sometimes, a dose of the clap would go with the service.

The hookers would then apply their make-up to attract the next mug, and so the night went on. Pimps would collect the money, and take their cut, handing the hookers a few dollars. The rest would go to men like Zuk. He, in turn, would give it to me to pay for the bootleg booze I was now shipping.

I had no feelings on the subject of hookers. It was their way of life. The protection from some of the more crazy mugs was left to the pimps. After all, a scarred and beat-up hooker would make no money for the bosses. A slack pimp was a dead pimp. Zuk saw his hookers as a production line. Get the mug in, get him done, get him out, get the next one in, and so it went on day after day. Customers who gave the girls a hard time would be treated the same. I had seen at least two mugs castrated for beating girls up so badly that they were unable to work. Hit them hard, and let them know what happens if they mess up one of Zuk's girls. Word soon got around the streets.

Even the cheap seedy motels that the girls used were owned by Zuk. A single lamp hanging from a tobacco-stained light fitting hung in each room. A wash basin sat in one corner so that the girls could wash themselves, as well a mirror for them to re-do their make-up. The beds were all the same – wooden frames placed in the middle of the room. Walls were stained yellow from a million cigarettes.

'It is not as if the men want to look at the walls once they are in there, is it?' This was Zuk's standard by-line.

Occasionally, one of the girls would fall pregnant. This was her problem. There were several doctors who could take care of it for her. Although, illegal abortions happened. The doctors might not like it, but give them enough money and intimidation, and they soon had a different outlook on things.

For those girls who wanted to keep their bastard child, they would work for as long as mug would pay her. Some of the punters got off on a girl being pregnant. After the kid was born, she was on her own. A rat-infested single room would be her life until she had no other choice but to return to the streets. Hooked on either booze or narcotics, it all brought them back to the streets. The kid would join the gangs as it got older, and so it went on round and round.

I had been against narcotics from the early days of getting involved with Zuk. It was fast-acting, deadly, and addictive to almost all of the users. Opium was shipped in from South America in its pure form. Once in the Unites States, it would be cut with things like sugar or flour, making a bigger profit for the mob bosses. Further down the line, the dealers would cut it again. They had to make their own profit from the deal. Some were not too bothered as to what it was cut with. Rat poison was one agent added to it. It then went out to the streets. The user would inject the drug into a vein for the quickest hit. Those poor bastards that got the rat poison suffered a long painful death in some toilet or back alley.

Unlike booze, the more narcotic you used, the more you needed. Before long, you would do anything to get your fix. Some of the hookers actually sold their kids for a fix. There was always someone out there willing to pay a price for a kid. For a small fee, Zuk would provide the kid with a loving family. The kid's mother would settle for a fix. Many a body had been found by the cops after an overdose of drugs. The purity of the drugs was not always the same, and the bad drugs injected gave a slow painful death to the user.

Narcotics were easier to hide as well. A hundred grand's worth of opium could be easily fitted into a single chest, and stowed in a ships hold. It was the one thing I would not allow on my ships. The profits for the mob were huge from narcotics, however.

In 1927, the shipping line grew from strength to strength. This was partly due to Zuk's influence. Many of his customers across the state of New York and beyond were rich powerful men. This meant that any hint of scandal could have been the ruin of them. Zuk played on these fears to secure the more lucrative cargos that came to us. As a share holder in the *Birket* line, it was also in his interest as well.

Copra from the Cuban isles and copper from the South American continents brought a small fortune on the stock market. America was going through a boom period during that year. Shares grew on the stock exchange at an amazing rate. Shares in the *Birket* line rose from an initial starting price of one and a half dollars. During the first quarter of the year, we were making large amounts of money.

Although, it did mean borrowing more money against the company, I felt the time was right to expand it even further. The cost of any new ship would be recouped in two years with the cargos we were handling. Each day, it seemed as if our share prices climbed as the reputation of the company grew. I'd decided that by investing more of my own money into the company, I would recoup a greater profit from it.

By late 1928, the naval architect, Henry Broadshaw, had submitted plans for the newest and fastest ship the *Birket* line possessed. At fourteen thousand tons, the *Bostonavia* would be ready for sea by the late 1929. She was to be built in the *Harland and Wolf* shipyard in Belfast, Northern Ireland. It was the same company that had built the *R. M. S. Titanic*. With the new steam engines he had designed, it would give her a top speed of almost twenty knots.

As for myself, I had no intention of being stuck in an office ever again. I appointed men far more suited to the job than me. Men who liked working with numbers, and sitting behind a desk day-to-day. I found myself happier at sea, and negotiating deals face-to-face. I enjoyed taking the odd watch, and keeping shift on board. It gave me something to do. I could also keep my eye on the crew. Not all were from Zuk's camp, most especially when we did the runs for Capone. The less Zuk's men knew, the better. For once, I found myself happy with being at sea again after so many years.

CHAPTER TWENTY-ONE

In September of 1928, I arrived home at my apartment in New York. There was nothing unusual about this as far as the hour was concerned. I'd spent the night with Rochelle.

All I wanted to do now was get some sleep before setting off again to meet another contact of Zuk's. He wanted forty thousand tons of iron ore shipped from the West Indies to the giant steel plants of Pittsburgh. At the rate things were going, it would mean more ships for the company. I was pretty happy about that. I had the same amount of ships as the *Nelson* line.

I climbed into bed, content and dreaming about the way things had panned out for me up until to now. I'd stopped worrying or feeling anything for the saps that had got in the way of business. That's the way I looked at it now. Just business.

I had been in bed for no more than an hour when the hammering on the door instinctively had me reaching for the Colt I now kept under my pillow. Although there was an uneasy peace between the mob gangs, I still slept better with it there.

Standing to the left of the door with the Colt in my right hand, I inquired, "Who is it?"

"Mister Birket, my name is John Pickwood."

The name had no meaning to me. I gently pulled the hammer back on the Colt. The empty chamber moved clockwise, allowing a round to move into the firing chamber of the gun. I always kept one chamber empty in case I squeezed the trigger during the night, and blew my brains out.

"Mister Birket, I am from the treasury department. I need to talk to you."

Lowering the hammer on the pistol, I took a deep breath of air. What in God's name did the treasury department want with me?

Keeping the safety chain on the door, I slid the bolt back. The door opened just enough for me to see outside. A tall, slim-looking guy stood there with half-moon glasses perched on the end of his nose. His hat was sitting squarely on his head, unlike most of the men I knew, who wore their hats slanted to one side. He drew his right hand slowly up to reach inside his coat. He would not be the first man to try the I–am-from-the-government card, and then kill the poor sap that opened the door. I was taking no chances. I pulled the hammer back again, ready to fire if I needed to. A small leather identity wallet flicked open for me to view.

I knew, at this point, that I could be in a world of trouble. The chain dropped from its latch as I opened the door wide for him to enter my apartment. Pickwood's eyes scanned the entire room as he made his way over to the mahogany dining table at the far end of the room.

"Make yourself at home, why don't you?"

My sarcasm was wasted on him. Dropping his hat onto the chair next to him, he settled down into one of the chairs to the right of the table. The small latch on his briefcase clicked open. A large file was placed on the table. My name was at the top of it.

Opening the file, Pickwood scanned it. Without taking his eyes off of the file, he asked me if I would survive life in prison or even the prospect of execution. Gripping the back of the chair, my mind was a blur. Unable to speak for several moments, I looked at him. If he had come to scare me, he had done his job. If he would not fuck off, that would be great. Somehow, I did not think he would. I had tried the poker face. I knew I looked shit scared.

"Oh, and I suggest you put the weapon away, Mister Birket. You don't want to have any nasty accidents, do you?" His voice now portrayed a southern drawl to it. "Sit down please, Mister Birket."

This was more of a command than a request. I did as I was told. Sitting opposite him, I continued to stare at him for several more seconds. My mind began to clear a little as he sat there scanning the file.

"What in God's name are you talking about man? Prison? I have done nothing wrong."

His eyes looked up from the file. "Please, Mister Birket, do not take me for a fool. We have it all here – the times, dates, and the who's."

I knew he was not joking. His face said it all. This man was deadly serious. Sometimes, it is better to let the other guy play his hand before you. With as much bravado as I could muster in my voice, I demanded an explanation.

For thirty minutes, he read from the file. Eventually, he sat back, resting against the high wooden back of the dining chair, allowing the smoke from his freshly lit cigarette to roll upwards. His eyes followed the smoke. It was time to play my cards.

"This is a load of crap. I know nothing of this at all. I run a legitimate business."

As my ace, I demanded that my lawyer be present before I said anything else to him.

"That is your right, Mister Birket, but as of yet, you're not under arrest. Please, bring your lawyer in. That would be Mister Brinkley, would it not? He is also the lawyer for Zuckerman, is he not?" Running his finger over a line of the page he was on, he confirmed it.

I don't think it was for my benefit, but more for his, and the effect it would have on me. I slumped back into my chair. With unsteady hands, I pushed a cigarette into my mouth. Pickwood leaned forward, offering me a light. I needed some time to get my brain working again. I blew smoke out of my open mouth.

The bastard had me.

"Why have you not gotten a warrant for my arrest?"

"Oh, I have, Mister Birket."

Folded white sheets of paper dropped onto the table. My hands were shaking uncontrollably now. I stared at an arrest warrant signed by Judge John Cummins, a district court judge from Washington D. C. I was being charged with conspiracy to murder, conspiracy for racketeering, breaking the *Falstead* act, as well as jaywalking.

"There is a way out of this, Mister Birket. If you want it."

Of course, I freaking wanted it! I screamed to myself. I did not want to go to prison for the rest of my days. Or worse, be plugged into the local power plant for ten minutes until I was a fried potato.

My eyes narrowed as I looked at him. "What do you want?"

"That's good, Mister Birket. I now have your attention. To put it simply, we want your boss."

"You want Zuckerman?"

"Oh, no, Mister Birket, we want Capone. We know you have been running contraband for him. There are certain men in the government who are now sick and tired of men like him, and we want him off of our streets."

"But I know nothing of Capone!"

"Don't mess with us, Mister Birket."

The pleasantries were well and truly over.

"You have been running booze for Capone for the past eight months. We have it all here. That alone is worth five years. You will serve every second of that term. I can guarantee it. The government can link you to the deaths of at least six people. That should be enough to get you the electric chair."

"You're full of crap!" I protested.

His little weasel eyes looked at me over the top of his half-moon glasses.

"I wouldn't count on that, Mister Birket. Remember, this is the

United States government you're dealing with now. We can pretty much do what we want. Accessory to murder is life without any chance of parole. We could, if we wanted to, pin any number of murders directly on you. For that, you would fry in the chair. Have you ever seen a person fry, Mister Birket?"

He did not wait for my reply. "No, I guess you haven't. I have. It's not a pretty sight, trust me. We don't have to go to all that trouble. We can throw you in Alcatraz. You do know where Alcatraz is, do you not?"

He now had a full head of steam up.

"Well, let me tell you, just in case. It is the nearest thing to hell on this earth that you can imagine. A dark and miserable rock stuck out in the middle of San Francisco bay. All we have to do is throw you in there, and let it slip that you're a rat for the government. I guess your life could be estimated in hours rather than days or longer. So, what's it to be?"

I started back at him blankly, my mind racing to find some form of response. All I really wanted to do was crap my pants right now. My head slumped forward. I had no choice but to listen to the guy.

"What do you want?"

My voice was nothing but a whisper now. I tried to keep the tremble out of my tone, but I couldn't. I sounded like I had the first time I'd been to the gun room back at the academy. I glanced at the floor. I had no wish to see the smug bastard's face. I could hear him shuffling in the chair opposite me. Papers began to rustle about on the table. I still could not raise my head. I knew if I had, I would have puked all over him.

"For now, Birket, names is what we want, and how much booze you're running for him. Destinations and dates, too. If I want more from you, I will contact you. Oh, and if you try to run or tip anyone off, I will happily execute this warrant I have here. Do I make myself clear?"

I nodded at him. I hated the sound of his southern drawl.

"I said, do I make myself clear?"

God, this bastard wanted his pound of flesh!

"Yes, very clear," I snarled.

I had a million questions swirling around in my head, but I was too numb to ask them all.

The only thing I could ask was, "Why me?"

Pickwood took his glasses off, and placed them on top of his leather briefcase. He fixed his stare on me for a few moments as he considered my question.

"You are the weakest link in the chain, Mister Birket. It's as simple as that. We know all about you, your background, and your family. Capone's men are all hardened thugs who would sooner go to prison or the chair than give him up to us. You are not like them."

He was right. I wasn't. I don't think I could spend my time in prison, especially at the rock Alcatraz was known as. I had heard about the place. Two of Zuk's men had spent ten years there. It left them broken men.

His voice broke my train of thought. It was softer now, perhaps even a tad compassionate.

"Make no mistake, Mister Birket. We are going to get rid of Capone. And when we have dealt with him, we will go after others."

He gave no names. Then again, he did not have to. If he could get Capone, he could get Zuckerman.

"Right at this very moment, your ship the *Clemmy G.* is being raided by the U. S. Coast Guard. She is one hundred miles north of the Hudson River. I can even tell you what she has aboard right down to the last case of Gin. If we continue to raid your ships, pretty soon, you will have nothing to run with. Your usefulness to the crime bosses will be over. As you well know, you are only useful to them as long as you make them money."

I felt sick to the bottom of my guts. He was banging on the button. The fact of the matter was, I was about to lose one hundred grand's worth of booze that belonged to me until it landed. Not to mention the thirty grand Zuk had paid out for it. I was in a lot of shit right now. I could afford to pay Zuk off the money I would owe him, but I had no

116

chance in hell of paying him again and again.

"We will allow some of your contraband ship through, but this is only to help us get Capone."

"If you have all of this information, why don't you just go, and get him?" My voice rose a tad as I spat the question at him.

He was well prepared. Pickwood did not even have to think about things before answering me.

"A paper trail, Mister Birket. We need that to gather enough evidence."

My instinct was to run, right there and then. I knew, deep inside, that it would be pointless. I also knew that I would be getting a telegram from the skipper of the *Clemmy G.* telling me the ship had been boarded by the Coast Guard.

With a tone of utter dejection in my voice, I gave way to his threats. I had no other option. None that I could live with, anyway.

"I want all paperwork that connects Capone to his operation by mid-day tomorrow. This is my number," Pickwood replied.

The small white name card dropped onto the table in front of me. It stayed there. I did not want to pick it up in front of him. The last thing I wanted was for this bastard to see my hands shaking as badly as they were now.

Even after Pickwood had left my apartment, I sat there, staring at the card. I tried to work out what I could do. Right now, it was a big fat zero.

I needed to go to the office right away. It was Saturday, so there would be no one there. The last thing I wanted was to be seen rummaging through months and months of paperwork. After I had showered and dressed, I stowed the camera in my briefcase. I was not going to hand over the documents.

In my mind, by doing so, questions could be asked about the missing paperwork. Things like that have a habit of finding their way into the bars and speakeasies of New York. The mobs had ears everywhere. Maybe I was being a bit paranoid, right now, but there was no chance in hell I was going to lead a trail back to me. I hoped that once I had handed over what I had on the Capone booze, I would be left alone.

I also knew I was being delusional. Once a rat for the government, always a rat for as long as they wanted you. After that, one of two things would happen. I could disappear, or the mob bosses would accidentally find out I had ratted them out. .

It was now twelve-twenty. I felt like shit, not only because of the fear coursing through me, but also because of the lack of sleep. It was stopping me from thinking straight. Each time I tried to come up with some way out, my mind fogged up. The light switched on in my head as I entered the office, and saw the safe in the corner of the room. I had twenty grand locked away in there. In my own mind, if I was to make a run for it, I would have to do it quickly. There would be no time to run around from one place to another getting stuff together.

At the moment, I had no place to run. Even if I did, Pickwood would have the ports covered. Hell, I might have been watched right now. I had no idea. I glanced out of the window, and looked down into the streets. Even for a Saturday, the offices and streets teamed with people. Pickwood's men could be anyone of them.

I downed a large glass of Scotch from my secret supply. If I was going to make a break for it, I would have to do it slowly. I planned to get some things together, and have them stored. I would then wait until Pickwood thought I was playing his game. Maybe he would relax a little. Until then, I had to assume I was being watched. I knew I was not being paranoid. The bastards were really trying to get me.

The contents of the safe went into my leather briefcase. Looking at my watch again, I found that it was twelve-thirty-five. God, I needed a drink! The bottle of Scotch in the safe was a welcome sight. The hot booze burned the back of my throat as I gulped it down. I don't think I had ever been so scared in my life before. I was in a world of shit, and I had no idea how I was going to get out of things alive.

After another slug of booze, I could feel myself relaxing a little. Twelve-forty. Picking up the telephone, I dialled the number on the card Pickwood had given me. It rang twice before he answered. He approved my idea of using a camera to photograph the paperwork.

"I will be with you in an hour."

I wanted to get this out of the way, then and there. A roll of film was just as bad as carrying papers around with me. After hanging up the phone, I walked down the hallway, and out into the sunshine. Looking around the street, I tried to pick out any sign of Pickwood's men. It was a waste of time. If I was being trailed, I could not see anyone. It would only draw attention to me, and I did not need that right now.

Pickwood's office was one block away. All I wanted to do was get this film to him, and get the hell out of there. I was there by ten past one. Dropping the roll of film on his desk, I turned to leave. I didn't want to talk to him if I did not have to.

"Mister Birket, I will be talking to you very soon," he said.

Hearing that was like being kicked in the guts. Frankly, I was not surprised.

CHAPTER TWENTY-TWO

I got back to my place, eager to sleep. I could think better once I'd slept. The phone ringing, however, cut into that notion. I wanted to ignore it, but knew I wouldn't.

My day got a whole lot worse. Jack Bent's voice was high and shrilled. He was one of our shipping agents based in Pennsylvania. I knew what he was calling about even before he began his excited chatter through the phone.

I tried to sound surprised about the *Clemmy G.*'s having been stopped, and boarded by the Coast Guard. I'd already lost a shit load of money on the deal, and I was now told that the ship itself had been impounded by the treasury. Could it get any worse? The way my luck was running right now, it had to. I let Jack have his rant, and hung up on him. My head was now spinning.

Pickwood picked the phone up as soon as I had finished dialling his number.

"I told you we would be speaking very soon, Mister Birket. You should listen to me more carefully," he said smugly.

The bastard was really enjoying this. I just knew he was.

"I shall be here for another hour, Mister Birket. I suggest you get here before then."

My brain felt fried as I climbed the steps again to his office. I could see the overhead light on through the glass panel on his door. Pickwood was sitting behind his desk. He was still signing papers. In fact, it was the same paper he had in front of him when I'd been there before. I knew it was a game to keep me on edge. It was working. I felt like the naughty school boy all over again.

"What about the *Clemmy G.*?" I demanded. "You have her impounded in some God damn port. That was not part of the deal!"

The asshole did not even give me a second glance as he informed me that it was now the property of the U. S. government. He even brokered a grin as he told me that as far as he was concerned, there had never been any deal. I was just doing as I was told.

Anger was boiling up within me. "If you keep my ship, how in God's name do you expect me to keep Capone supplied with his bootleg booze? How do you think I can keep track of him for you? Have you thought of that one, Mister Government Man?"

"You have other ships don't you, Birket?"

"It is Mister Birket, you God damn asshole! And yes I do, but if I use another ship, he might ask questions as to why. Have you thought of that one? And if he asks questions, do you not think that he might change shipping lines? From what I know of Capone's set up, it's that he likes continuity."

Placing his pen back in his pocket, Pickwood looked at me. A thoughtful look now settled upon his face.

"Very well, Mister Birket." Heavy sarcasm was now in order for him. He pointed to a chair at the rear of his small office. "Take a seat."

I stood my ground. I'd had enough of being ordered about by him. Picking the phone up in his right hand, he drew the pen from his pocket once more, and used that to dial. I could hear the ringing on the other end of the line. After two rings, a man's voice answered. He pointed to the seat at the back of the room, his eyes boring into me. I had made my defiance known, and I now settled back into the chair. Once Pickwood made known what his thoughts were, he listened closely to the voice on the other end of the phone.

Hanging up, he looked at me. "Very well, Mister Birket. Get back to your office, and call your lawyer."

My mouth fell open. Had I just dropped myself well and truly in the shit?

"You will be in front of Judge Freeman in Washington next week. I suggest you get a clean lawyer, Mister Birket. You don't want Zuckerman's lawyer in your corner, do you?"

He slipped a card across the desk for me. The man was full of God damn cards!

"Try this man. He is clean. You will be charged with breaking the *Falstead* act. He will plea bargain for you from a jail term to a fine. That should keep any questions at bay. Good day to you."

I stood up, and headed for the door. Ironically, he wasn't finished with me yet,

"Oh, and Mister Birket. Same time next month with more paperwork!"

I was now dismissed. His pen scribbled across more paper. I swore to myself that before I completed my disappearing act that there would be a bullet with this bastard's name on it. I hated him with a passion. He was doing to me exactly what I had rebelled on throughout my entire life. He was a smug, bullying bastard who knew he had me over a barrel.

CHAPTER TWENTY-THREE

I met with the lawyer Pickwood had recommended to me. Christopher Driscol was based in Washington. I was not happy about meeting an attorney I had never met before, and was less keen about the idea because Pickwood was the one who'd sent me to him. At the back of my head was the fact that the amount of people who now knew what I was doing was growing by the day. The ripples on the pond were now spreading outwards. I did not care how much of an assurance I was given. People always talked. In the racket I was in, when people talked, someone always ended up dead. In this case, it would be me.

For two hours, we talked over the case before the district attorney joined us. Pickwood had obviously told him what my involvement was. The case would be heard in the judge's chamber. At least I was not going to have to sit in an open court. I think my life would have been ended by the end of the day if that had been the case.

The formalities of the plea bargain had to be laid out in front of the judge. I was not sure if he knew about my involvement, but I had to assume he did. After, I pleaded guilty to every crime in the world, as well as the fall of the Roman Empire.

It cost me fifteen grand, including the cost for the court's time, as well as paying the impound fee. The booze sitting on the *Clemmy G.*

would be destroyed. I knew this was crap, as one of the mob bosses would most likely bribe the drivers to take a hit, and the booze would mysteriously disappear, thereafter, ending up in some bar or other owned by the mobs.

I was also sure that the days of the mob were coming to an end. I'd had time to think. I knew I had to get out of this racket. The problem for me was that there is no option of walking away from it. You either stayed with the mob until you died, or you stayed until a bullet killed you. The feeling of having to make a run for it grew deep within me now.

My plan seemed simple enough. I would start buying legitimate shares in other companies until I had enough money to cash them all in. When the end did come, I would still have a healthy income.

Whether the district attorney meant to or not, he let slip that the government was setting up a new department aimed at ridding the country of gangsters and hoodlums. By taking away their income, the money spent on buying protection from officials would be stopped. No money, no protection.

It all fell into place for me at that point. By taking Capone down, the biggest hood in the country, it would send a clear message to all the rest. If, and when, the prohibition ended. The booze racket would be no more. This alone would take millions of dollars out of the hands of the mob.

Back at my apartment, I packed a small case with the very basics of what I would need. When it was possible for me to do so, I would add more money to my stash. When my time to leave came, it would have to be quick.

I hid the case at the very back of a wardrobe, packing clothes and anything else I could find in front of it. I had no wish to let others see that I was planning on running.

I had plenty of friends in the financial district of New York all willing to give tips on long-term investments. What I needed was short-term gains. This meant making some illegal deals commonly known as insider trading. There were very few people I knew who did not have some inside knowledge of shares, and many were only too willing to share with friends. It is not something you can do over the phone, however. Share prices were on the up, and had been for some months now. Short-term gains with the right information should give me the cash I needed. In the meantime, I would carry on, making the booze runs I had to keep my life as normal as possible.

We sailed from New York on the 17th of December, 1928. I remember the day clearly. A hit was made on Governor Bill Twilly. He was one of the new breed of men who wanted an end to prohibition. Open and frank about his feelings, he took every opportunity to have his say in public.

Governor Twilly had taken to the steps of the Washington court building, the very same building I had been in only a short time ago. Two slugs fired from short range hit him. One in the guts, and the other high up on the shoulder. The gunmen were cut down by the local cops. It's one thing in turning a blind eye to illegal booze and racketeering, but even the cops could not let this one go. The bodies of the gunmen were never formally identified. Those of us in the know knew it was a mob ordered hit. The mobs did not want an end to easy money.

Governor Twilly survived the attack, and made great gains in popularity. The only thing the hit did was to increase the call to end prohibition. Other politicians jumped on the band wagon with him, creating a greater call for the *Falstead* act to be repealed.

CHAPTER TWENTY-FOUR

There was no real reason I had to sail on that trip. The operation was now pretty much back on track. Pickwood had kept his word, and left us alone. However, this came at a price to other gang bosses. Eight ships had been impounded in just over two weeks. None of them belonged to me. I knew I had been responsible for three of them being stopped. Pickwood and his weasels had to have more information coming in from other sources. This did not surprise me at all. He had the backing of the whole federal government.

The *S. S. Botany Adventurer* had tried to make a run for it from the Coast Guard ships. She was now lying in ninety fathoms of water out in the Atlantic. Most of her hands had gone down with her. Machine guns don't stick a cat-in-hell's chance against a four inch deck mounted gun. As each day passed, I knew I was getting deeper and deeper in the shit hole I was in. At least at sea, I could think clearly, and plan ahead. I had no idea how much time I would have to make my move. That all depended on Pickwood.

An Atlantic storm was raging even before we left the river estuary. We were constantly battered by the south westerly wind. The ship rocked back and forth like a shit house door. It did not help with us being in ballast. Normally, we would have a cargo to take to Canada, but this was a rush job for Zuckerman. When he wanted it done, he wanted it done, there and then.

I took several watches. This was more for my own benefit than anyone else's. Spending time in my cabin only made me think bad things about my own future. It looked pretty bad in every way. I had managed to amass forty-two grand in my hideaway. I had moved it from the back of the wardrobe to under the floor itself. With me being away on these voyages for so long, it would be easy pickings for any would-be thief. I still had no idea where I would run to. It would do no good staying in the United States. Once the shit hit the fan, there would be a contract out on me that would allow any hit man to retire on the hit.

I had thought many times about tipping Capone off. I knew if I had done so, one of two things would happen. Pickwood would have me in prison before I could take a crap. Or Capone would have me bumped off as a risk to his empire.

My thoughts came back to the ship as another wave smashed over us. I lost my balance for a second, having the grab a hold of the binnacle in front of me. There was not a murmur from the men on the bridge with me. Things had changed since I had taken some of the watches. I now had some authority. The slightest laugh or comment from the men on watch would have resulted in them being sent forward to check the mast head light.

Snow was being driven along on the wind. It was one of those sorts of watches you wouldn't turn a dog out in. At the moment, the sea was washing the snow off of the ship. If the wind dropped, and the snow kept falling, it would be a different matter. Tons of snow setting on the ship could make her top heavy. Many ships had been lost this way. A man's chances in the water in these conditions were jack shit.

Every muscle in my body hurt from being thrown about, and trying to hang on as each wave smashed over us. By the time I was back in my cabin at two in the morning, all I wanted to do was sleep. At least the exhaustion I was feeling would stop me from thinking, and I could get some sleep, after all.

We dropped anchor in the early hours of Christmas Eve. Snow was still falling heavily. At least the wind had dropped. With luck, we would be alongside by mid-day. What a way to spend the festive season, stuck out in the middle of a snow storm with a gale of wind blowing down your trousers.

At eleven in the morning, we began to haul the anchor, ready to slip alongside our berth. It would still be another hour and a half before we made fast.

CHAPTER TWENTY-FIVE

Mat Valente met me at the quayside. At least I would spend the evening and night in good company. It was good to see him again.

The night went as I had expected it to go. His place was filled with women and booze. Both ready and willing to make sure I was kept warm throughout the night.

It had to be close to midnight when Mat mentioned a name to me in passing. For several minutes, it played on my mind. I knew the name, but in the state I was in could not connect with it. It dawned on me who it was as I lay on the bed with some girl. Her name was of no interest to me. She was only too happy to have sex with me. That's all I cared about right now.

The name of the treasury man I had been dealing with coursed through my mind. I felt sick to my stomach. For some time now, I had wondered how the treasury department had caught on to me. It was falling into place. Mat Valente had ratted me out to them. There was no other explanation for it. How else would he know the man? Mat was in Canada. Pickwood was in New York. The way he talked about him made him seem like a long lost uncle.

I then tried to dismiss things from my mind. The reason being, I had known him for many years, on and off. He was not the ratting kind. But then again, neither was I. Yet, I had spilled my guts.

I hated Pickwood, and the way he was blackmailing me into ratting. Yet Mat drew his name like a gun. Could it be that he was under the cosh like me? Or was he just an unwitting stooge in all of this? Either way, I needed to know more.

I was distracted by Jenny who was, by now, naked again, and kissing my body all over. No matter what she or I did, I could not get rid of the thought that I'd been ratted on by a friend.

By three o clock in the morning, I had sobered up, and needed a drink. Jenny was still naked, fast asleep, her dark hair matted to her face.

Slipping my pants on, I left the bedroom, silently in search of a cold drink. The small light in the dining room was still on, so I did not bother turning any more lights on. Nearing the kitchen, I could hear Mat talking. To whom, I had no idea, but my suspicions from earlier got the better of me. As quietly as I could, I crept closer. Mat's voice was a lot clearer now.

"Sorry, Uncle, I know I have screwed up, but maybe he did not take it all in. He was pretty smashed, you know."

Mat grew silent. The other person was talking now. I did not have to hear the voice. I knew now my good friend was related to the treasury man.

Making my way back to the lounge area of the house, I deliberately kicked a small foot stool, letting out a loud curse as I did so. Quickening my pace, I stumbled through the kitchen doorway, surprising Mat.

"Yes, Mother, he is here now. Of course. I shall pass on your good wishes."

There was no doubt now. I knew who the rat was. But what was I going to do about it?

His blustering about his mother to me only deepened my belief that he was a rat. If it was not the hangover making me feel sick, the sight of him standing in front of me spouting off about his mother made me feel it.

I could only play the game calmly right now. What I really wanted to do was kill the bastard. Not only had he cost me my very life, but also a lot of money. I sipped my glass of water, looking at him. If he knew that I had tumbled him, he was very good at hiding it. However, his eyes gave him away. I had to find out more. I sat down at the table, the smoke from my cigarette spiralling upwards.

"Do you mind if I use your phone? I need to call New York."

He pointed to the phone he'd just used. "Help yourself. I won't be long. I might even take Suzie with me for company. If you know what I mean."

The confident grin was now back on the bastard's face. Waiting for him to leave the room, I fumbled about for my diary.

"Operator, I have just been cut off. Can you reconnect me to the number I had?"

The beauty of small telephone exchanges was that there were only one or two people on the other end of the line.

"I am sorry, caller. I shall reconnect you now."

I waited for several moments, and then the phone rang twice. There was a brief moment of silence.

"Pickwood, here. Who is it?"

I hung up. That's all I wanted to know.

If I could have gotten away with it, I would have put a bullet through the dirty rat's head, right there and then. That would have been too easy, though. He would be dead, but I would be in prison.

I then put a call through to New York, but it was to my apartment. If he was suspicious about me, he might try the same trick I had, and check on the number. By the time he came back, I was sitting back at the table, drawing on another cigarette. The familiar feeling of being kicked in the guts was back.

The giggling bitch, Suzie, followed the rat to the bathroom. The sounds of water running were drowned out by her annoying laughter, and squeals of pleasure.

Enjoy it, pal. If I had anything to do with it, this would be one of the last screws he had. I had pretty much made my mind up on that.

I sat there, listening to them for a few minutes. Not out of any sense of perversion, mind you. I was just too shocked, and pissed off to move right now. I felt betrayed by this man, yet somehow, I was not surprised, and that annoyed me more. He had put me in a world of shit that I could see no real way out of.

I had trusted him, and again, that hurt. I did not give my trust out so easily. This bastard had pretty much found out everything I was doing, as well as my plans for some time ahead.

I would not be sorry when he got his.

CHAPTER TWENTY-SIX

I stayed with Mat Valente for another two days. As each minute went by, my loathing for the bastard deepened. Each time he left the house, I found an excuse to stay. This gave me the chance to ferret about. I searched his drawers, cupboards, and any other place he might have information hidden.

Mat had not been very careful about hiding his tracks. Maybe he was still ignorant to the fact that I now knew all about him. The bottom drawer of his bedside cabinet had several contact numbers, and even department numbers, of the various government offices he was calling. I made notes of these. As soon as I got back to the United States, I would make it my business to call them. Several names of cargo ships were also on another list. I knew two of them, at least, had been stopped by the Coast Guard, including the *Clemmy G.*

To my horror, the date of our sailing and time had been underlined twice. I put everything back as I had found it. The knot in my stomach tightened with every second. If I was right in my suspicions, the *Clemmy G.* would be stopped again when we hit the United States territorial waters.

I began to hatch a plan in my mind that might work, but I needed to get back to the ship. I could not just leave. I wanted him to think that everything was normal. That was the understatement of the year.

By mid-afternoon, Mat invited me down the warehouse. He had some paperwork to prepare. This would give me the chance to slip back aboard. I readily accepted. I could do with picking up a change of clothing, I told him.

On the drive back to the ship, I tried to keep things light. Inside, I hated this man with all my heart.

Back aboard the *Clemmy G.*, I went below to my cabin before quickly calling in on the skipper. By the time I went ashore again, I had slipped him two envelopes. Mat was blowing his car horn.

I walked down the gangway, knowing there was no turning back now. I had no regrets about what I had just done. It was self-preservation, as far as I was concerned.

We sailed from Halifax on the 29th of December in one of the fiercest snow storms of modern times. Visibility was less than ten yards, at times. All available hands were placed on lookout duties. We were steaming at dead slow ahead.

The pier we had been berthed at was quickly out of sight. This suited our purpose. We would only be steaming for an hour. Two miles along the coast line was a warehouse I owned. It had been bought when I was going to go into the booze game with Mat on a bigger scale. Thankfully, he knew nothing about it. Now, it would pay for itself.

We steamed using the ships log as a navigation aid. It was the only way to see through the snow storm. The log is a metal torpedo-like device that is lowered over the stern of the ship. The torpedo turns in the water, and that in turn, makes a dial go around on deck. This can give you a reading of how far the ship has travelled. In this weather, it was the most accurate way for us. The rest of the navigation was down to the skill of the skipper and lookouts. We would have no chance of getting alongside in this weather, but we could lay off the jetty, and wait it out.

It was well after nightfall when the weather began to clear. The skipper of the *Clemmy G.* was good. He had reckoned us bang on our mark.

Within the next hour, we were alongside the *S. S. Ventura*. Her cargo hatches were already open. Throughout the night, both crews swapped the cargos from each ship.

By oh-six hundred hours, we sailed again. This time, we were carrying machine parts. The *Ventura* had the booze aboard her. She would sit at her berth for another twenty-four hours before sailing. If we were given the order to heave to by the Coast Guard, then I would have no doubts in my mind that Mat had ratted me out again.

For two days, we sailed south along the coastline, staying out of U. S. waters as if it was our normal routine. Just after dawn on the third day, the U. S. Coast Guard ship came into view. Her signal lamp flashed us to heave to.

Sitting two hundred yards off of our port beam, the Coast Guard ship began lowering boats. Several well-armed crew members scrambled down the cargo nets into them. Pushing away from the ship's side, the crew began hauling on the long wooden oars. The sea was still choppy. The bastards would get wet, at least, on their way over to us. It was not long before the small boats needed bailing out. Sea water was beginning to fill the bottom of the boats up. Bailing tins were now at full swing.

You had to give them full marks for their determination. It must have taken them a full thirty minutes to row across the short distance to us. Several of their crew members had parted company with their recent meals into the bottom of the boats. A whaler is no place to be when the sea is a bit choppy. It will make the most hardened sailor want to part company with anything in his guts.

The senior officer clambered up the cargo nets we had put over the rail for them. Falling on his arse as he landed on the main deck, I stifled a laugh while standing on the bridge. No one from our crew helped him up. He was not here to do us any favours. Brushing himself down, and checking that his side arm had not slipped out of its holster, he made his way onto the bridge followed by three of his crew. The rest of the men waited below on the main deck.

I'd perched myself at the aft end of the bridge. If he wanted to talk to me, he could see me well enough.

"Captain, I am Lieutenant Bryce of the U. S. Coast Guard. We have orders to search your vessel for contraband. Should we find any such contraband aboard your ship, its cargo will be impounded for breaking the *Falstead* act. Do you understand what I have just said to you, sir?"

The skipper took the paper from the lieutenant's outstretched hand. With a quick scan of it, he set it down on the chart table.

Lieutenant Bryce tapped the window of the bridge, signalling his men to begin the search. Taking two steps back, he quickly moved to cover over his side arm.

No one on the bridge moved. He did not draw his weapon. We all knew he meant business, though. On the main deck, canvas sheeting and deck boards were stacked neatly on the port side of the ship. Two ladders lashed to the port side rails were now lowered into the hold. With torches flashing, the crew of the Coast Guard ship climbed down. They knew exactly which hold they wanted.

For the next three hours, they checked box after box in the number four hold. The leading hand eventually came topside again, waving his left hand to indicate they had found nothing in that hold. At this point, Lieutenant Bryce left the bridge. It did not take a genius to work out what he was saying to his men.

The order would be to search the ship from stem to stern. Bryce stood at the port rail, signalling his ship. Again, there was no need to read his signal. His men had already started to uncover the forward hatch. This was going to be a long day for them. Another twelve hours passed before Bryce called an end to the search. Night had fallen, and the snow was now heavy on the decks. The running lights from the Coast Guard ship were only just visible to us.

I was not going to let the opportunity pass without comment.

"I shall be sending a bill to your department, Lieutenant. You have cost this vessel over a day in costs, and for what? Nothing. Nada. Zip."

I had no doubt that if I had sent a bill in for accrued costs, it would not be paid. Never-the-less, I felt better about having said it.

The irritation in his voce as he said his goodbyes was all too evident to those of us standing on the bridge. As soon as the last man had scrambled down the cargo net, the skipper gave orders for us to get under way again.

The wind had fallen off within the next hour to be replaced with even heavier snow. Once again, the deck hands were ordered out on deck to shovel snow off of the decks, and break ice from the rigging.

It had been a long day for all of us, and I was ready to turn in. My cabin was warm thanks to the heat coming up from the engine room. Lying in my bunk, I tried to sleep, but recent events would not allow me to. Mat had well and truly shit on me. Eventually, I fell asleep, knowing the slime ball would get his, sooner rather than later. I had no problems with that at all.

CHAPTER TWENTY-SEVEN

Following the *Clemmy G.*'s having been stopped and searched, I made a long distance call to Capone's man in Chicago. Ernest Coulton was his money man. Unlike most of the men who worked for Capone, he was well-educated and well-spoken.

He had received the telegram I had asked the skipper to post for me back in Canada. The personal touch of a phone call was always better, though. All bootleg trafficking through my shipping company had stopped since that date. It meant I would be losing valuable income, but if the ships were to continually get stopped, it was the only option. Capone's booze would now be brought in over land from other suppliers.

As for Mat, he would be getting a visit any day now from a couple of Capone's men. There would only be one outcome.

By late January of 1929, none of the ships in the *Birket* shipping line had moved any bootleg booze for Capone. Instead of using Mat in Halifax, Zuk had been using a supplier from the far southern states. The treasury men had no further use of me, at the moment. I had no problem with this at all, but I was wise enough to know that the treasury department never let go of a fish once it was hooked.

The news I had been waiting for came to me on the 31rst of January.

Mat had been killed. From what I had heard, it was not a pretty death. Most of his bones had been broken before he had taken a single shot to the head. As a final touch, a rat had been forced into his mouth.

The official line was that he had stumbled across a robbery at his warehouse. This would have held things up, seeing as most of the booze in his warehouse had been taken. To anyone who knew about mob punishment, the rat in the mouth gave it away. It was a clear warning to others. Not that Capone needed to send many warnings out.

One of his last acts before the government took action was on the 14th of February, 1929. Capone was in yet another turn war with a rival gang. He lured them to a nearby car park. Once there, he had them slaughtered. It was dubbed the St. Valentine's Day massacre by the press. For once, they had not sensationalized it.

Yet it was not until March of that year that Capone was taken into custody. It wasn't for the murder of the six, however. His usual tactics of bribery and threats failed. He even had a physician's note saying he was suffering from Pneumonia.

As he left the court of the grand jury in late March, he was immediately arrested for contempt of court. He posted his bond, and was released. By May of that year, he and one of his men were arrested for the crime of carrying a concealed weapon. So keen was the government to rid the streets of him that his case was dealt with within twenty-four hours. He was given a one year prison term.

The government had made their statement to the mobs. If they could get to somebody like Capone, then the rest were easier to get to. It did have the desired effect on Zuk back in New York. Although he continued to bring booze in against the *Falstead* act, he was also trying to become legitimate.

America was going through a time of boom. Even poor businessmen could make money on the stock exchange. The cost of buying judges and city hall officials was getting higher each week. Being legitimate cost nothing but taxes. The time of the big mob bosses was coming to an end. It was only the stupid who felt otherwise.

I did not consider myself a mob boss or stupid. I began investing in companies that had good short-term outlooks. At some point, I would make my move to get away from all of this. I knew it would only be a matter of time before the treasury went after Zuckerman.

With Capone, it had been fairly easy to get information to the treasury men. Capone did not really know me. Although, I had met him once or twice in the last year. Here in New York, Zuk had eyes everywhere, and very little got past him. The thought of having all of my limbs broken, and a rat shoved in my mouth before being shot, scared the crap out of me.

I continued to spend most of my evenings at the Green Parrot. Over the past several weeks, I'd noticed that the amount of city hall officials coming and going had dropped off. I pointed this out to Danny on one occasion. All he said was that they may be away now, but they will be there when we wanted them to be. He lived in a dream world.

Several judges had been given amnesties from the prosecution already. They may not remain as a judge, but they were left alone to continue in practice. I had no doubt they had spilled their guts in order to be given the amnesty they received. The price they would pay for their treachery would be high. There is no hiding place from the mob.

This feeling was confirmed when two of the highest ranking judges in the state met with so-called accidents. Judge Harvey Longmire was found dead, face down in the river. His body had so much alcohol in it that it could have pickled a Herring. The official line was that he was drunk while in charge of his vehicle. Having lost control of his car, he ploughed through a fence. The car was recovered, face down, in a quiet river upstate. Judge Longmire was still sitting behind the wheel. It was not the usual mob hit. This was meant to look like an accident.

The other judge to die was John Steel. The gas mains in his country home exploded one dark cold night. There was not much of him left to bury. The body of a young girl was found in one of the outbuildings. She had a syringe stuck to her arm. The post mortem carried out on her showed that it was narcotics that had killed her. The fact that she was on the judge's property and the syringe had the judge's dabs on it made for some raised eyebrows. Judge Steel was deemed to have committed suicide. The young girl found on his property was left as an open verdict.

Both judges had agreed to give evidence to the grand jury, indicting several local mob bosses. Zuk, being one of them. These were no accidents. It would have been easy to have them bumped off by one of his hit men. I had no doubt in my mind that it would have sent a very clear message to anyone else thinking of ratting him out. However, by doing that, it would have brought the government agencies into play. As we all knew, the government had far more powers to dig deeper in the shit pile than the local cops. Suspicions might be aimed at the local mob bosses, but they had no real foundations to them.

On the day of the funerals for each of the judges, Zuk, Jimmy Carboni, Johnny Duke, and Gino Campanelo attended the graveside. This was the first time these men had been in the same place at the same time in over six years. It was an uneasy meeting, but it was also a show of strength to all there.

Government men were there, taking photographs of the assembled mob bosses. This was more to annoy them than for public record. Their photographs had been plastered on every newspaper in the state over the past few years. The mob bosses held a silent dignity. The last thing they wanted was for any sort of drama to unfold that would bring the G. men down on them. Zuk even managed to dab a tear away from his eyes as he walked past the graveside.

Judge Steel's widow knew why the men were there, and took great delight in slapping Johnny Duke hard across the right cheek. Duke stood there for several seconds, the veins in his neck standing out as his rage grew. No one had done that to him in many years. The mourners at the graveside whispered amongst themselves at what had just happened.

As for Duke, he took the widow's hand, and shook it, whispering to her that he was sorry for her loss. Whatever else he whispered to her was not heard by anyone else. However, she recoiled in horror, taking two paces back before stumbling into the outstretched arms of her twenty-year-old daughter. Tears welled up in her eyes before freely flowing down her face.

It was no great surprise to anyone when the daughter ended up in the local hospital two days later, following a knife attack that left her scarred forever along the right side of her face. Johnny Duke had made sure he was in the company of the local police chief at the time of the attack.

CHAPTER TWENTY-EIGHT

By May of 1929, the days of the big gangster were coming to an end.

In April of that year, Jimmy Malone was gunned down by the G. men just outside of Charlottesville. He and his gang had tried robbing the second city bank. The G. men had waited for them to get into the bank before surrounding it. With a haul of thirty-two thousand bucks tucked into mail bags, they came back from the vault area in the bank's basement. The lookout man, Sol Perlman, had not seen the G. men waiting outside. The gang fired several warning shots at the bank staff, urging them to stay still for the next ten minutes.

The G. men opened up. Tear gas first blinded the gang. Alongside, the local cops opened up with machine guns and shotguns. The gang took cover inside of the bank, trying to use the staff as hostages. The cops were not going to negotiate with them. Hundreds of rounds poured into the bank. The gang was now well and truly screwed. They opened up themselves on the cops outside, and were now using the hostages as human shields.

Two cops fell early in the fire fight. This only intensified the fire going into the bank. Malone dragged a woman hostage to the doorway, threatening to kill her. He also threatened to kill someone every five minutes, unless the cops drew back, and gave him and his men safe passage out of the place.

A single snipers round hit him in the forehead, dropping him instantly. His hostage fell to the ground, screaming in a blind panic. Cops and G. men moved forward, using cars as shields. Heavy fire came from the bank for another minute or so. Seeing that Malone was dead, his gang soon gave up the fight.

At their trial, two of Malone's former gang members were given the death sentence because of the cops' murders. The rest were sent away to prison for various terms, ranging from sixteen years hard labour to life without parole.

Buck Leadbetter had been another of the big players for several years. He was taken at his mother's graveside on a quiet Sunday afternoon. Two G. men casually dressed walked up to him, and slapped the cuffs on him before he had time to cross himself. He was found to have two silver Colt's tucked inside his waistband. The G. men searched his car, and a Thompson sub-machine gun was found in the trunk, along with over ten grand in cash.

Buck Leadbetter had been instrumental in the killing of six rival men. He was tried In Washington D. C., and was sentenced to the chair. He left the court, threatening his revenge against the district attorney and the trial judge. They were the last threats he ever made. Two days later, during a failed escape from the jail, he was gunned down by a small army of cops. They chased him half way across the state, eventually cornering him on a quiet road.

CHAPTER TWENTY-NINE

More and more of the mob bosses had turned from the rackets and bootlegging to narcotics. Their reasoning was simple. There were greater profits achieved from this, and narcotics were easier to hide. A car could bring in as many drugs in one go than a fleet load of wagons could bring bootleg booze in.

There were no cops and judges to pay off with narcotics. Users would become distributors, taking a small amount of the top for their own use. To make up the amounts, they would cut the drugs with other agents. Talcum powder was a favourite used.

Private houses would become the new warehouses. Over a city as big as New York, that would amount to a lot of warehouses. Millions of dollars were being used for narcotics.

Some of the bosses had strict rules as to whom the drugs could be sold to. Some of the heavy users had begun selling them to high schools. Although the profits to the dealers were high, some of the bosses still had a moral code they stood by. Several dealers in Zuk's patch had been given broken knee caps for selling to kids.

Other bosses saw this as an ongoing market. It came down to money again. The effects on the users were devastating, at times. Some bosses sold cheaper narks to kids to get them hooked, and the kids would shop about for the best deals.

Going from one supplier to another had different effects. The dealer who cut the drugs with other agents made a weaker drug. So naturally, when a kid got stronger drugs, and gave him or herself the same amount, it was the same as taking an overdose. I had seen kids from rich well-to-do families turn to prostitution for their next fix. Families desperate to get their kids off drugs would throw them out on the streets with the thinking that by cutting off their money supply for the drugs, it would stop them from using. Little did they know, the high degree of dependency on narcotics would come at a great cost.

Danny Strain, from the Green Parrot, was a classic example of an addict. After a couple of months of taking the stuff, he became paranoid to the degree of keeping his gun sitting on the bar next to him. On several occasions, he became agitated by people's laughter, convinced they were laughing at him.

I had been on the receiving end of his paranoia once. I have no shame in admitting that I pissed my pants when he held the gun to my head with the hammer drawn back. There was little point in trying to talk him round, or to tell him I was not laughing or talking about him. If he was going to blow my brains all over the bar, he would do it, regardless of anything anybody said. For what seemed like a lifetime, I sat there with the cold metal pushing into the right temple of my head. Beads of sweat poured off of him, dripping onto the table as he snarled his death threat to me.

Another punter at the bar moved. Danny was convinced that the man was now out to shoot him. His attention turned to the poor bastard. The punter's first, and biggest mistake, was trying to laugh the situation off as Danny marched over to him. The veins in his neck stood out as the rage grew within him. Danny did not shoot the man. Instead, he turned his pistol around, and beat the poor sap to within an inch of his life.

No one in the bar moved. Your own mortality stops you from moving, and it is easy to reason that it is not your problem. As for Danny, he thought the whole incident was funny. A maniacal laugh came from him as he stood over the bleeding mess on the floor.

People began drifting out of the bar, quietly and quickly. Silent tears fell from some of the women's faces. Husbands and lovers urged them to be silent as they made their way towards the doorway. For two days, Danny sat around the bar in his bloodstained suit. Before he had gotten into the drugs, he would have worn a new suit every night. Now, he was a mess.

This went on for several more weeks. Then one night, Danny disappeared. His body was found in the Hudson River by the cops. It was determined he had died from an overdose of narcotics. My own feeling was that Zuk had seen enough of his one-time friend losing him business.

The one thing I learned about narcotics was that once it had you in its grip, it would never let go. A man's self–respect, thinking, and morals went down the toilet. The only thing you want is your next fix of drugs. It doesn't matter how you got them. You just had to have that fix. Self-respect was the last thing addicts were concerned about.

CHAPTER THIRTY

For the past few months, the *Birket* shipping line was growing. My time at the Green Parrot club was curtailed, as was to a certain extent, my time at sea. I was not unhappy about this. The Danny Strain incident had scared me. I have no problem with admitting that to anyone.

I threw myself into building the *Birket* line up. I still had to deal with Zuckerman on a daily basis. He had become a member of the board. If we were to expand, then I would need the approval of the board. I could have sold some of my shares of the company, but this would mean that I would lose control of it. I had no intention of doing that.

Zuckerman and his fellow board members loaned me money from their own personal stores to allow the expansion plans. Again, they would get the best end of the deal. The shares they held would soar in the current climate. The end-of-the-year dividends would also yield a good profit for them.

For me, it meant putting myself into a lot of debt with the mob, but I would get the extra money with a lower interest rate than any of the banks could offer. Zuckerman let it be known to a lot of his clients what the plans for the company were. This meant the share prices went up rapidly. Since I had started the new company, I had seen my own shares soar from an initial two dollars per share to just below four dollars per share. It seemed like the whole world had gone money mad. If it was an investment that would make a buck or two, then there was always some silly ass to invest in it.

I had borrowed a total of five hundred thousand dollars from members of the board. With the reckoning I had done, and the amount of money I had myself invested, I could be debt-free of the loan in two years time. Until that time, my ass belonged to the mob. The other side of the coin was that the members of the board knew how to bring in good profitable contracts that would see us expanding for the next five or six years.

CHAPTER THIRTY-ONE

I had not seen Pickwood for several months now. Perhaps this was partly due to the fact that the *Birket* shipping line no longer carried bootleg booze into the country. Or the fact that his rat in Canada had been dealt with swiftly by Capone. Several of our ships had been stopped in the past few months by the Coast Guard vessels. They never found any contraband on them.

It was one of those times when you think all is going well in your life. Yet as soon as that thought came to me, I knew the shit would hit the fan. I did not have to wait too long. Within twenty-four hours, I received a knock on the door.

Rochelle had spent the night with me. Even first thing in the morning, she looked good. The silk dressing gown she wore hung off of her shoulder. She looked at the door, and then at me. It was far too early for this to be a social call. Pulling her robe up over her shoulders, she sprawled herself out on the long leather sofa. Smoke drifted upwards as she lit her second cigarette of the morning. The smell of fresh coffee sweetened the smell.

Pulling my shirt on correctly, I opened the door. My mouth fell open as Pickwood stood in front of me. Alarm bells began to ring inside me. God, the last thing I wanted was for Rochelle to know that I was a rat fink for the treasury men.

Pickwood saw the look on my face. A small smile spread across his lips. Coffee and cigarette smoke blew towards the open door. Rochelle's purse sat on the table behind me. His eyes fell straight on it.

"Sorry, sir, I must have the wrong apartment. I was looking for the Jenks apartment." Holding his wrist up so that only I could see it, he pointed to the watch. "One hour. My office!" he whispered.

Turning on his heels, he walked away. I breathed a huge sigh of relief. At least he had some tact. I closed the door with a slight nod of acknowledgment to him. I felt sick to my guts again. I had hoped I'd seen the last of him. How wrong can one man be?

I slammed the door shut, cursing noisily. Rochelle had slipped her robe off, and was now lying on the sofa with that seductive grin she had about her. A short strand of hair covered her lips. Her right hand covered her breasts. Slowly, her hand moved down along her body. The smile on her face was inviting to me. She stroked her body several times, her head turning slowly from side to side. The strand of hair that had covered her lips had fallen back off of her face, and she was now slightly pouting. Her tongue snuck out, and she licked her moist lips. As much as I wanted her, right then and there, I turned, and went towards the bathroom.

I dared not be late for Pickwood. I knew he would come back. Maybe next time, he would not be so tactful.

By the time I had showered and dressed, Rochelle was sitting back at the table. A slight look of disappointment and annoyance was spread across her face. I doubt many men had left her feeling like that before.

I had no time to worry about her mood right now. I felt like one of Pickwood's lap dogs. When he called, I went, no matter what. I hurried from my apartment, still straightening my tie, and combing my hair as I made my way out into the hot day. My fear of Pickwood and what he could do to me at the stroke of a pen urged me to move my ass. The nightmares I had been having of me being locked in a prison cell for the rest of my life only made me move quicker. I knew I could never survive in jail. Pickwood knew this as well. The bastard had me over a barrel. I almost ran up the five concrete steps to the main door of treasury offices.

His office still had a musty smell about it. The familiar paperwork spread out across the top of his desk had not changed. I wondered if this was for my benefit.

As he had done on previous visits, he kept me waiting while he scanned a sheet of paper before scribbling his name at the bottom of it. This no longer had any effect on me. I knew this was all part of his game to keep me in suspense for a few seconds longer.

Without even looking up at me, he told me he wanted Zuckerman. I froze on the spot. It was one thing giving him information on Capone. After all, I had no real knowledge of the man, apart from what I'd read or had been told. Zuckerman was different. I knew loads about him. If I spilled my guts, it would be clear as to who it came from. I was as good as dead now.

"No," I protested. "I can't do it. Do you know that it will mean my death? Or do you not care enough about that?"

Pickwood looked up at me. His glasses slipped half way down his nose. He now looked like the headmaster of a school about to punish a pupil.

"Quite frankly, Mister Birket, no, I personally don't give a hoot about what happens to you, but the government does not work like that. Consider this. Life in prison is a long time for a rat like you."

The bastard was not mincing his words.

"But like Capone, we will get Zuckerman with or without your help. So the choice is yours. Now, sit down."

This was more of a command than a request. I did as I was told, and slumped into the creaky wooden chair opposite him. I hated this guy. If I had one chance, I would happily put a bullet into his scrawny balding head.

One look into my eyes, and he knew he had me again. I could taste the defeat in my voice. I hated it.

The small buzzer on his desk rang to the outside office. I could feel my whole body tense. Was he having me taken to prison now?

The door swung open. I was waiting for some of his friends to come in rough me up a bit to keep me calm, and then drag me out while I was puking up my last cup of coffee. Instead, a small middle-aged woman entered the room. I had not seen her before. She clutched a writing pad and pen in her right hand as she closed the door silently with her left hand.

Pickwood turned his attention back to me. "We shall begin with his shipments of narcotics. Miss Madison will take down what you say."

He knew I would spill my guts. I had no other choice.

Miss Madison sat in the third chair behind me. The faint smell of cheap perfume filled the room. I was not sure as to what was making me feel sicker. Whether it was her perfume, or the fact that I was now in a world of shit even bigger than I had been before.

As an act of defiance, I protested at her being there. "How many God damn people are going to know about all of this?"

I knew it was only an act in myself, but I had to make some form of protest.

"Get on with it, Mister Birket, and Miss Madison stays."

From behind me, the sound of her chair moving across the varnished wooden floor annoyed the crap out of me. I had no real idea about how much narcotics Zuk was bringing into the country or how. I had told him, time and time again, that I hated narcotics. Pickwood finally accepted this from me only after an hour of questioning, but I did give him the name of some of the buyers, and how he got the stuff to them.

Miss Cheap Scent was scribbling away behind me. I could hear her pen scratching across the paper as I spoke every word. Whether it was intentional or not, Pickwood let it slip that Zuk was bringing in over two tons of the shit each year.

"If you know how much he is bringing in, why don't you just stop his supply?"

He did not answer me. There was little point in asking him again.

After all, he was asking the questions. I was just the piece of shit on his shoe.

For five hours, I sat there telling him what I knew, or did not know. At times, I had to think on my feet. I was not going to put my head in the noose willingly, and connect myself to murders. My sense of own survival was still strong. At the moment, I was not under arrest so I had some freedom. If I had spilled my guts about the two killings I had been involved with, I would be held in custody, and would still have to rat Zuckerman out.

My thinking was pretty clear. If I was on the outside, I could run. Inside, I was dead. I might even be dead on the outside, but it was a chance. One, I had to keep to myself for now.

By the time I had left his office, I was beyond tired. My head was also pounding from the stress of it all.

It was not over yet. Pickwood would check out what I had told him so far. If it was correct, we would sit down, and talk again, as he put it. There was no mention of what would happen if I had filled him full of bullshit. Then again, there was no need to mention it. I knew already.

My apartment was cold and dark when I got back. Rochelle had obviously got pissed off with waiting around. The only thing left of her was the smell of her perfume. At least that did not smell sickly sweet. I slumped into the leather arm chair with a large glass of Scotch whiskey, almost drinking it in one gulp. The bitterness of it burned the back of my neck as it went down. Pouring myself another one, I sat there with the afternoon sun almost blinding me through the window.

I had very little option now, but to run, and to run soon. I needed money, and lots of it. In my head, I began hatching a plan. Slowly, I would begin selling shares. I knew this would take months. Until then, I would have to play the role of being the government's lap dog. I knew I would be able to get a false identity card from one of the many underground hoods with no questions asked. It happened all the time.

The one good thing was that at the moment, shares were being bought and sold for small fortunes. If I could ride this storm out with the government for the next month or so, I could make my run.

Any guilt about hanging Zuk was justified after downing the next three glasses of Scotch. After all, what was he to me? He deserved to get caught for his crimes. Scotch whiskey made a great friend. It was always ready to tell you that you are right in your thinking. It was in the morning when your friend had gone that your thinking and guilt came back to you.

I woke up with a pain in my neck. I had fallen asleep in my chair, the empty glass smashing to the marble floor. I lit another cigarette, and let the smoke drift up to the ceiling. The lock of the door turned, and the bright ceiling light hurt my eyes. Rochelle stood there, looking like a million dollars. The smile on her face was warm and seductive. For a few more hours, I could hide my thoughts and fears, and enjoy her just as she would enjoy me.

CHAPTER THIRTY-TWO

By September 1929, I had given so much information to the federal government that they could have fried Zuk in the electric chair several times over. They had not yet arrested him. As each day passed, I got more and more jumpy. My natural paranoia had pretty much taken over my life.

Teams of government agents watched him around the clock, gathering their own evidence on him and anyone he talked to. I freely admit that I was happy to dive into a bottle of Scotch for breakfast, lunch, and dinner. It made me feel better about what I was doing. It also covered the deep loathing I had for myself.

Many times, I wondered as to how many men would have given another man up so easily to save their own necks. Perhaps there were many, but the circle I had been moving in over the past several years told me very few would have done it. I had seen men take the rap for the likes of Zuckerman and other mob bosses, choosing to spend time on the rock or other hellholes. Some had died for the mob. Others came out of prison broken men. Maybe it was because of their loyalty to the mob, or fear of reprisals against their families. It did not matter where the family lived in the world. If a hit was ordered, then the hit was made. Perhaps the reality of it all was that family came before prison.

I knew I had very little time left to get away. It was only a matter of time before the G. men took Zuk off of the streets. He would then face the grand jury. It was at that point that he would work out he'd been ratted out by someone close to him. I also knew it would be at that point in which he would put out a contract on the rat. I also knew, deep inside, that the G. men would try to call me in as a witness for the prosecution. If that was the case, I would never see the witness box. Even if I did, my life could be counted in hours.

Money could buy anything and anyone if it was offered in big enough amounts. Zuk had plenty of it to splash out. If it meant the difference between freedom and the chair, he would spend his last cent.

I began investing in more and more stocks and shares on Wall Street. If I was going to run, I would do it with enough money to lose myself in some far off place in the world where no one knew me, or even heard of America and its gangland bosses.

Every dollar I could find was invested on the markets. As it happened, the markets were prime for plucking right now. It was almost impossible to make a bad investment. I would sell shares for a profit on a daily basis, reinvesting the money for more shares in other companies.

Steel, shipping, oil, and banking were my favoured options. Friends would give me tip offs as to who was doing what on the markets, allowing me to make better investments. This was called insider trading. Although this was illegal, it went on big time within the stocks and shares community. I did not give a shit about the legality of it all. It was my life I was raising money for.

Within a very short time, I had managed to pay a lot of my debts off to the gang bosses I had borrowed from in order to invest in my shipping line. I avoided buying too many shares within my own company. The last thing I wanted was for any of the mob bosses to see the amount I was putting into the company. I had no great reason to invest more money in the *Birket* shipping line. My profits were soaring from my original investment.

I could have led a very extravagant lifestyle, and shown the world how well I was doing. Many of the rich people in New York saw this as part of being wealthy with big cars and big houses. Yet I remained in my modest apartment. I also kept to my routine as much as I possibly could. The last thing I wanted was for the G. men to cotton on to what I was trying to do. They wanted me at the grand jury to testify when they finally pulled the plug on Zuk.

I had been told that once he had been taken in, I would be taken as well, and placed in what they called protective custody. In other words, I would be in prison some place, left to rot, while they did what they had to do to convict another mob boss.

Late September saw me amass a reasonable amount of money in my security box at the *Hudson and West* bank. My new identity card was also safely tucked away at my apartment. It had been there for several weeks now. I had made sure of that. My reasoning was that even if checks were made about fake identity cards I would not be on the list. Normally, a person gets a new identity card to make their run as soon as possible. Long-term planning was not an option for them.

I hoped my forward planning would help me when the time came. My escape would be via Argentina on a steam ship. A simple cabin with no fuss about who I was, or what my business would be. Booking passage on the bigger liners to the Caribbean would only bring my attention to those on board. Many of the people I knew often went to the Caribbean for months at a time to escape the harsh New York weather.

Many would also take bundles of cash to invest in the Cuban islands to avoid tax. My main reason for avoiding the big ships was that my name would not tally with the people who would surely know me. Word would get back to the mob. I would be dead before we ever hit land. A body can be easily hidden in ten thousand miles of ocean, and the sharks would do the rest.

The steamer, *Queen of the Pacific*, was due to sail on the first of November. Up until that point, it was all about amassing as much money as I could.

I had thought about taking Rochelle with me as I had become very fond of her lately. She was of constant support to me, but at this moment in time, I could not tell her. My biggest fear was that she would unintentionally let it slip to others. Secrecy was the key right now.

If I took her, I could soon buy another ticket. Her identity was not as important as mine. She could travel under her real name. I had already made sure she had one. We had talked of spending time in Mexico on a vacation, so she had no need to be suspicious when I asked her about her identity.

CHAPTER THIRTY-THREE

During the early part of October 1929, all of my plans were going well. I had decided that I would take Rochelle with me. I stuck to the idea of the vacation in Mexico, leaving my real plans to the very last moment. It gave her just enough time to pack a suitcase. I had managed to stash away thousands of dollars into my security box at the bank. I also had several thousand dollars in mixed currency in my stash at home. I had no real idea where I was going to end up. I wanted to be sure that where I went, I would have some form of currency.

The shit hit the fan on the 24th of October. There had been rumblings about share prices on Wall Street reaching a peak. I took no notice of the rumours. These often went around the block a few times. I sat in my office waiting for the market to close, the little ticker tape machine sending out share prices.

By the end of that day, there was an eleven percent drop on the market. I sat by the ticker tape machine in my office constantly watching it. I'd lost only a few thousand dollars. I can't say I was overly concerned by that. Shares did rise and fall.

In my mind, I rationalized that the weekend would bring some calm and stability to the market. I spent the weekend at my private club. Most of the members were men in the know about the markets.

Bankers, business advisors, and the like. I felt quite comfortable with what I was hearing. Like me, many of the club members were thinking that it was just a glitch on the market. The weekend would bring a little stability to the market.

Monday morning saw me sitting by the ticker tape machine. I had a niggling feeling deep within me that all was not well.

Trading on Wall Street opened with a glut of selling. Share values began to fall drastically. By mid-morning, my nerve had gone. I had thought I could hold out and hope for a recovery. I was losing money rapidly on all of my shares. At the end of business, I had lost a small fortune on the markets.

I was glad when the bell sounded for the close of business. I had lost over two hundred thousand dollars that day alone. The news that day called it Black Monday. I called it a disaster. I needed to off load as many shares as I could the next day.

That night, I slept in my office. I wanted to be first in line to get a hold of the dealers in the morning. It had been impossible to contact any of traders. Their lines were permanently busy. I should have guessed that would happen. Many people would be doing the same as I was. I even drove round to my good friend and stock dealer, Garry Bart. A slew of other people had come up with the same idea. A long line of people were gathering around his home. Garry was standing on the stoop of his home, red-faced, and appealing for calm. Maybe he was right.

I turned my car around, and went back to my office. The phone was already ringing as I walked through the door. Investors in the *Birket* shipping line demanded to know what was happening to their own shares. After the first ten calls, I took the phone off the hook, and left it buzzing on the desk.

The top and bottom of it was that like many other businesses that day, we were in deep shit. Some of the smaller investors had already lost their money and more. The company was worth only half of what its value was at nine a.m. that morning.

Outside, many people had gathered in the streets. Mainly, the small investors wanting to get their money back from the banks, and were trying to sell their shares in various companies.

It was pointless for them if, like me, bankers and stock dealers would be holed up with a massive headache of their own. The night was one of the longest I had spent alone. I was willing for the morning to come.

During the course of the day, I, like many other investors, poured money into the stock market trying to prop my own interests up. I could only hope the new day brought calm. By seven a.m., I knew it would be another bad day. Investors in the *Birket* shipping line were almost kicking the doors off of the hinges in their haste to sell their shares, and gain some form of information. It was pointless for them to hammer on the doors. I personally did not hold the stock certificates.

I looked out of the window towards the banking district. Lines of people, much longer than last night, were forming at the doors of all the banks. All of them wanted their money.

The markets opened to a massive run on selling shares. Cops lined the streets outside of the banks. Money made ordinary people turn into pack animals. Fights broke out.

At ten o'clock, cops fired several riot guns into the air in an attempt to bring some order and calm to the area. It had no effect on the panic at all. Several people had collapsed in the crush of the crowd pushing forward in their attempts to get into the banks. They lay where they fell. The urge to get into the banks took over any sense of human decency at all.

Replacing the handset on the phone, it began ringing instantly. The first three calls were from smaller investors. All I could do was refer them to the dealers who had sold them the shares. The worry in their voices poured out. Life savings were at risk. There was no real way to give a good explanation to them at all.

Two out of the three calls, I ended abruptly. I was not prepared to listen to the threats and cussing coming down the line at me. I had enough of my own shit to deal with. My personal diary had all of my contact numbers in it. In between fielding calls, I tried to call my own dealers. The line was always busy. I prayed that they would have the sense to sell my shares, and salvage what they could for me. This was more of a hope than anything else. No one would see a client's shares without permission.

My next call was from Zuk. I sat in my chair listening to him. There was no cussing from him, but he made sure I was under no illusions that he would be holding me personally accountable for the state of the company. My protests fell on deaf ears.

By mid-day, the whole country had gone crazy. The market kept falling sharply. Even the big companies were now in a new world of shit. I joined the madness on the streets below, lining up to get into the banks. I had to try and salvage something from the day.

Shit like this did not go away in one day. If today was an example of what was to come, then I needed out. I stood in line with the rest of the crowd, demanding access to my account. Some of the banks closed the doors early. They had given all there was to give. In effect, time had gone bust. I had no chance of getting my money out of the security box now. The banks could not wait to close their doors. Cops were deployed to stop the near rioting that was almost inevitable.

Back in my office, the phone lines had gone into meltdown. Miss Dewberry was almost in tears, as such had been the volume of calls she had listed. The abusive tone of many of the callers had taken its toll on her.

Three names I recognized at once. The first one was from Jimmy Baker, a long time friend of mine, and one of the principal players in organizing some of the loans I had taken out. I had a very private number for him, and knew I would be able to contact him.

I turned the radio on, and put my feet up. Kicking my shoes off, I poured myself a large Scotch. I needed to know how bad things were. As if I did not already know. It took several moments for the crystal set to warm up.

The headlines were as bad as I'd expected them to be. Billions had been wiped off the markets. The phone rang again. Without thinking, I picked it up. It was Patrick Neal. He was the second name on my list of callers throughout the day. He was also one of the New York mob bosses to whom I owed money. Forty-five grand, to be exact. He was in no mood for pleasantries.

"You owe me money, Birket, and I want it now."

Time to go into bullshit mode.

"Patrick, how are you? Good to hear from you. I just got back to the office. Your name is at the top of my list of people to call."

"Do not give me all that crap, Birket. Where is the dough you owe me?

"Well, I don't have forty-five grand lying about the office, Patrick."

I tried to put a little laughter in my voice. Ironically, he saw straight through it.

"It ain't forty-five grand, you dumb ass. It's fifty-three with the interest."

"Patrick, I will get to the bank in the morning, and draw your money. There is no need to get upset."

That was the one thing I should not have said to him. The tirade of abuse that came down the telephone was threatening and hard. I now had forty eight hours to get his money or else.

The phone line went dead. For several seconds, I sat there with the earpiece still stuck to the side of my head. I replaced the handset. That was another mistake. The damned thing rang again. If I wanted to use the phone to call out, I would have to answer it.

"Hello?" My tone was quiet and worried.

"Robbie? Zuckerman, here."

Oh, shit! My day just turned from bad to a fucking disaster.

"You owe me money, Robbie, and a lot of it."

I sat there, and listened. He was in the same meltdown pot as I was. The long-term loans I had with him were now very short-term ones. By that, I mean within the week. Add what I owed Zuk to the money I now owed Patrick Neal, and I was in the shit big time. Well over two hundred grand!

A wry smile settled on my face. Just how many times can I have every bone broken? I can only be shot once in the head, too.

Neither option appealed to me, however. I slammed the hand set down, and quickly picked it up again so that I could get a clear line. Looking at the number written down in front of me, I called Jimmy on his very private number. It rang three times before a very weary voice answered. Trying to put some energy in my voice, I nearly shouted his name out.

"Jimmy, I need to get rid of some stock."

"You're not the only one, my friend. The problem we have is that you don't have a lot left to get rid of. As you will have seen, everyone is selling shares. The markets are in meltdown."

That's not what I wanted to hear at all.

"In truth, Rob, you're pretty much broke."

I felt sick. "What have I got let?"

"Virtually nothing. All I can do is sell what I can for you in the morning, but if the market is like it has been today, then you are in a whole world of shit."

I hung up. I did not need to hear anymore. The phone rang again. I let it ring and ring.

I pulled the drawer open, and reached for the Scotch. My Colt forty-five stared back at me. It would be very easy right now to do the mob bosses job for them. A quick gulp of Scotch, a squeeze of the trigger, and it would be over. My right hand ran down the barrel of the gun. The temptation was strong to use it.

It was ok. Jimmy told me he might salvage something from this. Even if he did, I would not be able to pay what I owed.

The Scotch burned my throat as it went down. I filled my glass again, and took another look at the pistol staring back at me from the drawer.

The door to my office opened. Rochelle stood there. The look on her face reflected what I was feeling. She was not a stupid woman.

"How bad is it, Baby?"

I smirked at her. "About as bad as it can get."

I took another gulp of Scotch. The pistol stared back at me. I slammed the drawer shut.

Beckoning Rochelle to sit down, I explained what had happened during the day. I also told her what I think would happen tomorrow, and about Zuk. I had no chance of paying him the money I owed him. In fact, if I needed a public john, I don't think I would have the cent coin to pay for that, too.

Without thought, Rochelle began taking off her rings, and the diamond and gold necklace she was wearing around her neck. "That will raise about fifty grand. Take it. Use it to pay what you can."

I could feel myself chocking up. She owed me nothing. Yet, she was willing to give me all she had.

A single tear rolled down my face. Her arms went around my neck, and cradled me against her. The tears rolled freely now. She held me without saying a word. Gently rocking my head back and forth, her hand stroked my hair.

"We have to make a run for it, Rochelle. I am a dead man if we don't."

She was silent. She listened to what I said. Her hands moved away from my neck and head.

"Can you give me an hour? That's all it will take to throw some things in a suitcase. Then I will go to the ends of the world with you."

I stared at her through tear-stained eyes.

"You big louse, did you not know I was in love with you?"

There was no hiding from the huge smile that was plastered across her face. I'd had no idea.

Trying to force a smile, I pulled her in my arms, and kissed her. "Thank you," I whispered.

Maybe we had a chance now. I had a glimmer of hope, and the makings of an idea were spinning around in my head. I kissed her gently on the lips again, and then I moved her towards the door.

"Be back here in an hour or so. I have no idea how we are going to get away. I have no doubt Zuk and the others will be watching to make sure none of their money suddenly makes a run for it. I think if we can get to the port, we might be able to buy a berth on any of the cargo ships. It doesn't matter where we go. We just need to get out of here. I will go to my apartment, and salvage what I can. But Rochelle, be careful. You could be watched as well."

With a final kiss on the lips, she left the office. It was now eight-fifteen in the evening. With luck, we could be down at the port by midnight. It would have been total madness to take a direct route. Perhaps I was being paranoid. I honestly did not know right now, but it was better to be safe than dead. By taking the back streets, and making a few detours while doubling back on ourselves, it would tell us if we had a tail on us or not.

Leaving the office with the lights still burning, I also made sure that the phone was off the hook. Anything to make people think I was still there. I then took the back stairs. Ten floors down wasn't too bad. I was just glad I did not have to walk up them right now.

The lower level car park was draped in semi-darkness. Keeping to the shadows, I left my car. I would take a cab from around the corner. By leaving my car there, any prying eyes would think I was still here. At the entrance to the car park, I stopped, allowing my eyes to adjust to the lights outside.

A flicker of light came from a doorway opposite of where I was standing. Domino Joe had lit a cigarette. He was nicknamed *Domino* because of the fact that when he struck, people fell like dominos. I was right to be cautious. Zuk had already thought I might try to slip away. I hoped Rochelle had not been seen. Just in case, I would call her from the call box outside of my apartment. I slipped back into the darkness, and moved to the side exit. He would not be able to see me from there.

Slipping into the yellow line cab one block away from my office, I told the driver where to take me. He was not going to take me directly to my home, as I preferred to walk the last couple of streets. I would have a look around me, just in case there was a set of eyes watching my place.

I stood on the corner of Forty-Seventh Street after the cab dropped me off. Directly across the road from my home, two men stood watching and talking. I had not seen them before, but I could not take any risks now. The back entrance would be the best way to get in.

Slipping down back alleyways like a thief in the night, I slipped in and out of the dark, checking behind me and around me every minute or so. So far, so good.

There were several cars parked along my route. Because of the darkness, I wasn't able to see if there was anyone in them. It was a chance I would have to take. Pulling my coat further up around my neck, and my hat lower down on my head, I tried to act confidently as I made my way home.

The thought of trying to get home had, for a short time, taken my mind off of my worries. The knot in my stomach reminded me from time to time.

The rear door to my apartment block was open. Thank God for that. Slipping inside, I stood there, looking back out over the street for a few moments to make sure that I had not been spotted or followed. My luck was holding. There was no movement.

Instinctively, I went to switch the light on in my apartment, only stopping myself at the last moment. Beads of sweat poured down the back of my head, making me shiver as it turned cold as it dripped towards the small of my back. Leaning against the wall to catch my breath, I waited for my eyes to get used to the darkness. Fortunately, the curtains had been left open, so light from the street filtered in.

The holdall I had hidden in my wardrobe came away easily from under the pile of clothing. Crouching down, and making my way to the large window, I glanced at the street below. They were still there. Good! I had not been seen. My fortune was now what I had in this bag, roughly ten grand, and some personal papers I had put in the case several weeks ago.

There was no chance of me getting to my safety deposit box. It would be unsafe. Ten grand was not a lot to show for all that I had, but it would have to do.

Moving to the bedroom, I then cleared out the small box I kept my several sets of cuff links in. If nothing else, I could use them to bargain with, should I need to. There was very little point in taking anything else. We would have to travel fast and light on this part of the journey.

Once more, I slipped out of the back lower exit, continuously checking again around me. This would be the hard part. A man walking alone along the street was nothing out of the ordinary, but a man walking with a suitcase was another matter entirely. All I could do, at this point, was make it appear that everything was normal for me.

The call box two streets away was empty. I took a moment, and called Rochelle. Her phone rang and rang. Perhaps she had already left. Hailing a cab, I travelled back to my office, reversing my outward trip.

Domino Joe was still standing there. The glow from another cigarette shone in the darkness. I dared not take the elevator. This was at the front of the building, and in full view of the street. It was like climbing a mountain up those stairs.

The office was empty. I put the phone's handset back on the cradle. It rang instantly. There was no point in pretending to be out. I wanted people to know I was here right now.

"Hello, Birket," Rochelle spoke calmly. "I think I am being followed. What do I do?"

The only thing I could think of was for her to leave her case in the cab. We could get her some more clothes as soon as possible. If she was being followed, then whoever it was would surely see the case, and put two and two together. Reluctantly, she agreed to do this.

The phone rang again as soon as I put it down.

"Hello, Birket." The tearful, almost hysterical, voice of Martha, my stockbroker friend's wife was almost screaming down the phone at me. "He has gone. He has gone!"

She repeated the same line over and over again. My good friend and stock agent had taken his own life by throwing himself over the side of the Manhattan Bridge into the icy waters below. He, too, had been battered by the market that day. Unable to deal with the losses, he had seen no end to it. He would not be the only one to take that course of action that night.

The thought of the pistol in my drawer came vividly back to me. I was now glad I had not done the same.

I sat there, stunned for several seconds. Her almost hysterical voice was still screaming through the phone. I had no idea what to say to her. Instead, I hung up.

The door opened, and Rochelle walked in. Her hair was ruffled, and a small bead of sweat ran down the side of her face. Her last two steps were stumbling ones. Domino Joe quickly pushed her to one side, and held his pistol out in front of him. His legs were slightly parted, and he was ready to shoot.

His eyes scanned the room. "Who else is here, Fink?"

He could see there was nobody else in the room. I didn't even answer. The gun in his hands was aimed directly at me. I was not about to move before he ordered me not to.

Rochelle sat on the floor where she had fallen. The swelling around her right eye was already turning purple. I had not noticed the small trickle of blood coming from behind her ear. The bastard had really laid into her

"I had no choice, Robbie! He made me tell him!"

I didn't say anything. There was no point right now. I needed time to think.

"Your little friend, here, tells me you're leaving. Is that right?"

I remained silent. He was enjoying himself too much to not follow this up. I did not have to wait long.

"Zuk was right about you, Birket. He said you would fink out. That's why I am here. You can go on your way as soon as you pay Mister Zuckerman what you owe him. Do you have his money, Fink?"

He knew as well as I did that I did not. He was going to take great delight in blowing my brains out all over the office. The hammer slid back on the pistol. Rochelle screamed at him not to shoot.

"I have money in my purse take it. Take it all!"

He looked down at her. The sneer on his face told her he did not want the money. It was the kill he wanted now. My only chance was to get him before he got me. It was instinct that made me move. Self-preservation had that effect on men.

I grabbed for the drawer. It slid open, and I could feel the butt of the pistol in my hand. The first shot rang out. A pain in my left shoulder slammed me back into my chair. I clasped the handle tightly, cocking the hammer as I drew it up level with him. A second shot rang out. The bullet flew past my head, slamming into the painting of my grandfather.

My gun fired. The shot rocked him back. His free hand came up to his chest. Blood spread across his chest, and through his fingers. A look of total astonishment spread across his face. I fired again. The second bullet spun him around.

He got off another round before hitting the deck. The pool of blood spread across the deck as he lay there. His eyes looked up, yet they no longer saw anything anymore.

I could feel the warm blood running down my arm. The pain was not too bad. I had always imagined that when a person gets shot, the pain would be agonizing.

Rochelle was still lying on the floor. At first, I thought she had been hit.

"Rochelle, are you hit?"

Slowly, she turned her head to face me. Streaks of blood covered her face. It was Domino Joe's blood. He lay three feet to her left.

We had to get out of here, now and fast. I'd had no choice, but to shoot him. It was self-defence. A long enquiry by the cops would allow Zuckerman to send more men after me. I had been lucky this time. How the hell I had not been killed, God, alone, knew. Next time, he would send more men.

Rochelle stood up, and slid behind the desk where I was still sitting.

The pistol was clutched tight my hand. I was unable to let go of it.

She went into almost panic mode as she saw the blood running from my fingertips to the floor. A small pool of it gathered by the foot of my chair.

I started to take my jacket off. I pulled my good arm out first. It was one of those useless bits of shit I had learned in the academy, to always take to good arm out of a sleeve first. It is less painful. Whoever said that was full of shit.

I let out a shallow scream as my good arm slipped out of the sleeve. Rochelle helped me to pull the injured arm free. There was no time for the niceties of undoing my shirt, and taking it off. She ripped away the sleeve above the wound. The good thing was, the bullet had gone all the way through. There was no need for a hospital visit. This would have brought the cops along asking questions.

"Get some towels from the bathroom. We need to stop the bleeding."

As she hurried to the far end of the office into my private bathroom, I took a belt from the whiskey bottle. Closing my eyes, I poured some of the booze over the wound. Alcohol was meant to be a good antiseptic. All I knew was that it hurt like hell. Sweat poured from my head as the alcohol penetrated the wound site. Black dots formed in front of my eyes. The room was now spinning wildly.

I lifted my head from the desk. Rochelle was now tending to my arm. I had no idea how long I had passed out for. I didn't ask, as it was not the most important thing on my mind right now.

Soon, Rochelle had done a good job on the wound. Packing it with torn towels, and then wrapping a tight bandage around it, she began making a sling for it. I turned this down. A man with his arm in a sling would draw attention to himself.

I always kept several clean shirts in my office. Appearance was everything when entering a meeting, and it made me feel good knowing that I could change my clothes whenever I wanted to at work.

The clean blue shirt was hanging up in the store cupboard. My head began swimming again as I stood up. Grabbing the edge of the desk, I steadied myself until the dizziness left me.

This time, it was bad arm in first, and then the good arm. Whoever came up with this shit was a lying bastard. It hurt like hell.

Whilst I dressed, Rochelle began sorting herself out. She washed the blood off of her face, and reapplied her make-up. No matter what the situation was, she had to look good.

"We cannot take a cab to the docks, and I have no idea how we are going to make it to a ship. Are you still sure you want to come with me?"

The phone was ringing again. It could ring now for as long as it wanted to. If I answered it, it could be Zuckerman. He might expect to hear Domino Joe's voice telling him I had paid my debt. Better to leave it ringing.

We had to get out of here, and quickly. It was not normal for shots to be fired in this area. Someone was bound to have heard them. Late night cleaners were always about.

Rochelle stood there looking magnificent. It was hard to know that she had witnessed a death right here in this office.

"Do you have any other shoes?"

She looked at her feet. The high heels would soon slow us down.

"No, this is all I have. We should be ok, though. I can keep up."

To prove the point, she began to walk around the office at a quick march pace before coming face-to-face with Joe's dead body. His eyes were now fixed and glazed over. She stopped in her tracks, holding both hands up to her mouth. Delayed shock can do this to any person.

I rushed around the desk, wrapping my good arm around her. This was partly to comfort her, and partly to muffle any scream she might be inclined to let out right now.

"Time to go."

I could feel her head nodding in agreement as she dug it deeper into my arm.

Her purse sat on the desk. She picked it up, and opened it. Inside, was a roll of bills, which she handed to me. There was approximately four thousand dollars.

"This is to help us get away."

I could have cried myself, then and there. Self-pity and gratitude was a shit thing to deal with at the same time. I took another slug of Scotch to ease the pain. All of my possessions were contained in one small holdall. I guided her to the door with my good arm, and then picked up the holdall. With one final look at the body on the floor, I closed the door on everything I had.

CHAPTER THIRTY-FOUR

Although Domino Joe was lying dead in my office, we could not take the chance in taking the elevator down to the car park level. We slipped down the stairs instead. Each step jolted my arm, making me wince.

Rochelle's high-heeled shoes clattered down the stairs, making so much noise that it would have woken the dead. Sensibly, she took them off. Neither of us talked at all on the way down. I was trying to listen for any little give away that might alert me another of Joe's buddies in case he was on his way up to see what was happening.

From what I knew about Joe, his work was done with fairly quickly. A few minutes of torment upon the victim, and then *bang*! Two bullets to the head saw his day's work done. If he had a buddy outside, he would have heard the noise of the shots going off by now.

Once more, we slipped into the darkness of the car park, standing still until our eyes became used to the murky blackness surrounding us. Rochelle gripped my hand as if her life depended on it. She was not wrong. If we were caught now, she would get a bullet for Christmas as well as I would. Zuckerman did not like loose ends. She knew a lot of things about his organization. He would not want that getting out. For obvious reasons, I was not about to share this with her. I was happy that she was with me right now.

Moving slowly along the back wall of the car park, we then turned north towards the side door, and out into the side street. It was going to be a long walk down to the port. The less people that saw us, the better. It would not be long before the word was out on the street that there was a price, not only on my head, but that of Rochelle's.

Some of the cab drivers would be only too willing to make a few easy bucks from selling us out. This part of our escape would be fairly easy, as lots of people filled the streets. We could mingle with them. Up until now, I hadn't thought too much about when we got to the port, but it was becoming an increasing worry. We had to get to the right ship on the first time of asking. A man and a woman wanting to leave the country was no big drama. A man with a bullet hole in him was a different thing all together. There would be too many questions. Sailors would be only too happy to share the story in the side street bars and speakeasies.

Once the crowds of people thinned out, we would stop, and go back in the opposite direction for about a half of a block or so before turning again. If I could, I wanted to get us to around pier forty-two. Most of the ocean-going ships were berthed there. Right now, I would have taken an old schooner to Timbuktu if it had been available to me.

My arm was really hurting now. I could feel blood seeping through the bandage Rochelle had put on it. I would have to stop soon, and make some running repairs to it. Once we hit the lights again, I did not want blood dripping from my coat sleeve. Rochelle slipped into a corner drug store to pick up some fresh dressings while I stayed outside in the darkness. One woman alone would not make too much of a problem. In the semi-darkness of a back alley light, we put on fresh bandages. I was not worried about the blood on my shirt sleeve as I was not about to take my jacket off.

The cold October air was now dropping to below freezing point, and our breaths were turning to mist as we walked slowly hand-in-hand along the back streets of New York. I was lost, in truth, but knew that if I kept heading east, at some point I would hit the water front. Rochelle

184

took her high-heeled shoes off whenever she could to give her feet a rest.

We reached the bridge at Lower Manhattan at around two in the morning. The hustle and bustle of New York still meant it was busy. If we could get across the bridge, and head south, we would be at the port. All along the river, front ships stood at anchor or at berth. Many of these were coasters tramping around the coast and as far as Canada. It would have been easy to try and slip along the coast on one of these ships, but I knew only too well that the mob had many faces in many places.

It had always been my intention to get out of the country. Pulling my coat collar up a little higher around my neck, I urged Rochelle to do the same before crossing the bridge. She let go of my hand for the first time since we'd left my office. Blood began running back into my hand, making it tingle. She was not the only one who was scared shitless right now. The cold weather would make it look like a natural act for the both of us.

Cars sped past us in both directions. Most of the people who were walking had taken the inside walkway. Once again, Rochelle stopped to sort her shoes out again.

I did not even see the black sedan move alongside us, and slow down. The window opened, and a man's voice called my name. A shot rang out. I hit the deck, slamming my arm onto the ground. Pain ran through me. Rochelle fell forward with me still holding onto my hand. I held her close, my bad arm wrapped over her, trying to cover her body with mine.

The car sped up, moving quickly over the bridge. I lay there for a few seconds, mentally feeling my body over for pain. Rochelle did not move. I turned to look at her. A single shot to the side of her head had killed her instantly, the exit wound taking half of her skull of at the back. Her eyes looked blankly at me.

A mixture of fear, rage, and hate welled up in me. I reached into my pocket for the pistol I had put there from my office. By the time I had drawn it, the car had left the bridge. There was nothing I could do.

I had no time to think of Rochelle. At this second, they knew I had not been hit, and would surely come back to give me my early Christmas present. I had to get out of this fucking place right now. People were now beginning to stop, and observe the drama that was unfolding before their very eyes. There was no way I would be taken by the cops.

I wanted to stay with her, to tell her how I felt. I wanted her to be alive. Sadly, I knew I couldn't. I scrambled to my feet, and pushed against a steel girder on the bridge. Even if I could, I would not be able to pick that one car out. It was too dark.

Cars streamed over the bridge in both directions. I began running back the way I'd come until I found a side street. Getting out of the line of fire was my first priority. The time to weep over Rochelle would come later. The pistol in my pocket was banging against my hip as I ran. I would only use it if I had to. I did not want any Saturday night heroes screaming shooter, and then tackling me to the deck.

Darkness covered me as I slipped down alongside a rubbish dumpster. I had to think of myself now. I kept telling myself this, but no matter what I did, all I could see was Rochelle's body lying on the side walk. For the next twenty minutes or so, I huddled there, full of rage and sadness.

I now had a chance to check myself over. I was able to run, so my legs were ok. Although my arm hurt badly, I could feel no fresh blood running down my arm. The vision of Rochelle lying there with her head blown open came to me again, causing me to vomit all over the side walk.

A tear rolled own my face. I had never been one to look back over things. As far as I was concerned, what was done, was done. But now I could not help but to reflect on my stupidity over the past hour. Why the fuck had I gotten involved with the mob? I was now almost certainly a dead man. All I could do was to try to out fox them somehow.

I had to move from here, and cross the river. Checking that the gun had not dropped out of my pocket, I found that it was still there. I stood up again.

The alleyway ran from West to East. Heading west would take me back to the city. If I went back that way, at least I could lose myself in the night-time crowds.

Ditching my hat, I slipped an old woollen one onto my head that I found alongside the dumpster. It smelled of shit, but right now I was in it, so it would match the mood.

At the halfway point of the alleyway, there was an intersection. Two old men sat there drinking over an open fire to keep warm. Taking five dollars from my coat pocket, I offered it to them to swap the taller one's coat with mine. He was about the same build as I was. The thought of five dollars appealed to him, and the deal was done. By morning, he would have hocked it for a couple more dollars, and then gone along to see one of the booze distributors for another bottle of the cheap gut rot Gin.

The coat smelled of cheap Gin and piss, but it would do the job for me. I would not stick out like a spare prick at a wedding now. I was just another bum on the streets.

At the end of the intersection, I turned right again. This would take me back to the on ramp of the Manhattan Bridge. As I crossed the road, I realized that cops had flooded the bridge, along with a large crowd. Rochelle was still lying there.

Cars had stopped to allow the drivers to have a good look at the drama. On the far side of the bridge, an ambulance was trying to weave through the long line of traffic. Car horns echoed off of the bridge's steel girders, and annoyed drivers cursed at each other. When I got onto the bridge, I began to stagger slightly to make it look as if I was a drunk. My right hand was firmly on the grip of the pistol just in case

I mixed with the crowds on the bridge. Avoiding the blue light of the cop cars and ambulance that had now managed to fight its way through the traffic, I tried not to vomit again. Sweat promptly poured out of me.

I could hear the cops calling for witnesses to the shooting, but no one had seen anything. Then again, this was New York. Who would honestly give that information to the cops?

I shook my head as another vision of her lying there, and the blood pooling around her came into my head.

Get a grip! There is nothing you can do now, I told myself. I then saw myself as a complete bastard who had no sense of humanity at all. If I'd had any guts about me, I would have gone over to the cops, and told them everything.

Right now, I was scared, and knew I would never rat out on Zuk in an open court. I think he knew that as well, so I was, in many ways, the perfect target for him. I was an example to all those who owed him money.

My hand went towards my wallet at the thought of money. Once more, I ducked down a side street behind another friendly dumpster. I was not about to get mugged as well as shot. I had five grand and change on me. Rochelle had given me some of her jewellery, too, so I could hock that if I had to. There were also some clothes in my holdall. The smaller leather pouch had papers in them, a relic left to me by granddad, Robert. I was not bothered right now about them, as they were worthless. Maybe I could wipe my butt on them if I got desperate enough. I kept heading east, keeping the river on my left as I did so. No matter where I went now, as long as the river stayed to the east of me, I would find it. So far, so good!

The buildings began to change now. After several hours of walking, houses and tall apartment blocks became warehouses. Trucks rolled past, horns blowing at people mad enough to walk in front of them. Pedestrians were only too happy to curse the driver's family as well as the driver.

Intersections popped up very quickly now. Instead of taking the first one, I continued walking. If my guess was correct, I would come out near pier forty-seven. I would not have much time in the open.

Dock workers paid no interest in me as I made my way along the sidewalk. I fit in well, looking like shit.

Several ship whistles boomed out in the stillness of the early morning. It was time to make my move out into the open. Making a left turn, I hit the main street again with the river dead and centre ahead of me. It was now a case of you-pay-your-dough, and you take a chance on picking the right ship. I'd already made my mind up. I would not try an American ship. It would end badly if I picked one of the ships Zuckerman or any of the other mob bosses was running.

Language barriers put me off of looking for any foreign ships. There were several British ships lying at their berths. I did not want a ship that was being discharged. She would be here too long, so that cut my options down. If I could find a ship low down in the water, and ready for sea that would be perfect.

After walking along the waterfront for an hour or so, the ships began to thin out quite a bit. I had seen only two likely ships. Both were British. One was, I would guess, half loaded. The other was ready for sea.

I made my way back to this one. Slipping back into the partial light of the warehouse, I watched and waited. Several of the crew returned, worse for wear after a night out. I did not see any of her officers, but this was no surprise to me

They did not mix with the crew. Her funnel smoke billowed skyward, and her running lights were on. It was now or never. Slipping from behind the packing cases, I walked up the gangway, and on to the main deck. No one approached me. Making my way aft, I looked up at the bridge. A small light shone from the aft end of it. Steps on the port side of the bridge would take me there. The metal steps echoed as my feet climbed them. I don't know why I did it, but I began to tip-toe my way up the stairs making my footfalls lighter. Instinctively, I went to straighten my tie, although I did not have one on. I shoved the woollen hat into my pocket, and wrapped it around the pistol's grip.

Knocking on the bridge door, I waited. The small light grew brighter. Someone was coming from what I imagined to be the chart room.

The first officer opened the door to the bridge. The three rings on his neat clean jacket gave him the air of authority he would carry on board. There was no point in my trying to go around knocking on the doors of several houses nearby. I needed help, and I wanted him to know it.

"My name is Birket. I need to get away, and out of the country. I am willing to pay whatever it takes for your help."

Well, at least, he was under no illusions now as to why I was here, or what I wanted. I would drop him if he even looked as if he was going to call for help. God, alone, knew what I would do then.

I could see him blink at me in the glow of the chart room light. I stood there silently. I had learned that when you're trying to negotiate things, it was better to shut up after you have said your piece, and let the other person speak now. Behind me, a sea bird flew overhead. Dawn was coming, and I had to get under cover before then.

I still stood there, looking at him. After what seemed like a lifetime, he ordered me to wait. The door to the bridge closed.

Again, I waited. My arm hurt like hell now, and the cold was not doing me any big favours, either. He was gone for about ten minutes. I could see him walking back across the bridge, followed by a smaller man who was not wearing a uniform. His deck-working smock was covered in drips of paint. I guessed he was the boson.

"Come in."

This was more of an order than a request. I did as I was told.

"It will cost you five grand to get you out."

They were taking the piss out of me. I had travelled in luxury for far less, but they knew I was in no position to argue the point. Taking the wad of money out of my pocket, I handed over the two grand.

"Plus another five hundred to sign you on the ship's articles."

I hesitated. Then again, I was over a barrel. There was no point in arguing when your life was at stake. I rolled another five hundred off of the roll of notes. The boson tapped his first officer on the shoulder.

"Oh, yes, and two hundred more for your food."

The bastards were enjoying fleecing me now. I wished I had split the wad of notes up into smaller amounts. They could see I still had money left over.

How much is your life worth? I asked myself. I knew that was what was in their minds as well.

I stuffed the remaining notes back in my pocket.

"Get him down into number three hold, boson. Keep him there until we are at sea. The skipper will see you then. Mr. . . . ?"

"Birket," I replied. "It's Birket."

The first officer left me to the dealings of the boson. Meekly, I followed him back down onto the main deck, and the aft of the bridge. The small inspection hatch to the hold was under the ladders, out of the way of prying eyes. The metal dogs were knocked back by the hammer lashed to the cover.

"Down you go, Mr. Birket. Oh, and you owe for the bed. That will be another three hundred."

I opened my mouth to argue with him. The smile on his face said it all. Pay, or piss off. I paid.

"Here, man. You will need this to keep the cold out."

Handing me half of a bottle of Irish whiskey, I asked how much that would be.

"The Scotch is free," he said.

I thanked him.

"However the bottle is fifty dollars."

Now, he was really enjoying himself. I went to hand the bottle back defiantly.

"No, you have bought it, so now, pay up!"

I could feel my shoulders sagging. All I wanted to do now was to get out of sight, and sleep.

I pushed the fifty into his grubby, greedy hands, climbed over the hatch cover, and slipped down into the depths of the ship. I was given a small lamp to guide my way down, and was a bit surprised when I was not charged for that. From above me, the boson called out that I would get my cot as soon as possible. The hatch cover slammed shut above me. Its echo banged off the ship's hull for several seconds.

My only company was several hundred tons of grain in sacks, and the rats that were now scurrying for cover. A shiver coursed down my spine. I had never been a lover of rats. Though, I think we would become good friends before this voyage was done with.

The lamp threw some light around the hold. I was not going to search about the place for a sofa and double bed. Instead, I pulled the nearest sacks down to the ceiling, and settled against them. The mouthful of Scotch I swallowed helped to warm me up a little. Wrapping my hands around the lamp, I managed to take some of the numbness out of my fingers. The climb down into the hold had not helped my shoulder at all. I could feel blood oozing. Another belt of the Scotch would do the trick.

How long I had been down there, I had no idea. I had taken my watch off as soon as I was able to, hiding it under some of the sacks, as well as some more of the money I had with me.

I had the horrible feeling that I hadn't finished paying yet for my passage. I fell asleep with the assistance of the Scotch. It was the vibration of the ship that had woken me from my sleep. Muffled sounds from outside, and straining noises from the hull soon reached me. Metal on metal screamed out in protest. We were being pushed. It had to be the tugs moving us out from the berth. Below to my right, the sound of the engines was heard speeding up. I should have been happy, at this point. I was still alive, and was now on my way to God-knows-where. It is the one thing I had not asked. Most likely, because it was the one thing I was not bothered with.

I sat there, straining my ears for outside noises. Several minutes after the tugs had begun pulling the ship away from the quay, several loud shrills from the ship's horn told me the tugs had now let go of the tow, and we were sailing out of the river into the Atlantic.

I fell asleep again. Several more slugs of Scotch made sure I would get an hour or so, at least. I wanted to dive into the bottle, and not wake up for a very long time. My last thought before sleep took over was, how had I come to this point in my life?

I was running away on an old tramp steamer with a price on my head. Two people were dead as a result of my actions in the past day alone. I did not give a rat's arse about Domino Joe. He deserved to die. Rochelle . . . Well, all she'd done was love me.

The vision of her lying there haunted me once more. A shiver ran down my back. Whether it was fear or the cold, I didn't really know. Nor did I care as to what it was that caused it. I was safe. For a while, at least.

CHAPTER THIRTY-FIVE

I had no sense of time or date. It felt as if I had been down in the hold for a lifetime. My only companions were the rats. I had let the lamp go out, and had no lighter to relight it. The rats were scampering about my feet. I huddled my feet up around my chin to stop the little bastards running up my trouser legs.

The metal dogs on the hatch cover slammed back, and a beam of light peeked through, hurting my eyes. The rats scurried off to other parts of the hold.

"Mister Birket, you may come up now. We are outside the three mile limit. The captain will see you now," a voice replied.

Once more, this felt like a command, and not a request. However, it could have been God almighty making the command, and I would have run up the steps if I was able to.

My arm had stiffened, making it difficult for me to make it to the top of the ladder alone. No help was offered, and the only thing I had left was my pride. I was not going to lose that by asking for help. Gritting my teeth, I climbed every rung, cursing the day I was born. A bright cold day met me as I climbed over the hatch cover.

"This way, if you please, Mister Birket."

Sarcasm was not the boson's best weapon. Several of the deck hands stopped their work, and looked at me as I climbed out of the hold. The boson screamed at them to mind their business, and get back to work. Charm was not in his locker, either.

Instead of taking me to the bridge as I had expected, the boson took me through a small hatchway aft of the bridge, and then up two flights of steps. He stopped outside of a solid oak door. The brass captain's cabin plate was shining bright.

After two knocks, the command to enter was given. The boson shoved the polished brass handle down, and stepped over the threshold. The captain was sitting at his desk with his back turned to me. He was busily signing papers set out before him.

Without turning, he thanked the boson, and dismissed him. I stood there, feeling like a naughty school boy back at the academy. This wasn't the first time I'd felt this way. Normally, I would have snapped an order to the captain, and he would have said, 'Yes, sir, Mister Birket,' but now I was the one who had to wait for him to make the first sound.

His swivel chair squeaked as he turned to face me. My mouth fell open for a second as I recognised the man sitting in the chair. It was Captain Williams, the man I had sent off on the *Sarah M.* I had the feeling this was not going to be a happy reunion. The telegram I had sent him sacking him came vividly back to my mind.

His smile confirmed my fears in as much that it was not really a smile, but more of a, 'I now have you, you bastard, and I remember well what you did to me!'

There was no point in my trying to play the old friends card here. In his place, if I had tried that, I would have him thrown over the side of the ship. I stood there again, feeling like a naughty school boy, waiting to see what he had in mind for me.

"Mister Birket, I have looked forward to this moment for a long time. I still have your telegram here in my pocket."

I opened my mouth to say it was only business, but I thought better of it.

"You are, for all intents and purposes, a stowaway on board my ship. I should turn around, and hand you over to the port police."

Panic began welling up in me. If it would have helped me, then and there, I would have let my pride go, and begged him not to do that. Yet, I said nothing. He was dealing all of the cards, and all I could do now was to see how the hand played out.

"Or I could simply sign you on as one of the hands," he suggested.

I had wondered what he was signing when I came into his cabin. The ship's articles sat on his desk.

"All hands on a ship have to sign the articles. It is a matter of law."

I could not see my name on the articles from where I was standing, but I was guessing he hadn't pulled them out just for the fun of it. I could afford to bluff a little here. If he was waiting for me to say anything, he was mistaken. He'd already made his decision, and he was just getting his pound of flesh out of me. I could only hope that I was right.

Turning back to his desk briefly, Captain Williams picked up his pen, and began tapping the paper in front of him. Perhaps he was not getting the reaction he expected from me.

"I have decided to sign you on, Birket. Don't get me wrong. I have never liked you. You were always a snot-nosed kid, but I am doing this for your family name."

Gone was the Mister, but I could live with that.

"It takes money to feed my men aboard this ship."

"Captain Williams, I have paid out over two thousand dollars to get aboard your ship."

"Well, it is not enough."

The feeling I had that I would be paying more was about to be proved right. There is no point in trying to claim I had nothing left. His first officer had seen the notes I put back in my pocket.

"How much?"

"Just hand over what you've got in your pockets."

I stood there, looking at him defiantly. My hand was stuck firmly in my pockets.

"It is pretty simple, Birket. You can pay, and get away form here. Or two miles from our starboard bow, there is a Coast Guard ship. I can very easily contact them, informing them that we found a stowaway. It might slow us down a little, but it means you're going ashore. I am guessing you wouldn't really want that, would you?"

The tone in his voice let me know that he was not fooling around here. I was screwed. He knew it, and I knew it. Pulling the notes from my pocket, I peeled off two hundred dollars, and put them defiantly back into my pocket.

"Yes, ok, Birket. I am not a heartless man. You can keep that. Now, you will stay in the aft steward's cabin for now. You will eat alone, and not go out on deck unless I tell you otherwise. And twenty-four hours before we get to Liverpool, you will be put back down in the hold. If you're caught, we will still claim you're a stowaway. Do I make myself clear?"

I nodded my head meekly. The only consolation was that I now knew where we were bound for.

England. I had heard many stories from Granddad Robert and Great-Uncle William about England. My heart lifted a little.

The door to his cabin opened, and the boson stepped over the threshold.

"Take him to number four, steward's please, boson, and treat him well."

I was not sure what that meant, or if it would cost me the last of my money.

"Aya, aya, sir."

For some strange reason, I found myself thanking the skipper. It was more of an automatic thing, than a full meaning one.

Two decks down on the port side of the ship, the cabin door opened. The boson stepped in first, giving me the one cent tour. There was a cot, chair, porthole, and a bottle of Scotch on the chair.

"How much for that?"

"On the house, Mister Birket."

I stared at him for a few seconds, waiting for the BUT. It didn't come. Just that knowing smirk on his face. I would have loved to slap it off.

"The heads are down the companion way on the port side."

He left, slamming the door into the hatchway. Standing there, feeling like and looking like shit, I could no longer hold the tears back. For several minutes, I stood there, freely sobbing like a baby.

The Scotch burned my throat as I took a large mouthful. At least I was safe, for now, and that was all I wanted.

I looked at my refection in the glass of the port hole. I really did look like shit. I took another mouthful of Scotch.

Making my way to the heads, I could not remember when I had shaved last, or taken a bath. I had paid such a price for this trip I was going to get every cents worth out of it.

The water was hot and refreshing. The razor lying on the small shelf was blunt, but did the job, none-the-less. The hot water stung my shoulder wound like hell. I had to keep it clean, so I put up with the pain. The bruising had started to come out around the bullet hole, making my arm even harder to move. A trickle of blood ran down my body, and down into the scupper. It was not fresh blood, thankfully, just all the shit around the injury site. Dabbing at it with the towel that had been discarded on the deck, I would re-dress it in my cabin. Once I had sorted myself out, I would try to wash some of the shit out of my clothes. It was a start, at least.

Back in my cabin, I tore the towel from the heads into strips, placing fresh ones under the single pillow I had on my cot. The old dressing went out of the port hole. The wind carried them back towards the shoreline that was now falling astern of us.

Another mouthful of Scotch didn't seem too bad right now. After re-dressing the wound, I went back to the heads, and washed my vest. This went onto the warm deck plate back in my cabin. It would soon dry. I slipped my shirt back on. I didn't want anyone to see my wound. I don't know why, but it was just me.

My cabin door opened. I was ready to demand why the man had not knocked on my door before entering. I had to bite my tongue. A bowl of porridge and hot coffee was set down on the chair. No words were exchanged apart from me thanking him.

I could not remember the last time I had eaten, or had a cup of coffee. Most likely, it had been before we'd left my office. This brought back the vivid memory of Rochelle lying on the road with her head blown wide open. I cannot say I was deeply in love with her, or ever would have been, but she had been so loyal and loving to me. So much so, to the point of trying to run away with me, knowing I had nothing to offer her. She had not deserved to die like that.

More tears welled up in my eyes. More Scotch would soon dry them. Pouring a good measure into my coffee, I drank greedily. The bowl of porridge was hot and sweet, and tasted so good. It had been years since I had eaten the stuff. Right now, it was better than a big T-bone steak from Mario's. Putting the bowl back on the chair, I slipped back onto my cot.

Sleep overwhelmed me. If I dreamt, I did not remember it. I woke up to find that the sky was dark. Far off to port, I could see the running lights of two other ships. Both were heading to the United States.

The coffee cup and plate were gone from the chair. With some alarm, I went to my coat pocket to make sure whoever had taken the plate had not taken what cash I had left over. Panic welled up. The money was not in the pocket. Spinning the coat around, I checked the other side. I let out a big sigh of relief both. The money and pistol were still there.

My arm did not feel as stiff as it had earlier, though I was still reluctant to move it. Putting the now dry vest on, I went back to the heads, giving my shirt a rinse through under the hot water. This would now go onto the deck plates to dry.

I hadn't had to do this sort of thing since my academy days. I remembered thinking, back then, that it was a waste of time I would have people to do this sort of menial task for me for the rest of my days. It is surprising what sort of shit you can remember when your alone and scared. I was both, right now, and freely admitted it.

There was nothing else to do, but think. In many ways, by confining me to my cabin, the skipper had opened up a Pandora's Box within me. Maybe that's what he wanted for me.

I tried to think of all sorts of different things, but each time, I came back to seeing Rochelle lying there dead on the bridge. Maybe in my own way, I did love her. Maybe it was guilt. The Scotch would absolve me from all that for the time being, however.

My cabin door opened again. The same man who had brought me my porridge was now carrying more food to me. The smell of stew hit my nostrils before I saw what was on the plate.

"What, no wine?"

My attempt at a joke fell on deaf ears. He turned on his heels, and left just as quickly as he'd entered the cabin. My thank you to him was met with the slamming of the door.

With a full stomach, and another belt from my good friend, the Scotch bottle, I slipped back into sleep. I had taken the money and pistol out of my coat pocket, and put that under the pillow. No need to temp fate. If all went well, I would dump the pistol out of the port hole before I arrived in England. There was no point in getting picked up for having a gun on me.

I had not thought of a plan once I landed in England. Sleep stopped me from formulating one.

It was still dark when I woke again. The motion of the ship had changed. The sea had picked up. She was now pitching and rolling in heavy sea. With my feet apart, and planting them firmly on the deck, I rolled with the ship, looking out of the port hole. Waves as big as a house were rolling past us. The ship was bow on to the sea, making her pitch and roll even.

Wind whipped the tops of the waves, blowing them wildly ahead of the sea. White caps rolled over and over. Above us, the sky was clear.

Stars shone down now, and the spray would turn the stars into a rainbow colour for just a split second. Unscrewing the metal dogs to the port hole, I held it open, smelling the sea. It was fresh and salty. Up until now, I had never been a big lover of the sea. For some strange reason, I now found that it was beautiful.

My shirt was dry. I folded it up, and put it under the cot mattress. It would press it for me while I slept. This was just another piece of useless information I had been given at the academy.

The Scotch bottle was nearly empty now. My arm began aching all over again. All I could do was lie on my cot, and endure the storm that was screaming outside. The ship groaned as each wave crashed over her bows, shuddering in the water as the force of the waves tried to halt her forward motion. Somewhere along the companion way, a door slammed back against the bulkhead. It was several moments before anyone came along, and shut it tight. One of the deck crew hurled a curse or two at one of his shipmates for letting the door wake him up from his off-watch sleep. From another part of the companion way, his shipmate told him to fuck off. He was nothing but a dick brain.

I braced myself again as another wave crashed over the bow. The motion of the ship soon had me drifting off again into a deep sleep.

CHAPTER THIRTY-SIX

The storm raged for two days. Dark clouds hung over the ship, whipped along by the wind.

There was nothing I could do to make the time go faster. I showered as often as I could, mainly to help keep my wound clean, but also to distract me from thinking too much. I had never been one for self-pity. That was for other people. The confines of my cabin began the first stirrings of it.

I had tried to come up with a plan for when I got off of the ship. Providing, I did actually get off of it, and not be taken by the cops or custom men. Paranoid thoughts did enter my head, but at this point, there was no point in going down that route. If the skipper was going to report me, then he would do so, and there was nothing I could do about that.

I was hoping that my favoured plan would work. I planned to go ashore with the crew when they signed off of the ship, or went to the local bar. There was no prohibition in England, so the bars would be full of sailors all getting drunk and making merry.

I also needed to take stock of what I had left. Cash-wise, I had one hundred dollars, plus another fifty I had down in the hold, and my watch. That had to be worth some money on its own. I also had the personal things I'd put in my holdall several weeks ago. I needed to see what was in that. Then there were the small items of jewellery that Rochelle had given to me the day before we left.

I pushed any thoughts of her to the back of my mind as far as I could. I did not want to cloud my thinking by wallowing in her death.

The problem was, my holdall was down in the hold. Until I was back down there, I was not fully aware of how well off or how bad I really was. As far as the ship was concerned, I was being treated well. I was eating and drinking well enough. I had begun putting some of the Scotch into one of the empty bottles. If I could get past any security in Liverpool by pretending to be drunk, all the better. I would give my clothes a good dousing in Scotch just before I left the ship.

Where I would go after that, I had no idea. There was a place at the back of my mind. I could remember Granddad Robert telling me about his home in Westmorland. Where the fuck that was, I had no idea. I would head north, and see where it took me.

By the time we were one hundred miles east of Ireland, the storm had moderated to a strong wind. In some ways, this was worse than fighting the storm. The ship pitched and rolled in an even lazier manner.

My cabin door opened. The boson stood there.

"Time for me to go back into the hold?"

I picked the blanket up off of the cot, and followed him. It was going to be cold down there. I wanted to make it to Liverpool without freezing my rocks off.

The cold air made me shiver. I had been tucked up in a fairly warm environment for the past few days. I tucked myself behind one of the legs of the ship's derricks as a wave broke over the bows. Water rolled across the aft, soaking the boson. I couldn't help but to smile.

The metal dogs snapped back, and the hatch was lifted. There was no warm conversation between us as I climbed over the hatch cover, and began my climb down into the hold. Some of the bruising to my arm had begun to dissipate, so it was not as bad as the last time I had gone down there.

I had to hang there several times as the ship took another wave over her bows, lifting the ship skywards before crashing back down into the sea. The first thing I did when I touched the ceiling was light the small lamp. Several rats scurried away from the light, back into the darkness. My holdall was where I had left it, as was my watch. It would have been mad to put it back on. If this was seen by whoever let me out of hatch later on, they might take it as an extra payment.

The catches on the holdall snapped back with surprising sound. The clothes I had were still there. These, I put on the grain sacks. At the bottom of the bag was the envelope I had put in there. Bringing the light closer, I began to pull the delicate papers from within. Much of it was from my grandfather, Robert's, day. There were also personal things from my grandmother. One thing did grab my attention. It was the word land. Pulling the paper closer to me, and nearer to the light, I scanned the paper. Granddad Robert had left one acre of land to whoever could produce this letter. The certificate was real enough to me.

One acre of land in a place called Tebay in the county of Westmorland. Once again the name Westmorland came back to me. Things were picking up from being piss-poor to land owner in less than a minute.

There was a letter that went with the document that I found hard to make heads or tails of.

If you are a true Birket, you will know where to go. Once there, go to the place that you can smell the sea from. It is waiting for you.

I sat there, staring at the letter for a long time, trying to work out what the hell it all meant. The lamp began to burn lower. Setting it down beside me, I turned the wick down so that it went out completely.

With the blanket I had taken from the cabin, I curled up on the grain sack, and tried to sleep. I'd tucked the letter into my coat pocket. I kept going over its meaning in my mind. Where you can smell the sea from?

What did it mean? Perhaps it was just the ramblings of an old man.

CHAPTER THIRTY-SEVEN

The engines began to slow. I had no idea what time it was, or what day it was. It seemed like I had been down in the hold for a lifetime.

No food had come down, nor anything to drink. All I had was a couple of slugs of Scotch left. It would have to do. During my time down there, I'd made myself a small nest-like area amongst the grain sacks. If the hold was opened, I would have been seen easily from top side. The last thing I needed, at this point of the game, was to be found by dock workers.

After a short time, I could feel the ship being nudged. It was more of a vibration than a noise I felt. The boots of the men echoed down to me. All was going forward. The faint shouts of orders being given made my heart beat faster. Now was my most vulnerable time.

For what appeared like a lifetime, nothing happened above me. The loud roar of the main engines had stopped some time ago. Trying to work out in my own mind what would be going on top side helped to pass the time. I had been around ships long enough to know that customs men would be going over the manifest now, and checking the crew.

If they were diligent, then they would search the accommodation decks. The cargo the ship was carrying was not a sealed cargo. The cargo hatches didn't have an official seal on them. With luck, a cargo of grain would not be of too much interest to prying eyes.

I spent some time doing movements with my arm, swinging it back and forth ten times. I would also engage in a ten times forward to sideways movement. Though, it was still a little hard, and I didn't want to open the wound up again.

My holdall sat by my side, and my watch was tucked into my pocket. I was not going to have it stolen on the dockside by drunkards from any ship.

The hatchway above me opened. I remained hidden under the bags of grain. I could hear the rats scurrying away into the darkness. Footsteps sounded on the rungs of the ladder. Someone was coming down.

A whispered voice called out. "Birket."

I stayed still.

The voice grew a little louder. "Birket, come on, man. Time to move."

I slid the sacks of grain aside, and poked my head out. The boson looked irritated because of my delay. Topside, it was late afternoon. Rain was falling, and darkness was settling in. This could only help me now. The knot in the pit of my guts was as tight as a mooring line. It would not have taken a great deal for me to puke up all over the grain sacks.

The boson stood there, looking back and forth from me towards the deck above us. He was pretty irritated, and in a hurry to get me off of the ship.

CHAPTER THIRTY-EIGHT

Liverpool docks were nothing like I had ever seen before in my life. I stood on the gangway in the middle of a crowd of sailors, all itching to get ashore, and to the nearest bar. Ships stood bow to stern across the dock. Men called from one ship to another in all languages. My stomach was turning in circles.

Some of the men had kit bags with them. I didn't feel so out of place now as I stood there holding my holdall. I let it slip to my side so that it would look more natural than keeping it close to my chest. Looking back at the bridge, it was immersed in darkness.

I had not wanted to say anything to the officers. After all, the bastards had fleeced me. I wanted to see if they would be watching me. What was left of the Scotch, I passed around my ship's mates. This brought a loud cheer from them. Getting us on first name terms was important right now. I wanted it to look like a natural thing when I left the ship.

Some of the men had some cheap bootleg Gin brought back from the Unites States. A bottle of this was passed around, making everyone slip into a happier state of mind. No one bothered to ask me who I was. You don't always see all of your shipmates on a voyage. Some work down in the engine room as stoker's engineers, and the like. Others worked as stewards or cooks. As far as the men were concerned, I was just another hand going ashore with them.

It was several hundred yards to the big iron gates. It was the only way out. The red brick wall built around the docks was to keep stuff in, and people out. The walls had to be over twenty feet high in parts. Two iron gates barred the way. The old man who guarded them looked bored to tears. He must have seen thousands of sailors pour through the gates, and shared the same jokes with them a million times.

With a fixed stare on his face, he waved men through, only bothering to check the identity cards of the people coming back into the docks. We neared the gates, and I began laughing loudly. This was partly due to my nerves, and partly because I wanted to annoy the guard a little so that he would just get us through the gates, and on our way.

As we neared him, he put his right arm in the air, stopping our progress. One of the men called out to him to get a move on. He paid no attention. Getting up from his seat, and the warmth of the brassier fire sitting outside his little black hut, he glared at all of us.

"WAIT!"

He was used to giving orders. Stumbling on weak legs, he made it to the big iron gates. Pulling the holding bar from the ground, the first gate opened. Its squeaky hinges groaned at being pushed back. A set of truck headlights turned into the gateway, and halted as Grandfather Time worked the second gate open.

The driver of the truck handed a sheet of paper to him. Unable to see through the darkness, Grandfather Time took the paper back to the light of the fire, pulling it back and forth in front of his eyes to focus on it. This gave us the chance to pour out of the gates. I stayed in the centre of the group, but gave a little push to the two men in front of me.

"Come on, pop. We want a beer. We haven't got all night!"

There was no reply from Grandfather Time. We surged forward, and out of the gate. Grandfather Time was left cursing all sailors from everywhere.

The sign across the road said Scotland Road. I was no wiser, as I could have been in any place. To my right, I could see the tall Liver building. It was, at one time, home of the *White Star* line. I had seen photographs of it in the newspaper back home after the *R. M. S. Titanic* had sunk.

The thought of home brought a rude awakening to me. I now had no home, and I was probably wanted for murder on the other side of the Atlantic. A shiver ran down my back. There was no time to worry about that just yet. I had to get away from here as soon as possible.

The smell of coal and smoke drifted towards me on the gentle breeze. I also heard the faint sound of a whistle

Some of the men hurried off, heading to the first bar they came across. The Red Lion was heaving with men. Two drunken sailors were squaring up to each other outside. Both were hardly able to stand, let alone get into a fist fight. I carried on up the hill. My only thought was to get some distance between me and the docks. I turned left, taking a side street. I needed to sort myself out a bit. Doing this in the middle of the main street would definitely have drawn attention to me.

This was a big mistake. Footsteps fell in behind me. I tried not to look around me. I need to keep it simple, and carry on. My only action was to speed up a little. The footsteps behind me were keeping pace with mine. Alarm bells began to ring inside my head.

I crossed the road. The footsteps did the same. Stopping and taking my pack of cigarettes out of my coat pocket, I turned away from the breeze to light it. This would allow me to face the footsteps.

The blade of a knife glimmered in the light of the street lamp. I threw myself to the right, falling against the lamp post. The knife flashed a few inches past my face. I grunted with pain from my introduction to the lamp post. My injury had slammed hard against it.

The man was tall, about six-foot-two. He was four inches taller than me. The blade swung backwards, hitting the metal lamp post. Kicking out as he caught his balance, I managed to connect with his right shin. He yelped with pain.

The blade came down in a straight line this time. I could feel, and hear it, run along my sleeve. I knew straight away he had not cut me. I lashed out with my foot again, missing him. Taking a firmer grip on the knife, he now walked towards me. A slight grin spread across his face.

"Mr. Zuckerman said to say hello, Robbie."

My mouth fell open. This gave him the advantage. The knife surged straight for my guts. Pulling the holdall up to protect me, the blade stuck deep into it. Twisting and turning at the same time, the knife slipped out of his hand, firmly embedded in the holdall. This time, it was his mouth that fell open.

Not sure if he should stay to fight or run, he stood there, looking helpless. Without thought, I pulled the knife out of the holdall, and pushed it into the left side of his body. His scream of pain was almost deafening. Slumping to the floor, he grabbed the bone handle of the knife, and pulled it free. Blood pumped from the wound. Trying to get to his feet, he slumped back down. Kicking his right hand, the knife fell free. I aimed a kick at his head, and he stopped moving.

Picking the blade up, I stuck it into my pocket. I left him there. Panic was now running through me. It was not the attack that had panicked me, but rather knowing that Zuckerman had known my whereabouts.

The police would hopefully think this was a fight that had gone too far. I began to run with no idea of where I was. I turned left and right, making my tracks hard to follow. Every few minutes, I would stop, and go back on my tracks. This would tell me if I was being followed again. If Zuckerman could send one man after me, he would send another. Questions began to ring through my mind. Why hadn't he had me killed on the ship?

That one was easy to answer. There were too many witnesses on a ship, but here in a strange port, who would know me? Like the man I had just left, the police would think it was just another fight between drunkards.

I ran north, dodging down side streets, and then back onto the main streets. By keeping the breeze on my right hand side, I was sure that I was going in the right direction. I ran until I could run no further.

Slumping into a side street, I leaned against the wall of a house. Retching and vomiting, my chest hurt with the efforts of running. My eyes scanned the area around me as I struggled to regain my breath.

The big warehouse had been left behind me. I was in a street full of small terraced houses. Several lights were on in some of the bedrooms.

Over and over, I kept asking the question. How did Zuckerman know I was on board that ship? Each and every time, the same answer came back to me – Captain Williams. It bothered me as to why he'd been courteous to me on the ship, going as far as to giving me a cabin and booze. He wanted to be sure I did not die in the hold.

Zuckerman's man must have joined her as part of the crew to complete this one job on me. It would also explain why I had been questioned about what I would do once I was back in England. My mind tried searching deep within itself. Had I given anything away about my intentions? I was sure I hadn't, but it didn't stop me from mulling over the questions Captain Williams had asked me on the bridge.

Although I felt sure I had killed my would-be assassin. My great worry was that Zuckerman now knew I would be in England. I had to lose myself as soon as I possibly could.

My breathing had returned to normal. I set off at a brisk walk, making twists and turns as I went. The streets here were quite dead.

My plan was to catch a train from Liverpool, and go north. I couldn't be sure if more of Zuckerman's men hadn't come over with the corpse that was now lying in the side street. If they had, then the railway station would be surely covered. Next time, I might not be so lucky.

I badly needed to sleep right now. I was not going to find a hotel, unfortunately. I would have to find a dark corner to hide and sleep in. My pace slowed. My eyes scanned every nook and cranny for some place to rest that was out of the way.

After another hour of walking, I came across a workman's hut. The door was open, and it was dry. A duffle coat had been left on the bench to the right of the doorway. Slumping down onto the bench, I pulled the door closed, and wrapped myself up in the coat. It smelled of old tea and piss. Beggars can't be choosers, though. For all intents and purposes, I was a beggar.

I was exhausted, and shit scared. I thought my plan had worked pretty well, in all honesty. It kept coming back to me that Captain Williams had ratted me out to Zuckerman.

Sleep soon washed over me. It wasn't a deep sleep, as every movement from outside had me sitting bolt upright, and waiting for the door to open.

How long after I had gone into the hut, I had no idea. At some point, I must have drifted off into a more deep sleep. Bright light soon hurt my eyes. There were men talking nearby. I jumped up, fists clenched, and at the ready to fight whoever it was.

A young boy, possibly thirteen or fourteen, stood there with several metal cups in his hands. Giving him no chance to raise the alarm, I brushed past him. At least two of the cups fell out of his hands. I was off, and running again, still heading north. A frost had settled on the ground, making the going hard. The smooth leather soles of my shoes were not good on slippery roads.

I had to get my hands on some money. I did have the few dollar bills in my pocket, and a few English pounds. If I could change them, I could eat.

Several shops were on my right. The middle one had three large metal balls hanging outside. A hock shop/pawn shop, it was all the same. The three metal balls were a universal language. The small wooden sign outside informed everybody that they were open for business.

All I had was my watch, and the jewellery Rochelle had given to me. I could not take the risk of trying to sell the jewellery. That would make anyone ask questions. The shop window had several watches on display at various prices. I took a moment or two to sort myself out. It is hard to change your appearance when you look and smell like shit, but a quick run through my hair with my right hand, and a dust off over my coat would have to do.

A small bell rang over the door as I entered. The place was small and dark. Two small electric lights hung over the wooden counter top. The rest of the shop was filled with an assortment of goods. From blankets to prams, and even children's toys to jewellery. The jewellery was securely locked away in glass cabinets.

A head popped up from behind the counter. A cheery good morning from the middle-aged man greeted me. Behind the greeting, a suspicious stare was aimed at me. Most of his customers would be regulars. I was a total stranger. I forced a smile onto my face as I bid him a good day.

His right hand moved out slightly so that he could feel the black wooden policeman's truncheon on top of the counter. I took my hand from my pocket, and offered it in a show of friendship.

"Good morning to you, sir. I have an item I wish to sell."

His smile broadened a little as I lay my watch on the counter top. Taking the small eye glass from his pocket, he looked at the watch, turning it over and over in his hands. The fingerless gloves he wore almost polished it as he gazed upon it.

Taking several glances at me before glancing back at the watch, his suspicious mind was working overtime. I must admit if I had been in his place, I would have looked several times at me as well. The watch did not go with the clothes I was wearing.

Seeming to satisfy his own mind, he pulled the watch beneath the counter. Ten pounds slapped down on top of the counter. I looked at him in astonishment. I had paid a greater amount for it in the past.

"Surely, you can do better than that."

After several seconds of a stand off, he took another ten pounds from his pocket. "Take it or leave it, sir."

My stomach told me to take the money offered. Pride and bartering would not feed me. I knew I'd been screwed over. There was nothing I could do about it. I picked the money up, and put it in my pocket. He would make a small fortune in profit from it.

We also negotiated twenty eight pounds for all of my American dollars. I had no intention of going to a bank. Although it would be difficult to trace the money, I was too scared to even try to change American dollars, just in case.

The three pounds and ten shillings I paid for the coat hanging just behind me was a fair price. At least it was warm and clean, and I could look like a human being.

CHAPTER THIRTY-NINE

After I had changed into the last of my clothes I'd been carrying with me, I dumped the holdall. A man with a case was a man going some place. I didn't want that to be seen. I had to disappear.

The small diner at the end of the road I was on looked to be busy. It was as good a place as any to eat. Not one person looked at me as I entered. That was good. What I really wanted was a big juicy steak. God only knew what was on the plate. It was like nothing I had ever seen before. However, it did the trick by taking my hunger pangs away.

Several trucks were parked alongside the place. I hung around, waiting for some of the drivers to come out. Maybe I could bum a ride away from here.

Several of the drivers were heading east. Only two were heading north. My luck changed for the better. I picked up a lift from a middle-aged driver who was a happy-go-lucky man. He was only too happy to give me a ride as far as Lancaster. In the back of my mind, the place struck a cord. Grandfather Robert had once told me about Lancaster. He had started his life at sea from a place close to there.

For the next two hours, Bert Quigly told me his life story. From his childhood to his married life. I was happy to sit there, and listen to him, nodding from time to time as he made a point of something.

217

My ears pricked up when he told me about the two killings in the city last night. There was no need to ask him any questions. He was only too happy to give all the gory details.

"Murder it was, mate. Both of them stabbed beyond recognition."

Well, one of them might have been, but if the other was Zuckerman's hitman, I knew exactly how he died. I was not about to correct him, though.

Shaking my head in surprise, I did ask one question. "Have the police got anybody for them?"

It was another twenty minutes before he got to the point.

"No, no one. They tell me it was a mad man, or a robbery gone wrong."

I, for one, was happy to hear that the cops were thinking along these lines.

CHAPTER FORTY

My driver friend dropped me off at a place called St. Georges Quay next to the River Lune. It was like I had been here before.

To my left, and away from the river, stood the castle. As I turned back on myself, I was now facing the city. I was about fifteen minutes away from the railway station. All I had to do was keep the river on my left. If I'd walked the opposite way, I would have ended up at a place called Overton, and the place my grandfather had joined his first ship, the *Stemsi*. So many memories came flooding back to me from my childhood. It was like being home again.

A cold wind blew along the river. The leaves on the trees fell, making a rich red and copper coloured pathway along my walk. Several small boats were moored to the wall, and the smell of industry from the big factories mixed with the smell of the salt water.

I had no recollection of my grandfather telling me about the factories. Then again, it was over one hundred and seventy years ago since he'd left these shores. The small shipyard he'd talked of was still there. Men were climbing up and down wooden scaffolding, calling to the young apprentices to shift their lazy butts.

Wagons and trains trundled along the roads and tracks, whistles and horns blowing to warn workers to move. Several young men had fishing pole lines stretched way out into the river, each concentrating hard on the tips of the poles, waiting for the faintest twitch to indicate they'd caught a fish.

The road turned left sharply, taking me west for a short time before turning north again. I could now hear the trains pulling into the station ahead of me. Surely, I had to be safe now from Zuckerman's clutches?

Greenayre Station was not what I was used to in the United States. It was nothing more than a small village line. The small arched ticket window hid a larger room. Set back into the back wall, a coal fire blazed away, radiating heat through the grill. The ticket seller had his feet up in front of the fire with a hot drink in his hand.

I had no real idea of where I was going. Unlike the United States, this man was only too happy to oblige me. I could get a train to Tebay direct from platform two. I didn't have to look too far for the platform, as all I had to do was cross a small bridge, and I was there.

I now had two hours to kill before my train came in. Not wanting to sit on a cold platform, I left the station again. Directly opposite of it was a pub.

The Mechanics Arms was a workers pub, set on the corner of the street. The main bar was filled with tobacco smoke. Its walls were stained yellow from a million cigarettes having been smoked in there.

Apart from the station master and two other people, the place was empty. The man behind the bar looked at me over his Daily Herald. Folding it neatly, he put the paper under the bar.

I ordered a beer, and took it to the back of the bar. Sitting under the window that looked out at the railway station, it hadn't occurred to me to look further at the papers I had in my pocket. I now had a chance to look at the papers Granddad Robert had left me.

The white envelope had turned yellow over many years. Several sheets of paper slipped out onto the table top. The cryptic message I had read on the ship, I left to one side. Unfolding the others, I found the deeds to one acre of land in Tebay. I smiled. I was now on the up. Already, I had land.

There was also a letter of introduction to the law offices of Mr. Herbert Greeves. The letter was dated over seventy years ago. I doubted that Mr. Greeves was still alive even now. I could only hope that his law office were still open. The office's address was listed as Castle Chambers, High Street, Tebay.

Picking up the cryptic letter again, I read it once more.

Go to the place that you can smell the sea. If you are a Birket, you will know the place. Dig at the foot of the mound you sit on.

What in God's name was it all about? I lit a cigarette, and took a mouthful of the beer. I have never tasted anything so vile in my life. It was warm and cloudy with a definite bitter taste to it. The bar man gave me a steely stare as I gagged on the taste.

I pondered about the letter for ages, taking an occasional sip of the beer. This was more to wet my dry mouth rather than enjoying the beer itself.

The God damn riddle was playing hell with my brain. There was nothing I could do about it just yet. I could drink no more of the God awful beer. Instead, I ordered a Scotch. At least this was drinkable.

I could feel my muscles relax a little as the warming booze went down into my gut. The large clock over the bar told me it was time to go. I had ten minutes to catch my train. I had let the time pass me by. I raised my hand to the barman as I left in a wave of thanks. He didn't bother to look up from his newspaper.

CHAPTER FORTY-ONE

It was after dark when I arrived in the small village of Tebay. I did not have to ask directions to the local tavern. It was as if I had known all along how to get there. I'd left the station, turned right, and kept walking for about half a mile. It was far too late to begin looking for lawyer's offices, or the piece of land Granddad Robert had left me.

The Cross Keys tavern seemed like a pleasant enough place for me to stay. It was more of a stopping point for travellers going to Carlisle to the north, and of course, Lancaster to the south. From what I could see, the only things that flourished here were the God damn sheep. To the rear of the tavern, was the coaching and stables. It was as if I had known this all of my life.

The landlord was a very pleasant man who was only too willing to let me have a room. I could freshen up, and then have some food. It was only at this time that I realised I had not eaten for most of the day. The large Scotch I had ordered would be brought up to my room.

"Say hello to Mary, sir, won't you?

"Who?"

"Mary, sir. She is our resident ghost. Hung as a witch she was. She now walks the floors of this tavern. If you say hello to her, she will leave you alone, then."

Oh, God! I have come to a nut house! I told myself as I climbed the creaky timber stairs.

Right now, I couldn't have cared less as to who bothered me. I wanted to clean up, and eat.

I'd poured water from the jug into the bowl when the knock came upon the door. The landlord had brought up hot water and my drink for me.

After cleaning up, I felt more human now. Pretty much all thoughts of Zuckerman had left me. I was so far off the beaten track, I doubt my own mother could have found me with a map and compass.

I'd been downstairs for almost an hour when I noticed a man staring at me from the corner of the bar. My stomach tightened. He was between me, and the doorway.

Don't be stupid! I told myself repeatedly. Zuckerman wouldn't have some of his boys here before me. This old guy must have been eighty, if he was a day. I lit another cigarette, and sat back in my chair. The warmth of the log fire made me drowsy. The old guy who'd been watching me picked his glass up, and began walking towards me. For a second, panic welled up as I stared at him. He was dressed in old clogs and work clothes.

"Excuse me, young man. Would your name be Birket?"

I stared at him for several seconds. He couldn't be a threat to me.

"Yes, sir, it is."

"Would your father or grandfather be called Robert Birket?"

With a frown on my face, I nodded. "My grandfather was called Robert Birket. He was from around here."

A broad smile spread over the old timer's face. "May I sit down? I grew up with your grandfather."

For the next two hours, John Arkwright told me stories about my granddad, Robert's, childhood, and about the old place, as he put it. It was his son who now owned my granddad, Robert's, farm.

For me, this made my lie a little easier. I told him about the small plot of land that I had been left. For a moment, he had to think back a long way. Historically, he'd allowed his stock to roam the land, no matter where it was. There was no reason in my mind to change this. As the landlord called time on his regular customers, John Arkwright invited me up to the farm the next morning.

"Just walk to the top of the hill, young Birket, and then head left."

He had no need to tell me. I knew where it would be, but I thanked him anyway. A little unsteady on his feet, he made his way to the door, still chuckling to himself about the stories he'd told me. No doubt, the several glasses of rum I'd bought for him had helped as well.

I tumbled into my bed, feeling as if the weight of the world had been taken off of my shoulders. In my semi-drunken state, I even bid good night to Mary, the resident ghost.

The following morning, I managed to bum a pair of Wellington boots from the landlord. Spats and leather shoes were not the ideal things to be walking about a hillside in.

From my imagination, very little had changed since Granddad Robert's time here. The long gradient of the hill soon had me breathing like an old timer. From the roadside at the top of the hill, I could see the farm house I felt I knew so well. A hard frost had settled on the ground, turning the area into a picturesque postcard scene. White smoke came up from the chimney. The far off hills to the rear of the house only added to the scene.

I was greeted at the door by John Arkwright. His eyes looked like piss holes in the snow after last night's little session. His smile was warm and friendly, and he waved me into the house. Very little had changed from my grandfather's description of the place. The open log fire with the big wooden surround stood in the centre of the room. The polished wooden floor had a simple handmade blanket rug on it. I could also smell coffee coming from the kitchen.

I sat on the three-seater leather settee to the right of the fire. The single chair was his. A shouldering pipe lay in the ashtray. His matches and leather tobacco pouch sat next to it.

"Young John won't be long, young Birket. He is bringing the beasts down from the top fell."

He could have been talking in tongues to me. I had no idea what he was on about.

The door swung open, and a younger woman came in with a simple wooden tray held out in front of her. All the makings for a hot coffee sat on the tray. A strand of grey hair fell down over her face. Her smile was warm and welcoming.

"Pleased to meet you, Mister Birket. Dad has told us all about you."

I gave John a quick glance, and a smile had broken out on his face. I would have guessed her age to be about the late forties or so. There was no sign of any other woman in the house.

It was only a few minute later that the door opened, and John Junior walked in. His face was bright red from the cold outside. Once more, we went through the formalities of the introduction. I had to insist they call me Robert. The formality of being called Mister Birket had gone the day I had left the United States.

It felt good to be treated so warmly by good honest people for a change. It had been a very long time since I had been made to feel so welcome.

CHAPTER FORTY-TWO

We'd been sitting for about an hour now, I guess. The old man made small talk about my grandfather, and what he could remember about him. It was fascinating to hear so much of my family's history. However, what I really wanted to do was to get onto the small piece of land I owned. The riddle had been eating away at me ever since I'd first read the cryptic letter. We spent another hour with me telling him about what my grandfather had achieved, and how he'd died.

I was asked what brought me back to England. I told them I had wanted to see my ancestral home, and that I was on business. I wasn't about to tell these good people I was on the run from the mob and the cops.

John Junior could have been reading my thoughts. After standing up and replacing the woollen scarf over his ears, he asked me to join him. He had to go, and bring some more beast's down from the top ten. I stood there, feeling baffled.

"Sorry, Robert, for you colonists, it means I have to bring some cows down from the ten acre field. Care to join me? I can show you the plot of land you have."

I could not get out of the chair quick enough. John Junior offered me one of the spare scarves from the hallway stand. I was not going to turn it down.

We turned north from the house, and headed of up the hill. There was nothing but hills here. We made small talk on the way over to the fields. John wanted to know what my plans were for the plot of land. I had not thought about it really, beyond the point of finding whatever there was to find. I could not see myself settling here. It was far too wild for my way of life. I'd been used to the easy life in many ways.

It seemed to take forever to get to a small stone walled area. Looking behind me, I could still see the house very clearly. John had been grazing sheep on the land. I had no problem with that. I was happy it was being used. The boundary of the land was about forty yards across to the other side of an old oak tree.

"Have a look around, Robert. I will be back shortly."

What he really meant was, 'You looked shagged out, and are holding me back.'

I was glad for the break. It gave me what I wanted, the time to look around the land.

The easterly wind had already chilled me to the bones. Pulling my coat tighter around me, I began walking the boundaries. I had no idea what I was looking for. An hour later, I was almost back to where I had started. I was no further on in my search.

In the back of my mind, I heard my grandfather's voice.

"I sat there like I had done a thousand times before, and knew I would never return to England."

The small mound . . . That was it! Two hundred yards to the east was a small mound. I almost ran over the field to get to it.

It took me six steps to reach the top of it. A small flat stone had been placed there many years ago. Mould and frost were now covering it. Brushing most of the frost and mould away, I sat down, looking around me.

I could smell salt. No, I could smell the sea.

This had to be it. It had to be! I wanted to start digging now. My hand touched the ground. It was solid, like stone. Behind me, John was calling my name. How long he'd been there, I didn't know. I was not going to try digging with my bare hands. It would have been pointless.

I stood up, and smiled. Walking towards him, I looked back at the mound. It looked no different than when I'd first found it.

Good! That's how I wanted it.

"Not much is it, Robert?"

He was right. It was not much at all.

"Would you be willing to sell it to me? I will give you a fair price for it."

I hadn't expected that to come. Stopping in my tracks, I looked at him, and then back at the small piece of ground.

"Tell you what, John. Give me the loan of a shovel, and I will let you know later on. I would like to put something of my grandfather's in to the ground as a memorial to him"

I was thinking on my feet here.

"I am sure we can sort something out."

The fresh lamb stew with dumplings was a welcome sight once we were back indoors. There was no further mention of his offer of buying the land during that time. He was a pretty shrewd guy really. It's exactly what I would have done. Make the offer, and then say nothing.

By one o'clock, John Junior was ready to get out of the house again, and into the fields. Picking the long handle shovel up from the barn, he left me to it. I would meet him back at the house once I had done what I needed to do.

My heart was racing as I neared the mound once more. For some reason, I took a few moments to have a look around me, making sure there was no one watching me. Why, I don't know. It was not as if this was the heart of New York.

The shovel bounced off of the hard ground, making me slip. I cursed aloud, and instinctively looked around me again. All was still clear.

Short jabbing motions with the shovel moved the first covering of earth on the southern side of the mound. Once I had gotten through that, it became fairly easy digging. Sweat poured down my back, freezing again as it settled on my lower back.

I had no idea where I should be digging, so I just kept at it. I moved around in small circles around the base of the mound. Forty minutes after, I started as the blade of the shovel hit something hard. I held my breath.

Working around the object, I could see the shape of a metal box. I took a moment to look around me. I was still alone.

The box came out of the ground reluctantly. Soil had pretty much made it solid now. Two hard hits with the shovel blade soon had the top giving way. With fingers pressed into the small gap, I forced the lid open. Two envelopes were neatly creased in half. These I took out, and put them in my pocket. I would read them later. Below that, a small piece of sack cloth was wrapped around something. Pulling the cloth back to one side, the corner of a gold bar shone in the late afternoon sun. All I could do was stare.

Dear God! Gold!

I could have danced up and down. There had to be over a pound of gold in this bar. The how's and why's hadn't gotten to me yet. I was too excited. Picking up the gold bar, I re-wrapped it in the sack cloth, and put it in my pocket. I was wrong. There had to be close to two pounds of gold here.

There was nothing else in the box. Picking up a little dirt from the ground, I put it back in the box, and re-buried it. Prying and inquisitive eyes might wonder what I had been digging around for. I could say that it was a little bit of dirt from Grandfather Robert's grave in America, and he was now back in England.

I sat there with a million thoughts running around inside my head. This was no place to have them, or try to think through them. The sun had begun to set over the eastern hills. The sun rays bouncing off of the white tops of the hills made a thousand rainbows dance along the skyline.

Patting my coat pocket to ensure that the gold bar was sitting comfortably in it, I made my way back to the house. John was already there, taking his cows into the barn for milking. His smile was warm and friendly. I needed to get back to the inn so that I could think, and read the letters that had been shut away for so many years.

"Have you given any thought to my offer of buying the land, Robert?"

"Can you meet me in the bar tonight, John? I think we can do business."

His face lit up as the smile spread from ear to ear. Shaking hands, we agreed to meet at eight p.m. that evening. It would give me time to get back, clean up, and think.

By the time I'd reached the inn, it was dark. Another frost was settling fast on the ground. I ordered a large Scotch to take up to my room.

The landlord had lit the fire in my room. I sat on the edge of the bed, and threw the gold bar down alongside me. I could have wept for joy. The last time I had seen gold values, it had been running at over thirty dollars an ounce, there must be nearly a thousand dollars worth here. Taking a mouthful of the Scotch, I unwrapped the bar. It was marked with the American eagle. How did American gold get into a shit field here in England?

The letters might hold the key. As carefully as I could, I unfolded the letters, folding them flat on the bed.

My Dear Son,

The fact that you are now reading this letter means you are back in England where my life and adventures began. You will also have found the gold bar I buried when we visited England all those years ago when you were a child. The gold is part of a shipment that your uncle, William, and I carried from the United States to England.

The shipment was meant to be for the Prussian war effort. It was not until your Uncle William and I had landed it in England that we learned that the ship meant to be carrying it was, in fact, a fraud.

231

Your uncle, William, and I, along with the American bankers, set up a code word that had to be given prior to any transfer of the gold onto the appointed ship. The code word was not given, and as a result, several cases of lead were transferred to the ship. The ship sailed, and was followed by a Chinese vessel, who went out to waylay it. Sooner than let the Chinese take the gold, the American backers had the ship sunk with the intention of salvaging it so that it could be returned to the United States.

Your uncle, William, and I took one gold bar each from the hold of the Sarah M. We both looked upon it as a payment for the damage caused to the Brandon Sherman. She had been badly beaten up in a fight with raiders who tried to take the gold from us.

A German ship set sail, taking a northerly route around the top of the British Isles. The plan was for the ship to be scuppered in waters off of the Pentland Firth. However, somehow, the Chinese managed to get a hold of the plan, and attacked her east of the Isle of Skye. Both of the ships engaged in a sea battle. Both went down as a result of it.

The Nelson shipping line was charged to salvage her cargo. Three attempts were made. All were unsuccessful. Twelve brave men died in making the attempt.

The map on the flip side of this letter will tell you where she is resting. Bring it up, my son, and return it to its rightful owners.

May God protect you!

Your ever loving father,
Robert Birket

I sat there, stunned. The letter was obviously meant to be for my father. The *Nelson* shipping line had been built up on the back of that one voyage my father had told me about, time and time again. If the gold then had been valued at two millions bucks, what would it be worth now?

My head was spinning. Several minutes passed before I flipped the letter over. A pencil drawing of the *Isle of Skye* had been drawn. It was faint, but still readable. The Scottish mainland was also sketched, and a single cross lay in the middle of the paper. This had to be the wreck site. Several numbers had been written in the top right hand side of the letter. Navigation points, I would bet. A small house had been drawn on the *Isle of Skye*, and a light house on the mainland. The X was slightly to the top of the drawing. I had to get the navigation points somehow before I could do anymore.

For now, I put the gold bar back in my coat pocket. I had to take the risk that by leaving my coat in my room, it would be safe. It would look odd if I went down to the bar with a heavy coat on. I had to appear normal for now.

Normal? I thought. How could I act normal?

I'd just found out that there were a couple of million bucks' worth of gold in the waters not too far away. The thought alone was mind-boggling.

Quickly washing and changing, I went down to the bar. My thoughts were filled with the map I'd seen, and what two millions bucks' worth of gold looked like. I wondered how I would be able to get it off the sea bed. It would take a ship and men. I had neither right now.

In my excitement, I'd left the letter and map lying on the bed. With a smile, I folded them up, and slipped them into my wallet. It then dawned on me that I did have a ship. The *Sarah M.*, the old sailing ship. She was here in England. It would mean a trip back to the port of Whitehaven, the very port she had sailed into all those years ago with the gold aboard.

But I had no worries about that right now. I would hole up here for another few days. Perhaps I would even stop shaving. A beard would hide my features a little more.

I made my mind up that I would not be returning it to anybody it was mine. I did have one massive question running around my head. If the gold had not gone down on the German ship, where was it?

CHAPTER FORTY-THREE

I had already come up with a figure in my head for the plot of land. I had no need for it now, and knew I would not return to this area again.

John Arkwright was already in the bar as I entered. The back drop of the fire, and his warm smile, was welcoming, and a slight distraction from the thoughts running around in my head. A glass of ale sat on the table ready for me. I don't think I will ever get used to drinking the stuff. The small talk soon came around to the land. He was itching to settle a deal tonight.

"Did you bring plenty of money with you, John?"

The smile slipped a little on his face, until I began smiling myself. "Well, I tell you, buddy. I have thought about it, and I think we can do business. All I need is pen and paper so that I can make the deal legal for the two of us."

The landlord obliged with this.

I, Robert Patrick Birket, do hereby sell the one acre plot of land attached to Arkwright's farm on Top Dale Fell to John Arkwright. The fee paid for the land by John Arkwright will be the sum of ten shillings.

Signed, Robert Birket on this date of 30-10-1929

It was a jaw dropping moment for John Arkwright, but as I explained to him, I could do nothing with the land at all. I think my grandfather would have approved of my actions. We shook hands on the deal. He handed me the ten shilling note. This, I gave to the landlord, and asked him to keep bringing the drinks for as long as it lasted.

By the end of the evening, I had promised that I would return to visit his family as soon as I could. I knew in my own mind that this would never happen. But a skin full of booze made a person say all sorts of things.

I shut the door to my room, and made for my coat. I wanted to be sure that no one had been in, and helped themselves to the bar.

My train ride back to Lancaster the following morning was a sombre affair. This was partly due to the massive hangover I was carrying.

My first task was to go back to the place I'd been dropped off at, the quayside along the River Lune. There were ships chandlers and shipping agents based there. I needed a navigation chart for the west coast of the United Kingdom. I then needed to sell the gold bar. Walking into a hock shop would make more problems than I wanted.

No matter where you went, there was always a criminal element who would fence pretty much anything as long as there was a profit in it for them. I had lived amongst them long enough to see them on sight. The small back room bars would not be the place. These sorts of men liked to show their wealth and strength in wide open spaces. Let the little man come to them. It gave them that sense of even more power. All I had to do was find such a place.

The ships chandler was a very talkative guy. Who he didn't know wasn't worth knowing. We poured over the navigation charts of the west coast of England. During this time, he gave me several names of local villains, as he liked to call them. Hard men who took no crap from anyone.

John Bently seemed to be the main man. He would buy and sell almost anything, even his own mother if the price was right. His favoured hang out was a place called the Kings Arms.

"Take a left at the end of the key, go up the hill, and keep walking until you see it."

Bently hung around in the top bar. It was a little more private up there, and his men would stop unwanted visitors from entering unless he gave the ok.

I had the grand total of twelve pounds left on me. I needed some clothes, and a place to stay. If I was going to see this Bently guy, I needed to look a little presentable.

There were several little hotel type places around the city that were cheap enough. It was not what I was used to, but when you're in shit you need to adjust.

By the time, I got myself sorted, it was well past seven in the evening. The Kings Arms was less than a five minutes walk away from me. The lower bar was pretty empty. Ordering a Scotch from the bar, I drank it in one gulp. A little bit of courage never went amiss. Feeling a little more confident, I set off up the wooden stairs to the upper part of the hotel.

Two gorillas barred my way from entering the main bar upstairs. I had dealt with guys like this before. Be confident, and you usually get past them.

"I want to see, Mr Bently."

"Who, pal? No one here by that name. It's a private party in there."

This was a typical answer from a brain dead goon.

"Listen, pal, I want to see your boss, John Bently. Now, you can either go and get him, or you can piss him off after I have seen him. Believe me, he will want to see me."

I stood there staring at the two of them. Both were reluctant to make the first move.

"Oh, for God's sake! Move, you limey dick brain!"

I walked past them without being stopped. Two middle-aged men were sitting at a table next to the fire place. Several leaves of paper were spread out on it. The older of the two men began to shuffle the papers together as I walked over.

The two goons followed me in. The usual blustering apology came from them both to their boss. A small nod of the head from their boss had them both stand fast.

"Who the hell might you be?"

"My name is Robert Birket, Mr. Bently."

Better to start off very formal, and see where manners get you.

"I was told you are the main guy in the district to see." The small bit of flattery brought a wry smile to his face.

"What do you want, Mr. Birket?"

Looking over my shoulders at his gorillas, I looked back at him. Another nod of his head sent his two men from the room.

"May I sit down, sir?"

Bently's head seemed to do all his talking. A nod invited me to sit down on the opposite side of the table.

"What do you want?"

Straight to the point suited me. Pulling the gold bar from my pocket, I placed it on the table, unwrapping it as if it was a precious piece of glass. There was silence in the room for several seconds. I took a quick glance at Bently's eyes. They were wide open. I had his interest now.

"How much?"

The well-rehearsed look of boredom settled on his face. I had seen it, time and time again. He was trying to unsettle me a little by pretending not to be interested. It was a ploy I had used often. His eyes had already let him down.

After several minutes of negotiating, and his sending one of his goons for a set of scales from the kitchen, we managed to get down to business. I had been way off in my estimate of how much the bar weighed. It was double the two pounds I'd guessed.

The fact that I had gone to him told him I wanted to sell it quickly and quietly. This put him, to a degree, in the driving seat. He would try and use this to his advantage.

238

He was very obvious in his questioning. Where had I gotten the gold from? Was there any more?

I gave very little information away. Sometimes, it is better to keep your cards close to your chest. I did tell him that there could possibly be more a lot more. This was to make him think about the price he would pay me. Unlike many other units of weighing things, gold was weighed in troy ounces. This was a historical method of dealing with precious metals. So instead of sixteen ounces to the pound, in gold measurements, there were twelve ounces to the troy pound.

This, however, meant diddly shit when it came to the black market in gold. It was a case of getting the best price you could for it.

Bently's first offer was a test the water one. One hundred pounds sterling. I openly laughed at him, and picked the gold bar up, ready to leave. After asking me to sit down again, the price went up and up. Eventually, we shook hands on six hundred at twelve pounds. To be paid the following day.

The man must have thought I'd sailed across the ocean in a row boat. He would keep the gold for safe-keeping until the deal was done. I laughed all the way down the stairs at his suggestion.

Like all hoods, none of them could be trusted. The worst types were the ones like Bently, the smiling, friendly ones. As soon as I was out of sight of his men, the smile on my face disappeared. If he could get a hold of the gold for nothing, I was left with no doubt that he would.

The main bar downstairs was filling up nicely. If Bently was like many of the other hoods, I'd known, and I had no doubt he was, he would have a pigeon down here some place, keeping eyes on the place. The cops over here might not be as corruptible as those in the United States. He would want warning just in case the place got raided.

I got myself a Scotch, and sat down at the far corner of the room. I could see pretty much all around me from here. Someone had left a newspaper on the seat. I picked it up, and began reading. I had become pretty adept at reading, and seeing around me at the same time. News of the stock market crash in the United States had been big news even over here. During those two days, over eighteen billion dollars had been lost on the market. If I was in any doubt then, I had no doubt now. I would have been wiped out.

One of Bently's goons came halfway down the stairs. A small weasel-faced man with half of his face covered in a beard, and heavy rimmed glasses received a nod from him. I spotted the signal easily. Weasel Face turned his seat towards me. He could now see every move I made.

I continued to scan the papers. I needed a way out of here. To my left, was the john. Maybe there was a window or something I could climb out of. At the bar, I ordered another large Scotch. Placing it on the table where I'd been sitting, I made sure Weasel Face saw me as I asked the barman to point me to the john. I already knew where it was. I just wanted Weasel Face to know I was going there. He would have no idea that I'd spotted him. I put the empty pack of cigarettes on the table along with the matches. It was a sign that I would be coming back. Weasel Face would not know that the pack was empty.

The john stunk of stale piss and crap. Only one man stood there with his back to me. I waited for him to finish. The fire door was on the far end. I was in luck. The small latch snapped open, leading to a courtyard. This swung around to the left, and then onto the main road. Within two minutes, I was out of sight of the place, and on my way back to my hotel.

CHAPTER FORTY-FOUR

I had arranged to meet Bently at eleven the following morning. For my own peace of mind, it would be back in the upstairs bar of the Kings Arms hotel. Last night had proven me right. I suspect I would now be in the local hospital with cracked skull, and no gold if I had not slipped out the back door.

I called in at Lancaster's other railway station. This served two reasons. The first, I wanted to get ticket out of here as soon as my deal had been done. The second was a simple one of being out in the open.

Bently would not be a happy man if he had tried to set me up last night. If we had been back in New York, he would have men searching the streets for me. Perhaps I was being paranoid, but I wanted to be safe.

The hotel bar was empty. The lone barman filled his time with polishing glasses, and looking bored. He hardly gave me a second glance as I walked up the stairs.

The two goons from last night were already at their posts. There was no argument from them this morning. One of them even opened the door for me to enter.

Bently sat there with a hot cup of coffee in his hand. There was no one else with him this morning. As I had done last night, I sat down opposite him. A small leather briefcase sat between us on the table.

"Help yourself to coffee, Mr Birket." His matter-of-fact tone was obvious. Lighting a cigarette, he looked at me for several seconds. "I have been up for most of the night, Birket."

So it was what I'd thought!

"The gold you have, I know all about it."

It was one of those moments I'd thought about. Last night, I'd tried to work out every angle, and this was a possible one. I sat there looking at him.

"It is part of a shipment brought over from the United States some years ago, was it not?"

I sat there, and said nothing. He was doing the talking. Let him carry on. He could be making a good guess. There was no point in spilling my guts to him. Better to find out what he knew first. Until now, he was bang on the money.

The next ten minutes were like reading from a God damn book. He could bank roll me. He could be my partner. He wanted in on the action. His attempt at an American accent was pretty piss-poor.

The one thing that worried me was that he had found out so quickly about where the gold had come from originally. Some of the things he said did make sense. I would need to be able to get to the bottom of the sea. I could use the *Sarah M.* to get there, but she was not going to be equipped enough to do the work I needed. The few hundred pounds I had, or would have, any time now, would not be enough to charter a ship and men.

Could I trust this man to be fair with me? No, was the answer.

CHAPTER FORTY-FIVE

I had taken the chance to make my excuses, and make my way to Whitehaven. I wanted to check the *Sarah M.* out. In my own mind, I knew she would not be sea worthy enough to go after the gold, but it gotten me away from Bently for a couple of days.

His offer was a pretty straightforward one. He would put up the ship, the men, and all of the diving gear. All of this for a sixty percent share.

We eventually settled on a fifty-fifty split. Should I decide to take him up on his offer?

Regardless of what I'd decided to do, the venture could not start until the New Year. The west coast of England was no place to be attempting a salvage operation during the winter months.

I had enough money to live comfortably through these months. I would spend a few days in Whitehaven, and then return to Lancaster. The *Sarah M.* was berthed in the one main dock at Whitehaven, stuck in one of its far off corners. There had been a caveat on her when she came over. She had to be kept in reasonable condition. Looking at her right now, she was in a pretty piss-poor state when I first saw her. She looked nothing like the painting Grandfather Robert had of her.

Spending several hours crawling over every inch of her, it was more and more obvious that she would not be able to do the job. Making my way aft again, I sat in what would have been my grandfather's cabin. The once leather seats had faded. The old sea chest still sat there, battered and bruised.

Its lid slightly buckled. Curiosity got the better of me. Flipping the lid back, the name, *Robert Birket 1872*, had been burned into it.

I sat back down again, looking out of the window towards the aft end of the cabin as the sun set over the horizon. It was time to leave this old lady. I had seen all I needed to. I slammed the lid of the sea chest down, and began to move to the stairs. A slight noise stopped me. The chest had a small drawer at the bottom of it. The slamming of the lid must have slipped the mechanism on it. Many chests of the time had small drawers such as this. A leather bound spine of a book was still in there.

I sat back down in the chair, and opened the book. It was my grandfather's personal journal. The light was fading too much for me to read it here. I left the *Sarah M.*, knowing that maybe there was something in this book that would shed some light onto the secret of the gold.

CHAPTER FORTY-SIX

It was another five days before I met Bently again. I had to be sure, in my own mind, that what I was about to do was right for me. I spent most of those days reading my grandfather's journals and thinking. I stayed out of sight back in Lancaster, opting to stay a few miles out of the main city.

It was pretty close to the end of November 1929, when I made contact with Bently. There was no look of surprise on his face when I walked into the room. In fact, he looked pretty God damned smug about the whole situation.

We sat, and talked for several hours. Both of us agreed that it would be a pointless venture to begin before the New Year. Storms in the Irish Sea could whip up from nothing. Trying to drag several tons of gold up from the bottom in a one hundred mile-an-hour wind was not the best idea in the world.

Bently had a ship in mind berthed in Lancaster – the *River Loyne*. She was a small ship, only weighing around the one hundred tons mark. The one thing that went in her favour was the steam driven windlass and derrick mounted on her main deck.

The plan was for us to find some poor bastard just crazy enough to go down in a diving bell. Air is pumped into the bell, allowing the silly bastard inside to breathe normally. The downside of such a stunt is that the whole thing is only tethered to the ship by a rope and airline. A simple telephone type of thing was the only communication with the ship.

The great skill in it all is how much air to pump in. Too little, and the poor bastard inside was dead. Too much resulted in the same ending.

Underwater currents, especially around the area were we would be working, were an even bigger problem. I had learned that on some of the big spring tides, the water could run at over ten knots.

I kept the navigation points as close to my chest as I could. Certain things I had to divulge. This was mainly a rough heading for any skipper to work out his route. Fuel and supplies had to be worked into the plan as well.

I kept away from Bently most of the time, only meeting when we had to. I knew he would double cross me if he got the chance

CHAPTER FORTY-SEVEN

In March of 1930, the *River Loyne* sailed down the Lune, past the place called *Snatchems*, where my grandfather's story began. A misty early morning frost lay on the ground. The hills to the east still had snow covering them. Hundreds of lowland sheep were feeding off of the rich grass that ran inland, away from the noise of the ship as she navigated the twists and turns of the river.

The small port of Glasson had three ships moored to the outside wall. The sound of power machinery drifted over us from the dry dock. I had been there a couple of times during the winter months. It was a small port governed by the tides. Two big wooden gates barred the dock from drying out on the low tide.

The main channel of the river narrowed a little. The wash from the *River Loyne* broke some of the sand banks off. Ducks and seagulls took off in alarm. A mile or so on the river, it widened out into the Morecambe bay. We would turn north-west. This took us across the bay to the port of Barrow. The diving bell would be there waiting for us.

On the aft end of the *River Loyne*, a small lifeboat was mounted. This would be my key to getting away. I was now convinced that once I had given over the navigation points to the gold, I would be gotten rid of. For my plan to work, I had to sail with the ship. Once it was done, I would be free of everything.

The short trip over to Barrow would take three hours or so. It was time enough for me to bundle some belongings into the small boat. Most of the crew, if you could call them that, were below decks eating or sleeping.

The lifeboat could not be seen from the bridge. It was easy enough to get my stuff into it. The canvas sheeting hid it perfectly.

I had to try, and judge my run perfectly. Too soon, and they would figure out my plan. Too late, and I would end up dead.

The entrance to Barrow Harbour was narrow. We'd picked up the harbour pilot twenty minutes earlier. On the far side of the dock, I could see the diving bell. It was still on the flat bed of a truck. The steam driven crane was moving slowly along the railway track towards it. We would be here no more than two or three hours.

I slipped below decks, not wanting to raise any suspicion by hanging around the aft deck near to the boat. The starboard side mess room was facing the shore. Leaning against the bulkhead, I watched as the bell was lifted from the truck, and out over the deck of the *River Loyne*. From my left, a car came into view, stopping alongside us.

My heart skipped a beat. Zuckerman stepped out of the back seat. He stood there for a few moments. Bently walked down the gangway, and shook his hand as if they were long-lost brothers. Both of them headed up the gangplank.

I froze in place. This was one thing I had not reckoned on. I could hear footsteps on the deck plates above me. Footfalls soon came down the aft stairwell.

I had no place to run. The pistol I had was back in my cabin. Fear took over. How the fuck had he known? I needed to get my gun. The door to the mess room opened, and one of Bently's goons stood there with a knowing grin on his face. I had no chance of getting past him. I knew he wanted me to try.

Footsteps sounded on the metal deck behind him. The grin on Goon's face grew broader. He was armed. His right hand was tucked

248

into his coat pocket. He was either a very good poker player, or the gun was pointing right at me. I moved back to the far end of the mess room, and sat down with my back to the bulkhead.

I didn't have to be a genius to work out that Bently had ratted me out to Zuckerman. I had a big price on my head back in the United States. He would collect the bounty, and part of the gold. He would also make a good friend in the mob.

Thinking back, it had been Bently's idea to delay the salvage operation until now. That would have given him more than enough time to send a telegram to Zuckerman, and for him to come and take me personally, especially if he could get his hands on my share of the gold at the end of his trip.

I took a cigarette from my pocket. My hand shook as I lit it. Plan A had gone to rat shit already. I tried to reason that he would not kill me straight away. He needed what I knew.

The door opened again. Goon Face moved to the left of it. Bently came in first. His face was full of the joys of spring. His well-rehearsed line of, "I have a visitor for you, Robert," was wasted on me.

Zuckerman made his grand show. His long black coat hung over his shoulders, and his hat was tilted to one side. He had not changed a bit. At least, he did not waste time with pleasantries. I would have been more surprised if he had.

"You owe me two hundred and ten grand, dickhead. Where is it?"

There was no point in my trying to bullshit, or to even be pleasant to him.

"You know as well as I do that I don't have it."

The first punch to my face came only seconds after Zuckerman had given Goon Face the nod. Stars swam around my head as the force of the blow smashed my head against the bulkhead behind me. I could feel a small trickle of blood run down the side of my face from the new cut to my eye.

"A simple hello would have worked just as well."

I had never thought of myself as one of a life hard man, and I had no level of pain tolerance. I knew, in my own mind, that if I gave in now, I would be floating face down in the Irish Sea before the day was out. I tried to reason that he would not kill me now so that he could take what he gave and lived.

Another blow smashed into my face. Black circles filled the edges of my eyes. This was just the softening up party. I let my head slump forward, slamming down hard onto the mess table.

Goon Face's hands grabbed my hair, yanking it back hard. An open slap landed on my right cheek. Zuckerman was now standing right in front of me.

"So, if you don't have the cash, you're just going have to hand over the gold, then, Robbie. You cost me a lot of dough. I also know it was you who ratted me out to the G. men. So we can do this quickly or slowly. The choice is yours. You know how I operate."

A small speck of cigar ash was wiped off of his coat as he said it. The thing was, I did know how he operated only too well.

Say nothing, I kept telling myself.

I received another slap, and two more punches. The one to my gut made me double over. I fell into the space between the table and the deck. Instinct told me to stay there. Goon Face could not land any more blows on me while I was there.

I could hear Zuckerman telling his man to leave me alone for now. I was going nowhere.

He was right I was not. I could not stop my breakfast from coming back up. I lay there in a pool of puke and blood, gasping for air. The door slammed shut. There was no need for them to lock it. After all, I was going nowhere anytime soon.

They would be back. I had something they wanted. It was up to me right now to hold out for as long as I could.

***

I knew Zuckerman's method of terrifying a person. He enjoyed this bit. Fear was a great speech maker. I had to get my head on straight. Crawling out from under the table, I tried to stand up. Although it was painful, the bastard had not broken any ribs with his last hit.

I would have a couple of hours at best to stew in my fear. Then he would be back to dish out some more. I puked again, but nothing came up. I bent over, gasping for air.

Trying to get a clear head, I could hear noises, but my vision was blurred, and I could not see a great deal because of the blood in my eyes. The diving bell touched down on the main deck, metal-against-metal. Men shouted orders to each other.

"Get it lashed down, and get ready for sea!"

It was shortly after this that calls for the mooring lines to be singled up came. I was going nowhere just yet. *Bang!* went my theory of Zuckerman telling me I could go.

I doubted I would have gotten too far down the gangplank. Still doubled over, I made my way to the mess room hatchway. Turning right outside the mess room, I headed towards the stairway leading topside. Zuckerman was not that naïve. He had posted a man there. I went back to my cabin. I had to get rid of Grandfather's diary. I was surprised he hadn't taken the steps to search it already. Perhaps he had given Bently some degree of common sense.

I had all the information I needed in my head. The port hole opened easy enough that the dogs holding it closed gave no resistance. I watched the diary float astern of us before being churned up in the ship's wake. Dogging the port hole down again, I grabbed my holdall, and made my way forward. I stopped only to peer around the corner that would take me to the engine room.

CHAPTER FORTY-EIGHT

I was back in the mess room by the time Zuckerman came back. I still looked, and felt, like I was in a shit state. There was no point in cleaning myself up. I knew I was about to get another dose of New York hospitality.

Goon Face followed him in. The stupid smile was still on his face. God, this bastard loved to dish it out!

Zuckerman stood there, his legs spread slightly apart to counter balance the rocking of the ship as the open sea got a little rougher. "You ready to talk to me, then, Robbie?"

I glared back at him in defiance. "Screw you!"

I did not get to finish my speech. The fist landed on the side of my head, dropping me like a sack of horse shit. Blackness had already begun to swim around my eyes. I had to hold out for a while longer. I looked up at him. My right eye was closing quickly. Another kick landed on my rib area, and dropped me flat on the deck.

I could hear myself gasping for air. That was about the only thing I could do. I was unable to move. Pain was shooting through every part of me.

"Don't say a word. If you do, you will die, here and now! I kept telling myself this over and over.

Two more kicks to my ribs had me rolling about the mess deck in agony. My watch told me it was eight o'clock.

"The *Isle of Skye*," I mumbled, and the beating stopped. I had the bastard's interest now.

My head was yanked back from the deck.

"Where?"

"The *Isle of Skye*."

"What are the navigation points?"

"When we get there, and I am put ashore, I will tell you."

I was thinking on my feet here, or my belly, as it was.

"We could beat it out of you, Birket."

Bently was speaking now.

This was not Zuckerman's way. He would not allow any more beatings. He had some information, and he would use that for now. He would not want to risk my being beaten to death right now.

Goon Face backed off.

The door closed again. He had time on his side. I had to act now. Dragging myself to my feet, I made for the door of the mess room. I hurt all over. There was no one outside the mess room. Zuckerman had me where he wanted me.

My head was spinning, and I felt like shit. I bounced off another bulkhead whilst heading aft to my cabin. Pain shot through me. I needed to grab what I could. I had to get away from here right now. I could not stand another beating. I had given them some information. It was just enough for them to keep away from me for a while. But I also knew Zuckerman. He would keep up the softening up process.

I could not help but to wonder if Bently knew he was a marked man. There was no chance in hell Zuckerman would share the gold with him. It didn't matter a great deal now. If everything went according to plan, I would get away from here shortly.

The small aft stairwell was unlit. That was good. No sudden beam of light was spilling onto the aft deck. By the time I'd reached the top of the stairwell, I already had my coat on. The steel door creaked open, and I automatically closed my eyes against the noise. Not that it helped at all. The sound of the engines would have muffled the screeching sound.

The cold bit into the open cuts on my face. The sea did not look too bad. All I had to do now was get to the small lifeboat over the stern, and into the water. I would then be home free.

Pushing myself into the shadow of the starboard side bulkhead, I moved slowly towards the aft. A cigarette lighter flickered on.

Freeze.

Someone was there. Shit, this was all I needed. There was no point in staying there. Sooner or later, I had to move. It might as well be now. There was a piece of a four-by-two timber lying on top of the water tank just ahead of me. Two feet long, this would do.

Taking it firmly in my hand, and raising it slightly above me, I moved on. As I neared the aft end of the bulkhead, I could smell the tobacco smoke coming around the corner. I bent over so that I could take a look from a low angle at whoever was there. Pain shot through my body as I bent over. I had to bite my lip to stop a scream of pain from warning whoever it was smoking.

Goon Face stood there with his back to me as he cupped his cigarette in his hands. Standing tall again, I moved quickly around the corner. The timber glanced off of his head onto his shoulder. Before he could move or scream, I let him have another one. This time, I connected with the top of his head.

He fell to the deck like a bag of shit. I vented all of my pain and anger on the next blow. Just for good measure, I kicked him in the nuts. A low groan escaped his lips. I could not leave him there. I would have liked to beat his brains out, and leave him, but if he was found, a search would be made for me aboard the ship. It would not take long to work out that I had gone over the wall. My ribs hurt like hell as I dragged him to the starboard side rail. He slipped quietly into the Irish Sea.

The tarpaulin came away easily from the top of the boat. Before I could launch it, I had to pay out twenty or thirty feet of the painter line.

This would tether the boat to the ship until I could get into it. I then fed the line through the port side rail, making it fast to the bollard. I would be out of the way of the wake this way. Once the boat was launched, I would bring it alongside using the stern line. I made this fast to the bollard, and lowered it into the water.

The winding part of the davit was free, and easy to use. I had made sure it had been greased well even before we slipped our mooring back in the River Lune. The locking lines holding the boat in place had been slipped.

Don't rush it, I told myself. If the boat goes under, then I'm well and truly screwed. Take your time, at this point.

Panic might be a natural instinct, but that would only lead to mistakes. Deal with any problems as they come up. The piece of timber I had used to dispatch Goon Face was still by my side. If anybody came, I would have to do the best I could to fend them off.

Slowly, the boat lifted from its cradle, and out over the stern of the ship. I looked at my watch. It was ten past nine. The full moon was shining down. I could have done without that. The visibility was clear. The shoreline was about six miles away off of the starboard.

The boat hit the water. The painter line rolled out over the stern until it stretched tight. Pain screamed out as I hauled myself onto the thin line. Pulling a small boat against the fast flowing water was hard enough under any circumstances, but when you have just had a beating, and were feeling like shit, it was almost impossible to do.

Adrenalin took over. Slowly, the boat started to come back alongside. Feeding the line back through the stern cleats, I wrapped it around the winch handle of the boat, and began turning. The boat started to move up now. Another five minutes, and it was alongside. With my left foot on the bollard, my right foot swung over the rail. My leg nearly buckled as pain shot through my rib cage. Black stars began forming around the edge of my vision.

For God's sake! Don't black out now!

I would have fallen right into the ship's screws. I took a couple of deep breaths, and waited for the dizziness to go away. I grabbed the rope, and began lowering myself down. It was about ten feet to the boat. It seemed like one hundred feet right now. The pain was almost unbearable as I took the full weight of myself on the rope. My right foot felt out for the lifeboat below me. The ship's motion kept it from lying tight alongside. If I got this wrong, I would be going for a swim.

My whole body was screaming in pain. Wrapping my foot around the painter, I tried hauling the boat to me. The pull of the boat nearly ripped my leg off at the knee. Bad idea! I lowered myself a little further. I was now in between the boat and the ship. If my grip went now, it would be over. If the ship's screws didn't get me, the cold would.

As my foot touched the bow of the boat, I threw myself back, landing in the bottom of the boat. More pain rippled through me. I lay there, doubled over for several seconds. The blackness came back to visit me. For a minute or so, I was unable to move, feeling winded, and in so much pain. I had to move, but couldn't right now. I had to let it pass. Balancing on the thwart seat, I reached out to let go of the tether.

The painter line was tied in the bow, and it made it easier to slip that way. A wet knot with cold hands is a bastard to untie. A single tug, and the line was free. I let it run through my hands. The little boat began drifting astern of the ship.

As it settled into the wake of the ship, it did get a bit bumpy, and I had to hold onto both sides of the boat to steady myself. I sat, and watched the ship steam ahead of me for a few more minutes. A great sense of relief settled over me.

It was now ten-fifteen. The breeze had freshened a little. A single cloud covered the moon for a few moments.

The tide was pushing me along behind the *River Loyne*. She was still making headway against me. Placing the two wooden oars in the rowlocks, I tried to row. My ribs hurt so much that it was impossible.

I had seen some of the fishermen on the River Lune, using one oar over the stern of their small boats. Sculling was not the easiest method of getting about, but it did mean I could use one arm. Making small figure eight movements with the single oar did give me some head way. I allowed the boat to carry on, going with the tide, and using the oar to steer with.

There was no point in trying to punch against the tide. I would have gone nowhere fast if I had. Fast flowing tide and small boats don't work together. Better to let nature take charge at this time.

Ten-thirty. I was within four miles of the shoreline now. There were no lights or visible signs of activity. This is exactly what I wanted. Ahead of me, the stern lights of the *River Loyne* were still bright. I would have gotten worried if I had seen her port and starboard lights on. That would have said I had been missed. Digging the oar in deeper, the boat turned quickly towards the shoreline. Salt was getting into the open cuts on my face. I felt like shit.

The *River Loyne* was still steaming ahead. I could smell the smoke from her funnel blowing astern of her. I could now make out the sand dunes on the shore. The breeze was dropping off a little. With my good arm, I pulled the collar of my coat higher around me. I was shivering.

The keel of the lifeboat dragged onto the sandy bottom of the bank at eleven-twenty. Ahead of me, the port navigation light of the *River Loyne* was visible. I had now been missed. It didn't matter now. I was ashore. The onboard search light began scanning the waters around the ship, stretching out in a wider ark on each pass. I had no more use for the lifeboat. I pushed it out into the channel. It began drifting back out to sea. The tide was now turning.

Both running lights of the *River Loyne* were now visible. She was coming back. I slipped behind a small sand dune. I would be safe here. Her engines grew louder as she crept closer to the shore, and her light was now bouncing off of the shoreline.

She was close now, very close. The search light's wide beam threw a shadow around me. I was still out of sight. They would pick up the lifeboat anytime now. Maybe they would think I had gone over the side, and drowned.

I guessed she was about a mile off shore now, and abeam of my position. The slow rumbling sound was the first thing I heard, followed by the large explosion. A wall of flame lit up the sky for several minutes. Screaming and bending metal almost shattered my hearing.

I stood up. The *River Loyne* was down by her stern. Flames burned fiercely from her cargo hatches. Two men were on deck, their bodies burning. One lay on the cargo hatch, rolling around, trying to put the flames out. The other took the more direct route, and jumped over the side. Her accommodation decks were well alight. Flames burst through her port holes. Anybody who had been down there would now be dead.

Steam hissed out of her single funnel. Sea water would be rushing into the hole. The bomb I had put down there would see to that. The timer had been made from a clock. Five sticks of dynamite would have seen to the rest. Zuckerman would now die by the very method he had taught me on making a bomb. His death was just an added bonus.

I had always thought that Bently would try to take me out once the gold had been found. This way, I would keep the gold, and get rid of two people who would have happily seen me dead within the next twenty-four hours.

Screw them! Let them burn. I had no feelings towards them at all.

CHAPTER FORTY-NINE

I stood there in that little sand dune, watching as the *River Loyne* settled lower and lower in the water. Two or three distant screams of help from men in the water soon went quiet. No man would have been able to stand the freezing temperature of that water tonight. That's if they had not been killed in the explosion.

Fucking idiots! If they'd only known the gold had never been lost at sea.

My grandfather's diary had told me so. It was still aboard the *Sarah M.*

Both my grandfather and Great-Uncle William had put the gold into the bilges of the *Sarah M.* before leaving New York. The threat of being boarded, and having the gold taken, was a very real one. They had both been determined that it would not fall into the wrong hands. The shipment that had been moved onto the German vessel had been nothing more than lead covered in gold

Once the *Sarah M.* had berthed in Whitehaven, the gold should have been transferred. However, the German captain and his first officer did not have the correct password to carry out the transfer. With that, Grandfather and Great-Uncle William kept the gold on board. It had been their intention to pass the gold back to the consortium of

American business men as soon as they had landed back in the U. S.

With the sinking of the German ship on the *Isle of Skye*, it was assumed by all that the gold had been lost. Both Grandfather and Great-Uncle William made the decision to keep the gold.

I found this incredible. My grandfather had always been one of those men who had come across as totally honest throughout his life. It is also one of the things he had passed down to my dad and so on.

When the gold had arrived back in the United States, many questions were asked about it. Over the next year or so, the *Nelson* shipping line grew, but it also had many spies watching it. The gold remained in the bilges since that day. I could only think that fear had kept it there. The first showing of a gold bar marked with the stamp of the U. S. would have brought suspicion and possibly death to Grandfather and very possibly the rest of the family.

Uncle William had taken two bars of the gold, and sold them quietly in the new world when he was away on one of his voyages. The third bar that I had sold to Bently was the only other bit of evidence that it existed. Now that Bently and Zuckerman had died, so had the secret of the gold. I would have placed the odds on it that both would have told someone about it. It was a secret far too big to be kept alone.

According to my grandfather's log, the gold had been stored amidships on the *Sarah M.*, sealed into the bilges with oak planks. It was sitting there waiting for me.

I smiled inwardly. I had wanted to take the *Sarah M.* out and burn her at sea after my dad's death. Things began to fall into place a bit. It had been one of the final requests that she was brought back to England. At least, here she was out of the way of prying eyes. Even after all these years! Rumours had been around for quite some time that the gold hadn't gone down with the German ship.

There was the enormous row my grandfather had been involved with. It had started as harmless fun one evening. A friend of his had made the remark that my grandfather had hidden the gold. Grandfather had got into a hell of a state about it. I remembered Great-Uncle

William had taken him to one side. I don't know what was said, but Grandfather had calmed down, and the two men had shook hands. Great-Uncle William blamed the drink on my grandfather's outburst. Maybe it was that moment that stopped Grandfather and Great-Uncle William from getting shut of the gold.

I do vaguely remember Grandfather becoming edgy over the years. The relationship my grandfather had with Great-Uncle William did deteriorate as well. Some of the rows they had were almost legendary. Great-Uncle William had taken to sailing more and more with a fresh sailing master, leaving Grandfather back in the office, or to sail on the *Sarah M.*

I also remembered Great-Uncle William spending a lot of time aboard the *Sarah M.* each time my grandfather came back from one of his little voyages. Perhaps trust only went so far when it came to this amount of gold. I now had to get back to the *Sarah M.* Perhaps the gold had been moved over the years. Right now, all I had were my grandfather's words.

Robert J. Watson

CHAPTER FIFTY

I stood behind the sand dune until the last flicker of flames had gone from the *River Loyne*. It was hard to feel any sort of remorse for the bastards that had gone down with her.

I knew what they had planned for me. As soon as we had arrived on the wreck site, I would have been tied to a shackle, and thrown over the side. Zuckerman was never going to let me live. He had a reputation to keep up. If he had lived, he would have become just another hood in England. The G. men would have had a country-wide warrant out for him. I was doing them a favour, really.

Bentley would have joined me, soon after. I was sure of that also.

A south westerly wind freshened, hiding the moon behind the fast rolling clouds. Another blow was on its way. I had no idea where I was. All I could do was head inland until I found a town or village.

As for tonight, I would have to sleep rough. It would not be the first time I had done this since I'd come to England. I just needed to get away from the shoreline right now.

Walking inland, I stumbled from sand to grass. The land began to climb steeply. It was pitch black now. The wind had begun to blow harder. The first spots of rain began falling. The last thing I wanted was to be caught out in the open.

A mile or so further on, I found a barn bales of winter hay stacked high to the rear of it. There were no other buildings in sight.

Climbing up the bales, I fell into the corner. My ribs reminded me I had been beaten up only a few hours ago. I managed to move some hay about so that I had a small nest protecting me from the freshening wind. The tin sheets on the roof rattled as it increased in is strength.

Lying there, I tried to think of my next step. It was pointless, as sleep swept over me.

I woke up abruptly. It was still dark outside. The sound of rustling hay came from below me. A lamp was shining in the barn. Men were talking. I could not make out what was being said. I was tucked up too well in my little nest.

Keep still, and out of sight. No need to let every man on the planet know I was here. Someone might ask questions. I had to lose myself once more until I was out of the area. If I was seen, there would be questions.

The muffled sound continued for hours. I lay there, huddled up. Now and then, I would take a bite from the bread I had with me. I was sure that whoever it was out there would hear my guts rumbling, and demanding to be fed. I drifted off to sleep again. I woke up when my left leg screamed in pain from a cramp.

There was no light coming from the barn anymore. It was dark. Looking at my watch, I had been asleep all day long.

Moving the hay nest from around me, I managed to stretch my legs. I bit off some more bread, and took a mouthful of the Scotch and water I had stowed in a canvas bag in the lifeboat. I began to feel brighter. I would give it another hour before I moved just to be sure it would stay quiet below me.

Moving as quietly as I could, I climbed down the hay stacks, and out into the open. The biting wind hit me, chilling me to the bone.

I needed to make my way south to Whitehaven and the *Sarah M*. I would walk as far as I could tonight. I would see where I was in the morning. I had to be in the right area as it was. We'd turned north with the *River Loyne*. Whitehaven was on the west coast, so it made sense that I would not be a million miles away.

I found a sign post telling me I was fifteen miles away from Whitehaven. I needed to head north again. What I really needed now was some food. The trouble was, it was highly unlikely I would find any place to eat out here in the wilds. Stale bread it was for my next meal.

CHAPTER FIFTY-ONE

I went aboard the *Sarah M.* after dark. Taking the lit oil lamp from the captain's cabin, formerly my grandfather's cabin, I went into the hold. There was no need to go back out on deck for this. The forward bulkhead that was part of the accommodation led directly into the hold.

The pry bar landed heavily on the ceiling of the hold, echoing around in the emptiness. Rats had taken over the hold and bilges. Several scurried away as the pry bar hit the deck. I was looking for the third ship's rib just abaft of the beam. Years of shit and crap had filled the joints in between the boards, making it hard to get any purchase on the bar. Slivers of timber flew in every direction as I tried and tried to lift them.

Sweat poured down my face as I kept on trying to raise the board. My excitement grew the entire time. I was now so close to the gold, I could almost smell it. The pain was masked by the adrenalin flowing through me.

The ceiling board gave way reluctantly. Once that first one was up, I found it easier to get another five up. The stink of dark stagnant water made me wretch.

The oak planks below the ceiling boards were surprisingly in good order. After so many years of being soaked in this shit, it would have been expected that they would be rotten. I spent another hour getting these up. After lifting the final board, I lowered the lamp into the darkness. Nothing but the foul shit that lay in the bilges.

Sticking the pry bar into the shit, I probed about. It made a metallic sound. My heart was beating like a drum now. I dropped the first bar of gold beside me. The beam from the lamp made it shine around the hold. This one was even heavier than the bar I had sold. Rummaging about in the bilges again, I could feel dozens of bars. There was no point in taking them all out. I would only have to find a place to stash them. This was a good a place as any to keep them safe. After all they had been here for decades already.

This one bar of gold would get the *Sarah M.* ready for sea again. I went back to my cabin. From now on, I would be living aboard her. I could not only supervise the work, but I could keep my eye on my gold. I was now rich again, and I had no intention of being poor ever again.

***

The following morning, I began making contact with shipwrights. There were many of them here. All of them were eager for business.

Thomas Cunigham and Son undertook the work, and guaranteed her a certificate of sea worthiness. A whole army of men and boys descended upon the *Sarah M.* within ten days of us agreeing a deal. The ship would need to be dry docked, at some point, to make sure her planking below sea level was ok. This was no great shakes. I knew she was sound below the water line. The foul smelling bilges told me that. If they had smelt of sea water, then she would have a problem.

Most of her canvas sails were screwed. The rats had chewed the sails to bits. The effects of sea water on them over the years had also taken its toll. Mile after mile of rope came aboard to replace all the rigging. Fortunately, very little of her needed to be replaced. Oak was a pretty hard timber to rot.

By late July of 1930, she was ready for her first trip out to sea. She looked magnificent, and her decks shone with new varnish. Her sails sat squarely on the masts. Her hull had been painted the original blue. Standing on the dock's side, looking at her, I could now see why my grandfather had fallen in love with this ship. The low setting sun bounced off of every part of her.

Below decks, her galley had been refitted, and the cooking stove was still a coal burning one. The crew decks stayed pretty much unchanged. The master's cabin had been refitted, and the old leather seats had been replaced. The smell of fresh leather drifted though the whole deck.

I had spent the time while she was having her re-fit, looking for a crew who was well-practiced at working sailing ships. This was not as hard as I had first thought. Many men in the port had sailed when ships were under canvas. By the end of July, she was deemed fit as seaworthy. I had my crew. The only thing they did not know about the *Sarah M.* was that her secret was buried deep in her bowels.

We sailed on the late evening tide. By mid-morning the next day, we were out of the sight of land. I felt some excitement about my new life in the Caribbean.

CHAPTER FIFTY-TWO

By sun up the next day, we were well out to sea. The land was just a distant mark on the horizon. A slight breeze drove her along at over ten knots. Her bow wave pushed a perfect wave outwards, rippling away on the gentle sea. Timbers and ropes creaked at every movement she made.

I stood on the stern of the ship, looking out to sea. In many ways, I wished I'd followed my grandfather, Robert, to sea. Perhaps if I had, I would never have gotten into the world of shit I'd been in.

I found myself loving being on the water. The helmsman stood firm at the wheel. We were heading east. Our destination would be the West Indies, or perhaps the island of Jamaica. I could settle there in a life of luxury.

***

The next day, we had perfect sailing weather. A nice breeze blew us along steadily.

The thick dark storm clouds began gathering then. Slowly, the wind began to increase. White caps formed on the crest of the waves. The *Sarah M.* dug her bows deep into the oncoming waves. I had to put two men on the wheel to keep her on a steady course.

Within twenty-four hours, it had become a full storm. Water crashed over the bows rolling aft. Below decks, men were manning the pumps, as we had started to take water on. This was no great concern. There were no water tight doors on this ship. As a wave crashed over the bows, it made its way below decks. The on-watch crew was sent aloft to reduce sail. The amount of pressure on the mast heads was incredible. Being dismasted out here was not the best place to be. Her masts groaned under the weight of the wet canvas, and wind blowing against them.

The storm blew for a week. During that time, we never made more than two miles headway. After the seventh day, the wind began to ease, leaving just a heavy, rolling swell. The men below decks were still living in wet damp clothes. The pumps had held their own. The urge for me to get below decks, and check on the gold was strong. I had to resist it. I went back to what was my normal position for me, pacing the aft deck for hours on end.

The main masthead lookout drew my attention. "Ship ahoy! Two points off of the port quarter."

Several sets of binoculars turned to look out over the stern of *Sarah M.* Way out on the horizon, a single trail of dark smoke blew west in a long stream. The ship was noted by the first officer, Mister Clegg. He was tall, gangly man from Whitehaven. He was also one of the men who had worked on the *Sarah M.* during her re-fit. What he did not know about sailing ships was not worth knowing. The bow of the *Sarah M.* dug into another wave, making us all grab onto anything that was steady.

By late afternoon, the ship was in clear view. She had slowly been altering her course towards us. I began to get an uneasy feeling about her now. What reason had she to alter course?

Unless, she was out for the gold. Although, I was the only one who knew about it. I had made sure of that. Gold could make men do some shitty things to get a hold of it.

I stood on the poop deck, looking out over the stern at the ship coming closer with each passing minute. It suddenly dawned on me. There was another person who knew about the gold. Tomas Jeffries. He was the man I had sold the single gold bar to so that I could have her re-fitted.

Thinking back to the moment I'd dropped the gold onto his table top, his eyes had narrowed for a moment. The first thing he had done was look at the stamp on it. We had even talked about my sailing time. I had been so fucking stupid. He knew pretty much all of my plans. I had also been sure that I had been watched, though I had no clear proof of it. It was just one of those feeling I'd had.

I had dismissed the feeling as that of me being paranoid. Living aboard the *Sarah M.* would have told anyone that I was not bringing gold aboard her.

The following ship would be abeam of us within the next two hours at the latest. She was pouring on the steam. Whoever she was, she had no flag of recognition flying. It was not a good sign.

I needed a plan B now. Dropping below to my cabin, I laid the chart out, covering the Irish Sea. To the south-west of us was the *Isle of Man*, a small island stuck in the middle of the Irish Sea. If the following ship was heading there, she should have been heading west, and not towards us. She could be heading to Scotland. I set the brass dividers to work on the chart. If we made a course change now, and headed directly across her bows, we would hit the Manx coast in six hours. I went back on deck, and gave the course change. Now all we had to do was try to outrun her if she was coming after us.

At last light, we would darken the ship, and continue along the coast line. We could then slip through the *Calf of Man* sound. If he followed us, he would not get through there. He drew too much water as far as I could see. That meant he would have to steam another few hours around the headland, and back onto our course to catch up with us. By that time, we would be miles away in darkness. With a little luck, by morning, he will be searching an empty horizon.

It all seemed pretty easy to me. I went below again to check my reckoning. Back on deck, I ordered as much canvas to be put on her as possible.

The *Sarah M.* shuddered as her bow dug into another wave. The extra canvas being put on her was now forcing her faster into the oncoming sea. I clutched at the desk with both hand as her bows rose higher up on the next wave.

The masthead lookout called, "Land ho!"

There was no need to check anything. It was the Manx coast line he was seeing. The ship was still with us, and was now off of our stern. He had altered course when we had. My head sunk onto my chest. In my mind, there was no doubt now. She was after us. Heavy seas slowed her down a little. She was not as good as the *Sarah M.* at riding the waves.

"Starboard five!"

This would take us closer to the shoreline. Our speed would fall off a bit now, as the lee of the land took some of the wind away.

The steamer closed in on us. Several small fishing boats sailed past us. Their crew was only too happy to give us a wave. This alone would offer some protection. If it was the gold they were after, they would not take the chance right now. Too many small boats were about. Our luck held. Several of the fishing boats had come across our stern heading out into the open sea. The steam ship would have to give way to them. Steam always gives way to sail.

As the fishing boats fanned out across the path of the steam ship, I took us in as close as I could to the coast line without losing our wind. The *Sarah M.* protested as the sea hit our beam, straining the sails, and the wood screamed out.

The steam ship would have to travel several more miles north before it could make a turn to follow us. This would put valuable miles between us. We had twelve miles to sail before we hit the *Calf of Man* sound.

If the steamer made a turn south when she'd cleared the fishing fleet, then it would confirm she was after us. Right now, there was nothing else we could do, but watch and wait.

CHAPTER FIFTY-THREE

The steamer made her turn south forty minutes after we had. If I had any doubts before, it was now confirmed that she was tailing us.

With five miles to go to our turning point, we headed out to sea. The turn was tight, and the channel narrow, so approaching it was the important thing right now. The wind was backing in on itself, turning on our beam. This would be a great help to us. If it was on our stern when we made the turn, it would push us through the very narrow channel.

At two miles from the *Calf of Man* sound, I ordered a slow and steady turn. The *Sarah M.* would take almost the full two miles to make her turn, and even her keel up. We also had to reduce sail again. There was not a cat-in-hell's chance of us going through that gap with a full all sails set. As the sails came off, she slowed. This lost us some manoeuverability.

"Port twenty."

The helmsman was on the button. No sooner had he been given the order, the big wooden wheel began to turn. The ship's head slowly turned. Her bows straightened up again.

"Midships."

Once again, the helmsman reacted quickly, and the wheel came back to midships.

The gap we were going into was less than forty yards wide. Beneath the hull, sharp rocks jutted up from the sea bed. The cliffs now stood towering above us on each side. Tidal eddies took a hold of her, pushing her bows one way, and then the other. The water on each side of us swirled in great whirlpools. We lost almost all of our headway here. It was only the current pushing us along now. We had three or four hundred yards to go.

Long shadows settled over us as the sun began settling in the western sky. On the bow, the lead linesman kept taking soundings with his trusty lead line. The lead line is a long length of rope some twenty fathoms long. Each fathom is six feet long. Various markings are made from different materials. The lead itself is seven pounds in weight. The leadman throws the lead out in front of him. By the time it hits the bottom of the sea, the line is abreast of him. He can then shout out how deep the water is.

It looked simple enough to me, however I was not the one standing up there throwing the God damned thing over the side, and reading the markings. At one point, we got below one fathom of water under our keel. If we hit one of the jagged rocks now, we would rip the keel out of her, and founder.

Seals dived into the water on our port side, making the whole thing more menacing to us. Wind from the cliff faces whistled through the shrouds and rigging. The first officer ordered some of the men to stand by on each side of the ship with push poles. If needed, they would try, and fend us off of the cliffs with them. That's if the rocks did not rip the arse out of her first.

The channel narrowed even more. I could have reached out, and touched the cliff on each side. More seals took to the water. Their warning barks echoed off of the cliffs.

The helmsman was earning his pay now, constantly changing course as the orders changed every few seconds. Our stern was taken by a tidal eddy, almost turning us broadside onto the cliffs. Push poles were shoved out in readiness. Another eddy took our bow round, bringing her back on course. I hung on for dear life.

The light was fading fast now. All I could see in front of me was darkness. The last embers of the sun went down behind the sea as the bow of the *Sarah M.* pushed out into the open sea again on the western side of the Isle.

"Set all sails. Let the wind take her now!"

Men scurried aloft, unfurling the huge sheets. The breeze soon filled them, pushing them out in front.

One of the hands was sent below to shut off all of the dead lights on the ship. All of the running lights were covered around the ship to make sure there were no lights showing.

The masts of the *Sarah M.* were over one hundred and thirty feet high. I had never been keen on going aloft back at the academy. There, the ships mast was only a training mast of sixty-five feet. That was enough for me.

We would stay on this course for the next ten hours before turning south. With luck, the steamer chasing us would have no idea what we'd just done. By the time dawn came, we would be out of sight, and on our way across the Atlantic Ocean.

I made my way around the ship, checking every cabin and navigation light.

CHAPTER FIFTY-FOUR

The wind freshened again from the north-east. White caps whipped off of the sea, stinging my face with salt water. I was not going below decks. As the weather closed down, dropping the visibility down to less than a cable's length, I relaxed a little. Heavy seas now rolled over the ship, and once again, men were sent below to get on the pumps.

It was after midnight before I went below. I was soaked to the skin and hungry. The hot food was welcome, as was the hot coffee. Plates slipped across the mess room table as each wave made the *Sarah M.* dig deep into the sea. Loud crashing noises on the top side had not only me rushing up on deck, but the whole officer's mess.

The top twenty feet of the main mast had cracked, crashing down onto the main deck. Four men were trapped under it. All hands were struggling to get to the fallen men. Heavy seas and splintered timber were making the work hard. Axes and knives came up from the boson's store. As each bit of the mast was cut away, it was thrown over the side. Hundreds of yards of rope had to be cut through.

Two of the fallen men were dead, their heads crushed like eggs by the heavy pitch pine timber of the mast. The main sail itself had gone over the side, threatening to turn us over, and acting like a sea anchor. Some of the crew was taken off of the rescue to cut away the sail.

Waves washed across the aft, knocking the men off of their feet, time and time again. Each time, they raced back to the work.

The ship had taken on a heavy list. It was now a matter of life or death to get the damaged sail over the side. I grabbed a spare axe, and began chopping at the thick hemp ropes. As each one was cut, the strain on the next became tighter. Water sprayed off of them at each stroke of the axe.

Rope ends flew all over the deck as they whipped back on us after the cut had been made. Behind us, screams of pain from one of the men rose above the roar of the wind and sea. I took a quick look over my shoulder. His right leg was shattered. His shin bone was poking through the muscle of his leg.

No time to worry about him now. If we didn't get this freaking sail out of the way, we would all be in the water soon. As the last piece of rope was cut through, the ship began to sit upright again. There was no respite. There were still men trapped under the length of mast.

Six of the crew were sent aloft to check on the remains of the mast. It would all be over if that came down now. Several splinters of the mast were hanging loosely above us. Coming down from over one hundred feet would kill anyone below it.

The men who were trapped were jumbled up in rope and wood. Two of the crew had reached the man with the open break to his leg. He had gone silent now. It was not a good sign. At least if he was screaming in pain, he was alert enough to know it. How much blood he'd lost, no one really knew. The sea water washed it away as each wave rolled down the deck.

Men were pulled back from the mess on the deck as we neared the injured crew. Too many cooks, and all of that. We had no medic aboard. It was left to the boson to strap the poor bastard's legs together, and haul him out of the mass of rope and wood. He was in a shit state. His lips had turned blue, and he looked like death warmed over. Four of the men now carried him below decks to the officer's mess. The long table down there would have to do as an operating room.

I stayed on deck to help clear the way to get the other man out. It seemed like mile after mile of rope went over the side, and we were still no nearer to him. It was nearly dawn by the time we finally got to him. He hadn't moved for some time now. Water washed over him, making his limbs look as if he was swimming. A foot length of the mast had pierced his neck, slashing the artery. We hadn't seen it until we'd gotten close to him. He must have been dead as soon after the mast had come down.

CHAPTER FIFTY-FIVE

Gibson, the man who had the leg injury, was in a real shit state. Blood soaked through the bandages on his leg. The small amount of laudanum there was on board had been used to keep him out of it. That was now wearing off. The only other thing aboard was booze, and we had lots of that. Each time he moved, and we poured more down his throat until he went quiet again.

He needed medical attention. We were still two days out from the coast of Ireland. Men took turns in shifts, loosening the tourniquet on his leg. Each time they did so, blood seeped out. It would be touch and go as to whether we got him to land before he bled to death.

By mid-day, the wind had started to ease, and the skies cleared. Whatever sail was left was crammed on. It made little difference to us. Without the main sail, we would only make one knot at best.

Below decks, we were still shipping water. The *Sarah M.* had sprung several planks on the bow. Water was pouring inside. The pumps were holding their own, thus far.

Teams of men manned the pumps. The ship's carpenter was below, trying his damnedest to cork and re-seal the boards. His hammering vibrated throughout the ship. There was a sense of urgency in his work. It was just one of those things you could tell. The hammering was fast and furious, instead of a slow and steady knocking. The smell of melting pitch tar wafted heavily throughout the mess decks. Its sickly sweet smell made me want to vomit.

"Ship off of the port quarter!"

My heart sank a little on hearing the lookout's words. Perhaps it was just another cargo ship heading westward like we were. Perhaps it was our chasing steamer that had found us easily. After all, we were lit up like a Christmas tree.

There was nothing we could do. We had lost any advantage, and we had no way of outrunning her, if indeed she was the steamer.

I went on deck, and picked up the binoculars. She was ten miles away, at the most. Her green starboard light changed. She had turned towards us. Her mast head light was clear, and both the port and starboard light showed brightly. I knew it was her. They had found us.

At our present speed, she would be on us in less than two hours. The heavy swell would slow her down a bit, but if it was the steamer, then it would still only be a matter of time.

Her lights got bigger as each minute passed. We would have been in clear view for some time now. It was not as if a ship under sail was an everyday thing these days. Working lights flickered on the main deck of the steamer. From time to time, they would dim as men walked past them.

On board the *Sarah M.,* I ordered her hard to starboard. She turned so slowly that I think even she knew the fight was up. We had no arms aboard to put up any sort of a fight.

The steamer was two miles away, and catching us fast, coming in on our port quarter. She began to turn with her starboard light showing. Maybe she was not the steamer. Perhaps she was just some tramp ship who'd seen us late, and was now getting out of the way. I stood there, watching her, and trying to reason all sorts of scenarios as to why she would be here right now, and turning beam onto us. Her deck flashed a brilliant light. Ahead of us, a plume of water went skyward.

"Hard to port!"

For the first time, the helmsman failed to react to my orders. I called hard to port again. This time he obeyed me.

A second shot burst forth from the deck of the steamer. Smoke billowed from her deck as her newly mounted gun kicked back. The foredeck of the *Sarah M.* lifted skyward. A million splinters of timber killed anyone standing close by, and flames soon erupted. What was left of her mast came crashing down, ripping her decks open to the sea below.

Flames moved towards the aft quickly now. She was going to founder. There was no chance we could save her. Her bows were now dipping lower in the water. Water was killing her now. The steamer had been standing nearby, her gun silent now.

Men screamed. Some from the pain, and others with fear. It had to be a mistake. Why try to sink us? If it had been another warning shot, they had screwed up big time.

"ABANDON SHIP! Every man for themselves!"

Men clambered over the side. Some were crying for help. I stood on the poop deck, immersed in disbelief at what I was seeing. Flames licked around the aft deck area now, and I clung on for my life. As she slipped silently beneath the waters, she was taking me with her, sucking me lower and faster to the bottom of the sea.

I had to kick out. I had to get up to the surface. My lungs felt as if they would burst.

I was free. Free from everything now. I had no pain, nor fear anymore. I would be with the two things I had loved in my life, my grandfather, Robert, and his ship, the *Sarah M.*

EPILOGUE

The official enquiry into the sinking of the *Sarah M.* was inconclusive. There was evidence that a ship called the *Sarah M.* had been in the area. Wreckage from the ship itself was found spread out over several miles of sea. The depth of water in the area was such that her hull could not be found. One month after the incident, her name plate was found. The body of a male was found clinging to it. The body could not be identified. Personal belongings showed that the body could have been that of Robert Birket, owner of the vessel itself.

The *S. S. River Loyne* foundered due to her main steam boiler exploding whilst at sea. There was no hard evidence of this. Her wreckage was found strewn over one hundred fathoms of water. There were no survivors. Several bodies were found, but all had died due to hypothermia.

Al Capone died on the 21st of January, 1947, from heart failure. He had suffered a stroke prior to this. It is widely thought his demise was brought about by an advanced stage of Syphilis.

Lightning Source UK Ltd.
Milton Keynes UK
UKOW04f0900081013

218655UK00002B/39/P